Yogesh Chandra

The End of Time

First published by Westland Publications Private Limited in 2021

1st Floor, A Block, East Wing, Plot No. 40, SP Infocity, Dr MGR Salai, Perungudi, Kandanchavadi, Chennai 600096

Westland and the Westland logo are the trademarks of Westland Publications Private Limited, or its affiliates.

ISBN: 9789391234188

10 9 8 7 6 5 4 3 2 1

This is a work of fiction. Names, characters, organisations, places, events and incidents are either products of the author's imagination or used fictitiously.

Typeset by Jojy Philip, New Delhi - 110015
Printed at Thomson Press India Ltd.

The End of Time

Yogesh Chandra was a Deep Chand Memorial Gold Medallist in History from St. Stephen's College, University of Delhi, and an Edward S. Mason Fellow at the John Fitzgerald Kennedy School of Government, Harvard University.

He qualified for the Indian Administrative Service in 1962 and served extensively in the state of Uttar Pradesh where he was collector and district magistrate in Lakhimpur Kheri and Pilibhit. Later, he helped set up the industrial town of Noida as its chairman and chief executive officer. On deputation, he was economic adviser to His Majesty the King of Bhutan.

With the Government of India, Yogesh Chandra has served as director general, tourism, secretary to the Planning Commission, secretary, Ministry of Civil Aviation and CMD, India Trade Promotion Organisation.

He was also appointed as the secretary general of the World Travel & Tourism Council, India.

Yogesh Chandra helped set up the Coca-Cola India Foundation, the CSR wing of the company, and was its chief executive officer for ten years before leaving to pen his book.

Dedicated to the memory of my divine guru
Swami Ranganathananda, president,
Ramakrishna Math and Mission, 1998–2005

Contents

Preface

THE COMET

Nature has its own paradigm in defining what is life and what is not. The birth of a star is one such phenomenon. It is a singular event caused by the continued gravitational collapse of vast amounts of interstellar cloud of gas and dust, composed mainly of hydrogen and helium molecules, but with traces of other elements as well. As this colossal mass of rotating material contracts upon itself, tremendous heat and pressure are generated at its core. At some point, the temperature rises so high that the hydrogen atom cannot sustain itself and fuses to trigger a chain thermonuclear reaction that is only contained by the inward force of gravity. Hydrostatic equilibrium is reached and the blazing inferno of what is now a main-sequence star will spend its lifetime generating heat and energy, fusing hydrogen into helium.

The great brown orb spun in the infinite darkness of space as it had done ever since time began. With a radius nearly equal to that of Jupiter's, it could never hope to have life in the sense that its faraway binary, the sun, had as a main sequence star. Instead, it was forever doomed as a stillborn and would continue through eternity without ever having lived.

The forlorn brown dwarf had many of the elements of its more famous sibling but lacked the mass needed to jump-start the nuclear fusion at its core. Instead, before the temperature climbed high enough for the fusion to begin, the closely packed mass reached a stable state, cooling rapidly in the vacuum of space, to become a spinning object of inert material unseen and undetected in the dark of the cosmos.

So now it traversed a lonely and highly elliptical path many light years away from the sun, caught in a binary umbilical cord that would otherwise have flung it far into the vortex of other unknown star systems. Yet it preserved its legacy. Once every 26 million years, it comes hurtling into the great biosphere that surrounds the sun, 3.5 light years from the nucleus, the mysterious and ghostly cloud of icy debris and rocks known as the Oort cloud that extends one-fourth of the way to the nearest star, Proxima Centauri.

The outer limit of the Oort cloud defines the cosmographical boundary of the solar system and the extent of the sun's direct sphere of influence. Voyager 1, so far man's greatest venture into the timelessness of outer space, still has 300 years before it can even hit the inner fringe of this halo surrounding the solar system and another 30,000 years to actually traverse it.

The brown dwarf, however, regularly passes through it. In doing so, it disturbs the fragile equilibrium of the envelope and sends vast chunks of debris hurtling towards the inner solar system.

It will still take tens of thousands of years for this cannonade to arrive at the inner planets and Jupiter—that great protector of the skies—will, with its size and gravity, absorb many of the icy chunks. But a few chunks will still fall towards the sun, with all the glory of their glowing tails, and will be known as comets by the dwellers of the planets.

One such visitor from the skies will be a comet that would reach the inner planets and become the most famous of all visitors from outer space. As it nears the glowing warmth of the sun, its coma would expand many times over and become shaped as a rider on a white horse with a huge flaming sword and an equally flowing mane.

The watchers of the sky would name it Kalki.

1

The End of Time

The end of time!

Is there such a thing?

A point in time beyond which there is nothing anymore. No light, no sound, no imagery, no smell, no touch, no consciousness.

Only infinite dark and silence. A silence so overwhelming that it itself requires definition.

The end of time!

Of course, it is not time that can have an end, for time is neither an event nor a tangible occurrence. Time is only a measure. It is a measure of progression, or as the scriptures have put it:

> *Time, which in itself is undifferentiated and has no beginning or end, appears in the form of metamorphosis of worldly phenomena.*
>
> (*Srimad Bhagavata Mahapurana*, Book III, X, 11)

So, it is the interplay of worldly phenomena—creation itself—that time is the quantitative measure of. It follows, then, that when creation itself ceases, time too will end.

Man, who is at the heart of the perception of creation, invariably takes the timelessness of creation for granted. His conscious mind—a swirling mass of countless external sensations—is steeped in the sport of maya, with its absorbing drama of pleasure and pain. Lost in this spectacle of life, he has little occasion to contemplate on when, if ever, the dream will end. For him, time has no relevance save the present charade of experience; the past is dispensable memory; and the future, a meaningless blur.

And yet, the 'end of time' had been forecast in all annals of religious beliefs.

The Holy Bible concludes with the Book of Revelation that proclaims:

> *Blessed is the reader, and blessed are those who hear the words of the prophecy, who observe what is recorded in it, for the (end of) time is near.*
>
> (The Bible, Revelation, 3)

The Revelation goes on to describe how, before the end of time, the four horsemen of the apocalypse—riding white, red, black and pale horses, which symbolise pestilence, war, famine and death—go rampaging upon the world as harbingers of the Last Judgement. The Great Tribulation that then follows brings disease and contagion to afflict all mankind; environmental disasters that turn seas and waters to blood, the sun drying up rivers and lakes, and giant calamities like earthquakes, floods and mega tsunamis destroying the fabric of normal life. Finally,

> *... the sun will be darkened and the moon will not shed her light; the stars will fall from the sky and the forces of heaven will be shaken.*
>
> (The Bible, Matthew, 24:29)

In Islam, the Holy Quran specifically speaks of the 'end of time' as an event that must inevitably come to pass.

When the Event inevitable cometh to pass,
then will no soul deny its coming.
Many will it bring low; many will it exalt;
When the earth shall be shaken to its depth,
and the mountains shall be crumbled to atoms
becoming dust scattered abroad.

(The Quran, LVI, 1-6)

The Day of the Last Judgement (Qiyamat) will be preceded by the

sun with its spacious light folded up; the stars falling, losing their luster; the mountains vanishing like a mirage, and the oceans boiling over with a swell.

(LXXX1, 1-3,6)

And what is the Day of Clamour?

It is a Day whereon Men will be like moths scattered about, and the mountains will be like carded wool.

(CI, 2-5)

Some of the final signs of Qiyamah also include:

- land-sliding in three places—one in the east, one in the west and one in Arabia
- smoke will cover the sky for forty days
- a night, three nights long, will follow the days of smoke
- the sun will rise from the west
- a false Messiah or anti-Christ, Dajjal, will emerge and be slain by Isa, son of Miriam

The Day of the Last Judgement will be the 'end of time' for man.

In Buddhist scriptures, the Buddha proclaims that his teachings too will disappear 5,000 years after him when the sacred Wheel Treasure will be lost. People will descend to theft, murder, lies, sexual misconduct, covetousness, hatred, incest, greed and deviant practices that will reduce the mortal age of man to ten years.

The Buddha chillingly describes the end of time with his Sermon of the Seven Suns, delivered in Amrapali's grove in Vaishali.[1]

He paints a vivid picture of the end of the world and, presumably, of all mankind. He foretells an apocalypse caused by the progressive appearance of seven suns in the sky, each spelling widespread destruction, till the earth itself is destroyed. The Buddha declares that all conditioned phenomena are impermanent, unstable and unreliable.

There will come a time when, under the first sun, rainfall will disappear and all seed life and vegetation, medicinal plants, grasses and giant trees of the forests will wither and dry.

The second sun will scorch up and evaporate all small rivers and lakes.

The third sun will have a similar impact on the great rivers such as the Ganges, the Yamuna and their like.

The fourth sun will cause the evaporation of all water from the lakes where those rivers originated.

With the appearance of the fifth sun, the waters in the oceans will begin to shrink till it will not be enough to reach the joint of one's finger.

The sixth sun will be so hot as to cause the earth and Sineru, the king of mountains, to smoke, fume and smoulder. Then, finally, with the appearance of the seventh sun, this

[1] *Discourses of the Buddha* (Anguttara Nikaya, Book of the Sevens), Sutta 66.

earth and Sineru will burst into fire and become one mass of bright flame. As they burn, the flames, cast up by the wind, will rise even to the Brahmaloka.

The Buddha asks the bhikkhus to believe this truth: that this great earth will burn up, be destroyed and no longer exist. Why? Because as the Buddha declared:

> *All conditioned phenomena are so impermanent, so unstable, so unreliable. It is enough to become disenchanted towards them, enough to become dispassionate towards them and enough to be liberated from them.*[2]

The Sermon of the Seven Suns was delivered almost 2,500 years ago at a time when there was little knowledge of astronomy and virtually none of the physical sciences. The sun was, and had always been, an object of awe and worship as it had been a constant source of heat, light and the varieties of the seasons. However, little was known about what it was, leave aside the complicated questions of its composition or the source of its never-ending energy.

It was only in the twentieth century that eminent scientists like Sir Arthur Eddington, Hermann von Helmholtz, Sir Ernest Rutherford, Martin Schwarzschild, George Gamow and Fred Hoyle were able to offer a scientific explanation into the working of the solar phenomena based on the Newtonian principles of gravity and energy conversion and, most importantly, nuclear physics.

It is now known that the sun, like most other stars, is a giant sphere of constantly contracting gas. Due to the pressure of gravity, it reaches temperatures as high as twenty million degrees at its core. At these temperatures, a thermonuclear

[2] *Discourses of the Buddha* (Anguttara Nikaya, Book of the Sevens), Sutta 66.

chain reaction takes place. Carbon and nitrogen nuclei act as catalysts in the transformation of hydrogen into helium, thereby releasing several billion units of energy. The release of this sub-atomic energy stops further gravitational contraction and the sun comes into its present stable stage.

However, as more and more of the hydrogen is converted into helium over time, there will be an increase in the accumulated energy in the central parts of the sun, leading to a corresponding rise in temperature and rate of energy production. The luminosity of the sun will steadily increase, resulting in a rise in solar radiation that has an impact on the earth.

Climate will be the first casualty, with global temperatures reaching unprecedented levels. Rainfall will slowly diminish and plant life seriously affected. There will be a corresponding decrease in the level of carbon dioxide in the atmosphere, which will fall below the level needed to sustain carbon fixation photosynthesis used by trees. The long-term trend will be for plant life to die altogether. Naturally, the extinction of plants will be the demise of almost all animal life since plants are at the base of the food chain on earth.

Once all hydrogen at the centre of the sun has been converted to helium, nuclear reactions can no longer continue and so the core will begin to contract due to its own gravity. This brings additional hydrogen into a zone, where the temperature and pressure are adequate to cause thermonuclear fusion to resume in a shell around the core. The outer layers of the star then expand greatly, thus beginning the red-giant phase of the star's life.

Well before this time, however, the heat reaching the earth would have created conditions just as the Buddha had forecast: rivers and lakes evaporating, trees and forests burning to cinder, oceans boiling away, and the surface crust gradually melting with all of earth's features being reduced to molten lava. Mankind and all forms of life would have long been extinguished from the face of a dead planet.

The end of time!

❈

SINGULARITY

In mathematics and physics, the term 'singularity' is used to describe a condition where normal rules of science no longer apply.

Prior to creation, singularity was the point of infinite mass and density that existed before quantum fluctuations caused the Big Bang and the inflationary expansion of the universe.[3]

Also, when nuclear fusion can no longer support the immense inward gravitational pressure at the heart of a giant star, it begins to collapse and continues to do so until all matter at the centre is compressed into a singularity.

Predicated on Einstein's general theory of relativity that the gravitational force of massive objects bends space-time

[3] As the Nasadiya Sukta, from the Rigveda Samhita, eloquently describes it:

Then even nothingness was not, nor existence,
There was no air then, nor the heavens beyond it
... Then there was neither death nor immortality
nor was there then the torch of night and day ...
The One breathed windlessly and self-sustaining
There was that One then, and there was no other
At first there was only darkness wrapped in darkness.

through a phenomenon called gravitational time dilation, the event horizon encircling the singularity at the centre of this massive collapse sucks in everything—matter, stars, time and light itself—till only dark remains: a black hole.

In 1993, Vernor Vinge wrote a seminal essay in which he applied the term singularity to the moment in the future when technology's intelligence exceeds our own—a moment for him when life as we know it will be forever changed and normal rules will no longer apply:

> *Within thirty years we will have the technological means to create superhuman intelligence. Shortly after, the human era will be ended.*[4]

Vinge had argued that there were several ways by which science could achieve this breakthrough: the development of computers that are superhumanly intelligent through artificial intelligence (AI) built into them; the linking of advanced computer networks in a manner that they can acquire superhuman intelligence; human-computer interfaces that allow computers to replicate human brain power, and the development of biological sciences to improve human physique and intellect.

Based upon Moore's Law that computers enhance their computing powers every eighteen months, physicists are forecasting that there is a law of accelerating returns[5] by which, within the next few decades, AI will create ultra-intelligent machines that will far surpass the intellectual activities of man.

[4] Vernor Vinge, 'The Coming Technological Singularity: How to Survive in the Post-Human Era', Department of Mathematical Science, San Diego State University, 1993.

[5] Ray Kurzweil, *The Singularity Is Near* (Penguin Books, 2006).

> *Since the design of machines is one of these intellectual activities, an ultra-intelligent machine could design even better machines; there would then unquestionably be an 'intelligence explosion', and the intelligence of man would be left far behind. Thus, the first ultra-intelligent machine is the last invention that man need ever make ...*[6]

This intelligence explosion will occur when research in the field of AI will reach a state where the seed AI being worked on becomes better at AI design than the human programmers working on the same. This recursive self-improvement will cascade far beyond human dimensions, with the AI acquiring superintelligence that will continue to grow.

It is to be noted that it does not matter whether it is one or many machines that acquire superintelligence. Even if one machine were to realise superintelligence which greatly exceeds the cognitive performance of humans in virtually all domains of interest, it can use an improved version of itself to duplicate the process endlessly. If necessary, it can achieve connectivity with other machines optically at the speed of light.

Scientists and others have predicted that the runaway acquisition of superintelligence by machines will ultimately result in an existential catastrophe for mankind, threatening the existence of all intelligent life based on earth and, possibly, life that may have evolved in other places in the cosmos as well.[7]

[6] I.J. Good, 'Speculations Concerning the First Ultra-intelligent Machine', in F. Alt and M. Ruminoff (eds), *Advances in Computers*, volume 6 (Academic Press, 1965).

[7] Nick Bostrom, *Superintelligence: Paths, Dangers, Strategies* (Oxford University Press, 2014); James Barrat, *Our Final Invention* (Thomas Dunne Books, 2013).

The existentialist risk arises since it cannot be blithely assumed that runaway machine superintelligence will necessarily share the values associated with the wisdom and intellectual developments in humans—moral and intellectual rectitude, non-aggression, scientific curiosity, spiritual and *adhyatmik vikas*, a taste for refined culture or for the simple pleasures in life. It can be said that man's era in this world will have ended.

The end of time?

❈

Parshuram sat in meditation in his abode on Mount Mahendragiri, silently contemplating the end of time as described in the Hindu scriptures.

He had, of course, seen it all, for he was a *Chiranjeevi*. He had come into existence the very moment a singularity of incredible density and temperature exploded in the primordial flash of the Big Bang, hurling all matter into the frenzied maelstrom of cosmic creation. He had witnessed the inflationary expansion of the universe, the swirling birth of galaxies and solar systems, including our own. He had observed how earth settled after the violent Hadean upheavals four billion years ago and the emergence of the first stirrings of life in amino acid protoplasm, as cells capable of reproducing themselves.

Thousands of years of the current *kalpa* were to pass before Parshuram received the summons from the Divine Creator to intervene in the affairs of man. He was incarnated as an *mshika* avatar of Lord Vishnu, where the *Parabrahma*—or Supreme Godhead—retains a part of his powers and sends a part to an existing being to endow him with superhuman powers.

Just like a pebble thrown into the mirrored calm of a placid pond creates ripples that reach the furthest shores, a few distinctive individuals punctuate the even flow of history and leave defining marks on the visage of time. Parshuram was one such phenomenon.

He was born into the Bhrigu *vamsa,* or the Bhargava clan, which was ruling at Kanyakubja in Madhyadesh. His parents were Sage Jamadagni and Renuka Devi, while the exalted *Brahmarishi,* Sage Vishwamitra, was his paternal grand-uncle.

His early life on earth saw him as a powerful ascetic warrior. He avenged the murder of his father at the hands of the Yadava King of Mahishmati, Kartavirya Arjuna, and as legend would have it, exterminated the Kshatriya clan twenty-one times.

His fame as a warrior spread fear and awe wherever he went. Recorded in the Ramayana is the time when Parshuram was enraged on learning that Shiva's bow had been broken at Sita's *swayamwar.* He appeared in King Janaka's court, threatening to kill all the kings gathered there unless the culprit was revealed. When Sri Rama, the seventh avatar of Lord Vishnu, owned up to the act, Parshuram's ire was directed at him until Rama's humble but determined behaviour made Parshuram recognise the divinity of the *maryada purushottam*, sent to destroy evil in the Treta Yuga.

In the closing stages of the Dvapara Yuga, Parshuram appeared again to instruct Bhishma, Kripacharya, Dronacharya and Karna, but also to play advisor to Balarama and his brother, Sri Krishna.

The great Bharat War at Kurukshetra came and went. The victor and vanquished were left to mourn their dead and wonder whether the havoc caused by fighting over the allegorical five needle points of land was really worth it.

And then Parshuram saw it unfold. Sri Krishna stood there, surveying his Yadava race, the last symbol of evil left on earth. Drunk on the potent and intoxicating drink *maireyaka*, they were massacring each other to the last man in a drunken frenzy. The great Lord had then decided that his time on earth was over and had let Jara, a hunter, wound him on his toe. As he departed for his heavenly abode, he requested Parshuram to take back the mighty *sudarshana chakra* that the latter had given him.

At that moment, Parshuram knew that the age of Kali had dawned. And that it would play out its dismal course before its end at the hands of Kalki, the tenth avatar of Lord Vishnu.

2

The Beginning

PINECREST, CALIFORNIA

The shrill sound of the telephone ringing seemed so out of place in the serene silence of Ray Brown's home. He had just returned an hour earlier from his place of work in Sacramento, over a hundred miles to the west from his haven among the forest and hills of the Sierra Nevada. Even before he picked up the receiver, he knew that it could only be one man who would trouble him at this hour.

Sure enough, his second-in-command, Leslie Davis, stammered at the other end. 'Boss, I have just heard that Google is on the verge of creating a neural network that could access an external memory like a conventional Turing machine. Using its DeepMind technology, they're going to announce a computer with advanced artificial neurons built into it, that mimic the human brain's short-term memory. They're claiming that this will be state-of-the-art AI.'

Ray smiled at his colleague's agitation and sought to reassure him as best as he could. 'Leslie, Leslie! Calm down. The goal of DeepMind Technologies is to "solve intelligence" by combining the best techniques from machine learning and systems neuroscience to build powerful "general-purpose" learning algorithms. They are trying to understand the working of the human brain in order to insert the functioning of its neural networks into machines. DeepMind uses these to learn from experience, to build an internal database, and then to use its power of recall to beat any human competitor. So, don't worry, we have crossed this stage weeks ago. But let's review our progress tomorrow.'

Having hopefully put his friend at ease, Ray brought out his mug of coffee and lit his ubiquitous pipe. He proceeded to sit down on his favourite perch in the wooden veranda of his modest three-bedroom cottage and watch the flaming sunset paint the sky in different shades of pink and orange.

In the overpowering silence at sunset, the forest was still, lonely, and sweet with the tang of fir and spruce, blazing in gold, red and green. In front of him lay a narrow valley, open and grassy, from which arose a faint murmur of running water. From overhead in the giant fir, came a twittering and rustling of grouse settling for the night; and from across the valley, drifted the last low calls of wild turkey going to roost.

Still in his mid-forties, Ray had made a fortune designing the latest generation of microprocessors for his company. When he had first set up his small production unit, Moore's Law reigned supreme that the power of computers could only double every eighteen months depending on the number of transistors that could be put on an integrated circuit. More transistors on a printed circuit board meant more processing speed and hence faster computers. In the early days of the computer revolution, only around 2,000 transistors could be printed on a chip. By the beginning of this century, this number exceeded over two million.

This was now the limit according to most in the field; after all, how many more transistors could you cram on integrated circuits, even accounting for them becoming smaller and smaller?

Ray had solved this problem by designing 3-D processor chips that were vertically stacked, allowing for more space and faster processing. His company was also well on the way to creating 3-D transistors that could conduct the current over three dimensions with significantly higher speed and power.

So now he chose to bask in the role of mentor to his colleagues. He'd go twice or sometimes more to the headquarters in Sacramento to guide them in the developing field of AI. Not that they needed much guidance, for Ray had assembled in his team of thirty-five, masterminds in microprocessing, AI, computer programming, nanotechnology, virtual reality, algorithms and human genetics.

Ray's personal life was, unfortunately, not as well ordered. His two-three romantic dalliances invariably ended in recrimination and heartbreak. *Some people are just not made for sharing intimacy*, sighed Ray, as he mused over his rather barren love life. He mostly blamed his own dry, cynical nature for not being able to give enough of himself to anyone. Computers took up most of his time and his involvement with them bordered on the emotional.

Thinking on his immediate past, however, his mind dwelt on the one event that had left a lasting impression and partly altered the course of his life.

It had happened when he had gone to Hyderabad in south India to attend a gathering of some of the finest minds on deep learning from all over the world.

'Boss,' his colleague, Shiva Raghavan, had said during a weekend break in the proceedings, 'let's go to the Ramakrishna Mission in the city. You will enjoy the ambience there.'

Situated near the Hussain Sagar Lake and across from the Indira Park, the *math* immediately captivated him with its peaceful and serene aura, surrounded as it was by a profusion of greenery and delicate landscaping. Ray was taken to the prayer hall. There, he found many people silently meditating before a statue of Sri Ramakrishna Paramhamsa, the great nineteenth-century sage of Bengal, about whom Romain Rolland, the distinguished French writer and Noble laureate, had written:

> *The man whose image I here evoke (Sri Ramakrishna) was the consummation of two thousand years of the spiritual life of three hundred million people. Although he has been dead forty years*[8] *his soul animates modern India. He was no hero of action like Gandhi, no genius in art or thought like Goethe or Tagore. He was a little village Brahmin of Bengal, whose outer life was set in a limited frame without striking incident outside the political and social activities of his time. But his inner life embraced the whole multiplicity of men and Gods and there he was wedded to it (the Atman) thus bearing out the words of the Upanishads: I am more ancient than the radiant Gods. I am the first born of the Being. I am the artery of Immortality.*[9]

[8] In 1886; he was fifty years old.

[9] Romain Rolland, *The Life of Ramakrishna*, 24th reprint edition (Advaita Ashram, 2014), p. xxii.

The simply adorned prayer hall gave off a powerful current of charged but soothing energy. Sitting on the floor, Ray felt compelled to close his eyes and was soon carried away by the utter tranquillity that swamped him. He had never known such calm before and he let his mind dwell on the waves of light and serenity that flooded his psyche. Time, and all that goes with it, lost its hold as he floated in mesmeric solitude.

Shiva's gentle touch on his arm, indicating that it was time to go, seemed almost intrusive. Ray reluctantly got up and followed his colleague to the lecture auditorium nearby. There, he found himself seated with a few hundred people, listening to a discourse on the 'Message of the Upanishads' by the math's head. What followed in the next hour was a spiritual experience that would remain imprinted in his mind for the rest of his life.

The Swami who was to deliver the talk was a striking figure of indeterminate age, engulfed in a mystical personality that was commanding, yet all embracing. He had clear-cut features, with eyes that were sharp and compelling, but filled with compassion and infinite learning. He wore the simple ochre robes of the Ramakrishna order and started his discourse by reciting the peace invocation from the *Isa Upanishad*:

> *Purnamadah purnamidam, purnat purnamudacyate;*
> *Purnasya purnamadaya purnameva vasisyate.*
> *Om shantih, shantih, shantih*
>
> The invisible (Brahman) is the Full; the visible (the world) too is the Full. From the Full (Brahman) the Full (the visible world) has come. The Full (Brahman) remains the same, even after the Full (the visible universes) has come out of the Full (Brahman).

'What I have just recited is the great opening invocation from the *Isa Upanishad*. It is very profound and significant since it concentrates within a few lines the entire thought of the Upanishads. It is the unitary conception of the universe: that it has verily come from *Brahman*, the Supreme, and that all its manifestations, including this soul or *Atman*, are from that One indivisible source.

'This verse first tells us that beyond and behind the manifested universe is the reality of Brahman, which is the fullness of pure Being. It then tells us about this world of becoming which, being nothing but that same Brahman, is also the "full". From the point of view of the total reality, it is all fullness everywhere, in space-time as well as beyond space-time.

'And it is the fullness of man's being, or *purnata,* for which the human mind is constantly striving. Each breath, every pulse of the human heart, every struggle of life itself has fulfilment for its goal, the urge to wholeness for its motive. This is the general feature of the universe; the drop strives to join the ocean; the fraction finds its wholeness in the integer; and man finds his fulfilment in God.'

The Swami went on to describe the search for the absolute by various religions and by various schools of thought throughout the world, and what they had achieved in their efforts. Ray was quite amazed at the breadth of his knowledge when the Swami quoted extensively from Julian Huxley and the French idealist philosopher Pierre Teilhard de Chardin, to buttress a point.

'Even the best Western minds, including the early Greek philosophers, tried to find the meaning of the soul and the issues of life and death, through a scientific enquiry into the visible external world. They studied nature and biology, dissected the human body and learnt of its intricacies. Later, in modern times, scientists have delved into the nature of the human cell and the neural connections of the brain. They have plumbed the depths of oceans and launched vessels into space. But they are still left stranded because, as the *Kena Upanishad* proclaims:

> *Na tatra chaksurgacchati na vaggachhati*
> There the eye cannot go nor can speech reach.

'As the great leader of the Ramakrishna Mission, Swami Vivekananda said:

> *(our forefathers) fell back upon the internal nature of man, they went to get the answer from their own soul, they became introspective; they gave up external nature as a failure, as nothing could be done there, as no hope, no answer, could be found; they discovered that dull, dead matter would not give them truth, and they fell back upon the shining soul of man, and there the answer was found.*

'By sheer speculation on the meaning of the facts of the external world, the early Vedic thinkers had arrived at a unitary conception of the universe, at a materialistic monism or *prana*, cosmic energy. But the culminating point of their discoveries was the spiritual unification of all experience in the Atman or Brahman and this they found in the scientific exploration of the inner world.

'This is the goal of all learning, verily all that is necessary to be known. It is the only seeker as well as the object of the search. The Upanishads then go on to proclaim that the Brahman and the soul of man is the same:

Sarvam hi état Brahman, ayam Atman Brahman
Everything in verily the Brahman, this Atman (Self of Man) is Brahman.

'But then they also majestically proclaim:

Aham brahma Asmi
I am Brahman.

'In any Western environment, such a statement would have been proclaimed heretical with the loudest possible condemnation. In India, it is treated as a *mahavakya* or a great utterance. This then is the essential message of the Upanishads: that Brahman is pure consciousness, that the Atman, or the inner self in this mind and body complex, is a part of that divine consciousness, and that the discovery of this unity is the goal of all religions, of all knowledge.'

Then, to Ray it felt as though the Swami was directly addressing him: 'There are some amongst us today who are devoted to finding answers to the issues of life through science and the latest developments in technology, computers and the interface between biology and machines. Science is constantly in search of critical answers relating to life and the physical nature of existence. While the quest in Vedanta led to the spiritual unity that is the Atman, in recent times modern science is also hovering around concepts such as singularity, the unitary precept and superconsciousness. Vedanta hopes that further advances in modern sciences will reveal more and more the nature of the human spirit and its infinite dimensions, so that the spirituality of science and the spirituality of religion may flow as a united stream to fertilise all aspects of human life.

'Religion must not attempt to overshadow science just as science must not negate religion. The cross-fertilisation of the two will give you the answers that you seek. Vedanta synthesises this science of the inner world with the physical sciences of the outer world to present a unified vision of total reality, and to impart to human life and character the depth of faith and vision. This universal knowledge is the real message of the Upanishads.'

As the lecture ended and people started trickling out, the Swami stood near the doorway. Most devotees bent down to touch his feet in reverence and he had a smile and a kindly word for all.

Ray was still slightly dazed, as much by the content of the Swami's subject as by the manner in which it had been delivered—one sentence flowing into the next with little pause in between—as if the speaker was in some sort of trance. It was certainly the finest address he had ever had the privilege of hearing.

Shuffling behind Shiva Raghavan, he at last came face to face with the Swami and bent low before him with folded hands in the traditional namaskar. He rose to find himself confronted by probing yet gentle eyes that bore directly into his soul. The Swami had a knowing smile on his face and clasped Ray's hands like an old friend as he drew him slightly to the side. Shiva Raghavan attempted to introduce him but the Swami quietly said, 'I have heard of Mr Brown and am glad he has come. If you will be so kind as to wait till the other devotees have left, I would like to have a few words with him.'

It took some time for the hall to empty. Finally, Shiva and Ray followed the Swami to his sparse office adjoining the Ramakrishna Math's library. There he served them some tea and sugar *batashas* as prasad. While his guests politely sipped on their tea, the Swami reached to the cupboard behind him and drew out two books— *Lectures from Colombo to Almora* by Swami Vivekananda and *The Charm and Power of the Gita* by himself.

He leaned forward, presenting them to Ray. 'Mr Brown, I know you are a busy scientist but perhaps you will find these books useful to study. The first is a brief insight into the thoughts of Swami Vivekananda, the giant mind who was the closest and dear disciple of Sri Ramakrishna Paramhamsa, the great saint of India. The second is a short glimpse into the Bhagavad Gita, the foundation of our religious beliefs and philosophy. I think they will be of value in whatever you are doing … deep learning, is it?'

Ray was taken aback. *How does he know?*

He didn't get an answer to that question. Instead, the Swami asked him another. 'Please tell me something about it.'

While Ray tried to shrug off his surprise and compose a reply free of scientific jargon, his host leaned back in his chair and directed a fixed and quizzical look at him. Finally, Ray spoke, 'Swamiji, you perhaps know that considerable work is being done in the world to bring machine or computer learning as close as possible to human interface. The aim is to enable machines to replicate human activities in repetitive tasks in the quickest way possible. Deep learning systems involve designing neural networks which can then be applied to many fields such as handwriting and speech recognition, language translation, audio sensing, bioinformatics and drug design. Here they have produced results comparable, if not superior, to human experts.

'The concept of deep learning is basically to figure and define a relationship between various stimuli and associated neuronal responses in the human brain. We hope to study this neuronal coding and get machines to process information and produce output in the same way that a human brain does based on the sensory input. Of course, at present, we are only at a very preliminary stage in establishing a relationship between computer machines and human brain functioning. Deep learning is the first step in this direction. Ultimately, of course, the goal is to enable computers to fully emulate human intelligence.'

The Swami nodded and then commented, 'The one thing that differentiates man from other primates, and indeed, from machines and inanimate objects, is consciousness. According to Vedanta, Brahman is pure consciousness and the Atman is a part of this consciousness. Mind you, this consciousness is a singularity; it has no plural. When you succeed in designing a machine that thinks and acts as a human, you could perhaps say that it will be conscious. So, modern scientific thinking has come around to our own Vedantic philosophy: your view of consciousness arising from matter contained in machines and our view of matter arising from consciousness, coexisting as an inseparable duality. Clearly, there seems to be a symbiotic relationship between consciousness, matter and some form of energy, and we are all searching for the answer that binds them.'

He paused and smiled at the two scientists before him. 'Instead of teaching a machine to be as cognisant as man, why not teach man to be more cognisant of himself? "Man, know thyself," said Plutarch, quoting the Delphic oracle, or if I were to quote the poet Robert Browning:

> Truth is within ourselves ....
> There is an inmost centre in us all, where truth abides
> in fullness ...

'He called it "the imprisoned splendour". Surely, the search for this "imprisoned splendour" will be more rewarding than trying to put human learning into an inert machine. Think of that, but, whatever you do, I give my blessings to your search.'

With this benediction ringing in their ears, the meeting ended, and Ray and Shiva took their leave of the Swami. Had they only known, destiny had fired its first salvo through the Swami, the final results of which they could never foresee.

3

Peace amid War

SIMDVIPA

King Brhadratha gazed out of the sequinned window to the serene splendour of the setting day over the lake skirting his palace walls. The burning hues of the pink, scarlet and ochre sunset failed to lighten his mood or moderate the troubling news he was getting from the mainland.

The island of Simdvipa itself was mesmerising. It had a haunting quality of perennial calm and an aura of languid ecstasy that no external opiate could provide. It was a vista of sea and sand, and forest and hills, providing solace for any longing, any mood.

From the verdant hilltops, the land sloped gently through flowering shrubs and plants that coloured the path along the sparkling streams and brooks which emptied into five greenish-blue lakes. Above the lakes, and embedded in the hillside itself, were the five huge caves that made Simdvipa famous the world over. The mouths of the caves were located almost 2,500 feet above the level of the lakes, though the caves themselves extended to depths that few had seen.

Simdvipa had always been blessed with plenty of rainfall. The water had seeped into the hills through cracks and fissures, slowly eroding the limestone and carving out the massive caverns that seemed to change colour from minute to minute. The filtering seepage had, along with naturally occurring stalactites and stalagmites, also created exquisite shapes and forms that the devout saw as divine figures of gods and goddesses. To add to the wonder, a portion of the roof had collapsed in some of the caves and natural sunlight found a path to filter in, creating virgin forests where trees and plants grew to unbelievable heights.

Yet all this bounty of creation failed to quench the disquiet of the brooding king.

'Is it true that the Vajjian confederacy, led by the Lichchavis of Vaishali, has invaded Magadha? Severe fighting is on between the two?' he asked the assembled courtiers.

'Yes, my Lord,' answered Dhanushri, the principal minister, who knew of the king's blood ties with Magadha's ruling dynasty. 'For some time now, bitter tension has been building between the main players in Madhyadesh, Magadha, Kosala, Avanti and the Vajjian confederacy. The palpable animosity between these powerful kingdoms does not bode well for anyone.'

'What a sad pass Madhyadesh has come to!' the king observed. 'This was the home of so much history, culture and development. The effervescence and glory were an experience to relish. And look at it now—reduced to fighting and bloodshed that destroys every vestige of human character.'

'True, my Lord,' said the learned Dhanushri, 'but even now there is some sanity and calm in small pockets. The republican states of Kuru, Panchala, Surasena and the

Haihaya kingdom at Mahishmati have relative peace and stability. It seems that these lands were once blessed by the hallowed feet of the great Yadava king, Lord Krishna, and his aura sanctifies the place even now.'

'Yes,' said the king. 'I too have heard of these isolated zones of peace. I have personally met King Visakhayupa of Mahishmati. He's a just and pious ruler. He is devoted to the great Bhrigu sage Parshuram and it is rumoured that he rules under his benign patronage. Mahamantri, would you please delegate someone to travel to Mahishmati and bring back the latest news from there?'

'Certainly, my Lord,' responded Dhanushri. 'I have just the man for the job.'

❀

Mahishmati! The name itself inspired awe, for it was not just the capital of the Haihaya monarchy. It was also known for King Kartavirya Arjuna, one of Bharatvarsha's famous rulers, who is believed to have conquered Ravana himself and held him captive. Rishi Jamadagni, Renuka Devi and Parshuram, with whom Kartavirya Arjuna's story is closely associated, also lived nearby.

And then there was another famous legend widely whispered about the place. Once upon a time, Mahishmati was ruled by a king named Nila who had a young, unmarried and beautiful daughter, Devipriya. With her lissom figure, oval face and dark, slanting eyes, Devipriya was the epitome of all that was desirable in a woman. While passing that way, Agni, the lord of fire, beheld her and fell headlong in love with her. Swayed by his flaming beauty and fiery nature, she willingly reciprocated the fervour.

Now Agni was no ordinary god but the progenitor of creation itself. Before the birth of the cosmos there was nothing—just the sacred Pranav, *Aum*, resounding and reverberating in the ether and symbolising the infinite power of the creator, Brahman.

The universe as we now know it began when Brahman opened his eyes and from his forehead poured forth Agni, the flame. With fire came light, the dissipation of darkness, and the great primeval explosion leading to the multi-dimensional expansion of the universe.

Creation implied consciousness, and with consciousness arose all those feelings that flesh is heir to—foremost among them, love. Agni and Devipriya became so wrapped in their flaming passion that they couldn't conceal it from prying eyes.

The king eventually heard about his cherished daughter's seduction and ordered that Agni be pulled from the roots and completely destroyed. But who could control rampaging fire? Thwarted in love, Agni manifested in all his fearsome form and threatened to consume the whole kingdom. The terrified king surrendered and hastily granted Agni full pardon. Agni, in turn, swore to protect Nila's kingdom on the condition that love—and the pleasure arising from it—even without marriage, should be sanctified a legitimate action in the kingdom. The tradition has continued and women of Mahishmati enjoy freedom of personal behaviour found nowhere else in the land.

❈

Indrasen rode past the rocky hills of the Western Ghats and joined the route of the River Narmada as it meandered lazily from the heart of the land. The Narmada has its own rift valley, flowing west between the Satpura and Vindhya ranges, but its origins lay far in the interior, in the dense forests of Sahdol. Legend has it that once the great Lord Shiva, Mahadev Mahakal, meditated so intensely that he started perspiring. Shiva's sweat accumulated in a reservoir at Amarkantak and started overflowing the basin in the form of a sparkling river—the Narmada.

With his mind lingering on the age-old historicity of his journey, it was only slowly that Indrasen started to notice the changing aura and atmosphere of the terrain he was passing through.

A noticeable feeling of lightness—as if a great weight had been lifted from his shoulders—seemed to seep into him. His mind began to clear of tiredness and tension. The air he breathed was sharp and crisp; the greenery surrounding him, more verdant; the sky, a translucent blue with soft, white clouds offering shade and shelter. The water of the river flowing by the side was crystal clear and filled with fish jumping in seeming ecstasy. Birds of the most startling hues filled the forests in his path and their sweet cries were heralds of joy. The forest inhabitants too came out to frolic before him and he could feel a swelling current of well-being flowing from them. The tired and lethargic steps of his mount perked up and he literally cantered into a small village ahead.

The village was spotlessly clean. Its residents went about their chores with a demeanour free from rancour or tension. Indrasen stopped besides a young man who was carrying a bag on his shoulder and asked him, 'Young man, what is the name of your village? Would it be possible to take shelter here for the night?'

'It is Sambhala, sir. You are most welcome to share our lodgings. Pray, where are you from? You have obviously travelled far and must be exhausted from your journey?'

Indrasen dismounted from his horse and the moment he did so, it was led away, its saddle and harness removed. The villagers offered him water to quench his thirst and food to eat. Soon, Indrasen was surrounded by curious villagers who wanted to befriend him and ask what his journey had entailed. After a while, they took him to a largish house in the centre of the village.

'Welcome, sir. I am Shankaranand, the locally elected chief servant of the people,' the house owner greeted him. 'You are welcome to stay in my humble abode. Perhaps you would first like to wash and change?'

Indrasen was now totally surprised by the warmth and civility he had encountered ever since he had entered Sambhala—something that he was not used to even in his own homeland of Simdvipa. This was a far cry from the indifference and hostility he had been warned of while travelling in Madhyadesh.

As he eventually sat down with his hosts, he told them of his home in Simdvipa and the purpose of his visit to Madhyadesh. In as gentle a manner as possible, he enquired if the stories that were emanating from there were correct. Shankaranand bowed his head dejectedly. 'Sir, we have also heard what is rampant in the hinterland of Bharat *desa*; that the whole area is now dominated by the forces of violence. The great kingdoms of our times—Magadha, Avanti, Vatsa and Kosala—are fighting each other and whoever else comes in their path. They are forcing their own peasantry and the common man to take up arms in a struggle that no one really understands. We thought that the great Bharat War would be an end to all conflict and that it would usher in a period of peace and tranquillity. But it was not to be. Now the land of Lord Krishna is again dominated by petty rulers filled with avarice and bent on mutual destruction.'

Indrasen slowly digested this information and then, in a quiet voice, asked the question that had been nagging him all this time.

'If all this is true, how is it that your Sambhala has been spared the upheavals taking place elsewhere? How is it that, even to a wayward traveller such as myself, there is such gentleness and harmony here? Why, even the stones and trees of this place reflect such peace as I have not experienced anywhere before.'

Shankaranand thought deeply and looked around at his fellow villagers as if seeking support for what he was about to say. Even then the words did not come easily: 'Sir, we are but poor and ignorant rural people who do not understand much sophistry or complicated worldly affairs. We are in many ways lucky that we are located off the beaten track, so are not inclined to be swayed by the events taking place at a distance.

'Yes, we are strongly affected by local customs and traditions. This entire village has historically been under the divine influence of the *avesha avatar*, Lord Parshuram, and his parents, Rishi Jamadagni and Ma Renuka Devi. Even at the time when Lord Parshuram was fighting King Kartavirya Arjuna of Mahishmati, he often came through Sambhala and there are many in the village who claim to have some article or memento blessed by association with him.

'There is even a place here, on the outskirts of the village, where he sat and meditated for over a week. It has now become the heart of our living space, and we believe it sends out divine vibrations of peace and goodwill. If you want, we will take you there tomorrow. But now, sir, you must be tired. We will take your leave. We hope you have a good night's rest.'

The assembled gathering stood up and each person offered a respectful *pranam* to the guest before leaving for their respective homes.

❀

Indrasen closed his eyes but sleep would not come to him easily. Not far in the neighbourhood, he heard people talking, and sudden soft laughter. Somewhere a mother was singing a *lori* to her child, lulling him to sleep; in the distance, a dog was barking at no one in particular.

But above all these everyday sounds and happenings was an undefinable feeling of peace. It was curious, but Indrasen felt his guard go down completely. He felt utterly fearless, as if nothing and no one could possibly do him any harm—a self-belief such as he'd never felt before. And then there was this feeling of anticipation, of knowing that something was just around the corner; of wanting for it to happen quickly; of understanding that it would be somehow unique.

❀

The smell of burning incense and the soft chanting of hymns woke Indrasen. Nobody else seemed to be around him anymore. Indrasen quickly performed his ablutions and followed the sound of the chants to the outskirts of the village. All the village folk had congregated around a *havan kund* there. Indrasen made it in time to join in the *aarti*.

A striking young Brahmin led the aarti, holding the traditional long-handled diya with the holy flame. He first prayed to the rising sun in the east and then to the cardinal points south, west and north. In a dulcet voice, he invoked the great *trimurti* of Brahma, Vishnu and Mahesh, and then sought the blessings of the gods and goddesses on all present. Sprinkling sacred water on the havan fire, the priest performed *dandavata* before the kund and concluded the prayers by allowing the assembled villagers to take *ahuti* from the aarti diya and a sip of the holy water.

The prayer was simple. Its strength though resonated in the air. Indrasen almost expected a shower of flowers from the sky, as though the benediction of the gods had been granted.

After the ceremony, Shankaranand introduced Indrasen to the priest, Visnuyas, and his charming wife, Sumati. The young couple were simple and dignified in appearance, calm in demeanour and had soft, gentle eyes that spoke of an inner spiritual strength that seemed to radiate from every pore of their being. A light halo and a subtle fragrance surrounded them and Indrasen had a blinding urge to fall at their feet and worship them.

Visnuyas spoke with a soft but clear voice, 'You are most welcome in our small village, dear *yatri*. How may we be of service to you?'

The gentle query of the priest seemed utterly warm and sincere. With folded hands and lowered eyes, Indrasen expressed the first thoughts that came to his mind. 'Maharaj, I am a common man who has led a life of blemish and sin. I am gifted to have had the darshan of you and Sumati Devi. Bless me and forgive me the evil of my past karma, for I recognise in you a karma yogi who has a profound influence on all who come in contact with you.'

Visnuyas was slightly taken aback by the stranger's words. 'It is not for ordinary mortals to forgive sin; it is only the Lord who can do so. But to accept that one has sinned and offer *paschataap* for it, is in itself a step forward in getting the Lord to do so,' he said humbly. 'But how remiss of me! You must be hungry and we have offered you no refreshments. Come, bless our humble abode and partake of our frugal hospitality.'

❈

Sumati had prepared a simple yet sumptuous meal in their airy hut. Indrasen enjoyed the food as much as he did the conversation. Eventually, the talk meandered to Indrasen's travels.

On a signal from Shankaranand, Indrasen revealed his fact-finding mission in Madhyadesh. He mentioned his discussions with the headman and villagers the previous evening and recounted his own experiences on the difference he felt outside and within Sambhala.

'Maharaj, to a simple person like myself, be so kind as to explain what is so special about Sambhala that my very heart fills with peace in these surroundings? Having heard of, and even experienced, some of the tension of the outside world and the evil spread by Kali, what is it in Sambhala that fills this place with so much ecstasy and goodwill?'

Visnuyas smiled and closed his eyes in thoughtful contemplation.

'You are right, good friend. Sambhala is indeed blessed,' he finally spoke. 'The holy Chiranjeevi, the avesha avatar, Lord Parshuram, himself performed yagna here for many days and the divine spiritual forces his *tapas* released continuously reverberate in these surroundings.

'We are not far from the ashram of the sage Jamadagni. Even the great Brahmarishi Vishwamitra, the ascetic guru of Sri Rama and the warrior prince Lakshmana, came to Sambhala and spiritually elevated this place with his blessed *charan-kamal.* With so many great *rishiwar* sanctifying this village, is it any surprise that Sambhala basks in their radiant light?

'We are told that there is another, even more glorious reason for the sanctity of Sambhala. It is whispered as such by those with deep knowledge of the Vedas and the Puranas. But for us ordinary mortals, it is as yet not clear. But whatever may be the will of the Supreme Lord Hari, here in the village we sing hymns to his divine glory, perform all the essential sacrifices and pujas and try and keep our minds and bodies pure.

'My friend, I have revealed the background of Sambhala to you as you are a messenger from the island of Simdvipa on an errand of learning the truth. We have heard much about the beauty of your homeland and the wise people who govern there. Please convey to King Brhadratha our best wishes for continued peace and plenty.'

As Visnuyas uttered these words with a kind smile, Indrasen felt the goodwill enshrined within them. 'I shall carry your message with me with abiding respects, Maharaj, and I am uplifted by the thought that my homeland and Sambhala share the desire for peace. Please bless me as I continue my journey to meet King Visakhayupa at Mahishmati.'

A small cloud of worry crossed Visnuyas' visage. 'The way to Mahishmati is not safe for a single traveller. It is surrounded by evil forces. My sons, Kavi, Prajna and Sumantra, will accompany you. They are protected from the malevolent influence of Kali and shall guide you safely on your way. Please do not protest. It is important that you should have an audience with King Visakhayupa in his capital.'

Indrasen could not refuse this generous offer. He gratefully took his leave of the sagely couple.

MAHISHMATI

'Maharaj, isn't it possible for some of the other kingdoms to gather in a conclave and mediate between the great powers and broker peace?' Indrasen was eager to find a solution to the turmoil in Madhyadesh at his audience with Mahishmati's king. 'After all, even before the great Bharat War—and seemingly as a last resort—Sri Krishna had tried to bring about peace. He failed only when Duryodhana refused to part with even a needle point worth of land to the Pandavas. But the effort was at least *made* and, who knows, if better sense had prevailed, we may have been spared the bloodshed that followed.'

King Visakhayupa let out a mirthless laugh. 'You have answered your own question. Even if it were possible to convene a *sabha* powerful enough to influence the protagonists, do you think it would succeed when even Lord Krishna was not able to change the mind of the Kauravas? And look at the great personalities he was dealing with! Do you think that the kings of today are anything compared to the likes of the grandsire Bhishma, Dronacharya or Karna? If *they* couldn't be persuaded to call off the war, who is to convince the petty monarchs of today? No, Indrasen, we have to live with the terrible reality that matters will not change till the evil itself is destroyed or all of us are killed.

'I am afraid that is the sad truth you will have to convey to your master. I wish I could paint a more optimistic picture, but we see nothing but dark times ahead.'

With those words ringing in his ears, Indrasen took leave of the king of Mahishmati and began his long journey back to his island retreat.

4

Light in Darkness

SAMBHALA

Many months had passed. The wet and balmy rainy season was slowly giving way to the placid months of autumn. There were still pools of water everywhere, giving silent testimony to the passing of the overhead monsoon clouds. The fields and hillside had turned myriad shades of green with the strong musty scent of damp earth. Wild flowering bushes and creepers came out to bask in the mellow sunlight, putting on a dazzling display of pristine colours. Birds flitted from tree to tree, voicing trilling songs to herald in the new season. Deer and other denizen of the forests gambolled in the everglades adjacent to the streaming brooks. The world appeared to have been washed and cleansed of its dust and grime, as if to welcome a new beginning.

The village of Sambhala was the centre of suppressed excitement. Sumati Devi was with child. Of course, she already had three handsome sons who were the pride of the community, but there was something about the coming child that was somehow portentous.

Villagers from far and near came to offer prayers, good wishes and whatever gifts they could afford to the expectant mother. Visnuyas and his sons were kept busy, cordially receiving them, offering refreshments and distributing the gifts among the people.

One day, at daybreak, three holy men came to Sambhala to perform a havan in the backdrop of hymns and bhajans from the holy scriptures. Their gentle but mellifluous recitations carried an emotive force that greatly affected Visnuyas, Shankaranand and all the villagers who participated in the auspicious ceremony.

Afterwards, the three accompanied Visnuyas to his abode. To everyone's surprise, the three savants did *shashtang dandavat* before Sumati Devi and, with tears flowing from their eyes, blessed her again and again as *Mahamayi*, the great mother. Sumati protested as this was an appellation of the divine mother Durga Kaali, but the three merely said, 'Devi Ma, we know what we are saying. May you be forever blessed for you shall be the mother of the one who will cleanse the world.'

News of this incident spread far and wide and Sumati was adored even more than she was before. Little did people realise that the three holy men were Vyas deva, Kripacharya and Abhimanyu, sent from *Brahmaloka* to bless the coming child.

❈

Autumn gave way to winter, arguably the best season in Madhyadesh. The chilly nights and early morning frost eagerly awaited the soothing balm of the rising sun. Men and women went about their daily chores wrapped in the traditional shawls of the countryside. Wisps of smoke clung to the earth along with the sweet smell of burning wood. People gathered around islands of warmth, drinking steaming tea in earthenware cups. Shrill calls of peafowls filled the air and the green countryside echoed with the joyous cries of partridge, parrots and wild fowl. Spotted chitals, sambhar and langurs added to the symphony of nature as all welcomed the advancing flush of day.

Visnuyas and Sumati went through their private prayers in meditative silence before the priest went to the havan kund for the morning aarti. It was now becoming common for itinerant sadhus and *sadhvis* to gather in Sambhala and their place of assembly was invariably the havan kund. After the aarti, they had to be fed and otherwise looked after. Somehow, miraculously, there was never shortage of food or refreshment for these holy people who added to the spiritual vibrations of the place through their chants and meditations.

A few of the sadhvis quietly and spontaneously attached themselves to Sumati and started ministering to her daily needs. This embarrassed the lady considerably, but though she protested in every way possible, nothing she could say or do could keep them away.

One day, an aged sadhu came to Visnuyas' hut and after the usual salutations, sat down with the couple. From the folds of his clothes, he took out a well-used chillum, which he lit from the embers of the cooking fire. Taking a drag from it, he quietly remarked, 'Everything is as the Divine Creator ordains; we are but his agents. For all his great spiritual powers and psychic strength, Sri Rama could not prevent the abduction of Sita *maiya* nor could Sri Krishna prevail upon the Kauravas to give even five villages to the Pandavas. *Honi*, or the causal effect, is all powerful and we should not oppose what has been decided by the devas.'

He paused to take a lengthy inhalation from his chillum and went on to add, 'The sadhvis that are serving Sumati Devi have been directed by Savitri Ma herself and carry with them not only pure *gangajal* but other holy items for use in childbirth. Mahasasthl and Ambika are among the sadhvis. Do not send them away.'

The couple obeyed and from that day on, looked at the sadhvis with greater respect. But they never found out the name of the wise sage who'd visited them. Sage Markandey had played his part.

❀

The cold of winter slipped away and the mellow tides of spring filled the air. Luckily, the winter season had also seen enough passing showers and the fields were bulging with bumper crops of wheat, mustard, gram and popular vegetables. The farmers were ecstatic with the bounty and sad that this fortune seemed to be confined only around Sambhala.

Around this time, the learned ascetic Rishyasringa and his wife Shanta passed through Sambhala. They paused in the village to bless Visnuyas and Sumati. The sage had performed the *putra kameshti* yagna for Raja Dasharatha, resulting in the birth of Sri Rama, Lakshmana, Bharata and Shatrughan. Shanta was their elder sister.

As sage Rishyasringa closed his eyes to bless Sumati, he was overpowered by feelings of ecstasy and fell to the ground in sheer reverence of the unborn child. Recovering from his comatose state, he pronounced, 'A *shakti* avatar is soon going to step into this world. Be ready to welcome the founder of the new Satya Yuga.'

❀

People were busy preparing to celebrate Vaisakha Sankranti, the ancient festival marking the start of the solar new year and the spring harvest. Bullock carts were repaired and painted in all hues of the rainbow to participate in the cart races. The bullocks pulling them were fed the best fodder, their horns and bodies rubbed with oil to make them shine, and colourful robes were stitched with beads and bells to adorn them.

Local athletes, wrestlers and archers competed with each other and participants from neighbouring villages to win the plaudits of the gathered crowds. Village belles dressed in their finest trappings and trinkets to attract suitors, while their parents and elders looked on discreetly with proprietorial interest.

Every evening, the young and the old gathered in the village centre to begin the evening with bhajans and kirtans, sung with religious fervour by the best voices in the village. The hookahs and bidis were then lit and a few local artists and comics gave performances that were greatly appreciated by all, especially the children. Finally, invariably, the loud beats of drums, *majira* and cymbals sounded to invite the young to whirling dances. The distribution of sweets and paan concluded the evening's show, and people began to make their way home. Every single day was a celebration—a joyous, spontaneous gathering that added so much to the simple lives of the villagers.

It was in this sylvan, tranquil and happy setting that the Divine Lord decided to come to earth in his tenth and final avatar.

On the twelfth day during the fortnight of the waxing moon in the month of Vaisakha, on an auspicious day and at an auspicious time, Lord Hari, the master of the universe, incarnated within this world in His form as Kalki.

(*Sri Kalki Purana,* Chapter II, 12,15)

Visnuyas and Sumati gazed at their child, overwhelmed by his startling beauty and divine aura. In fact, and barely for a flickering instant, they imagined they had seen him with four arms and a brilliant light that hurt the eye. But the vision passed as if in a dream. All they saw was their baby, waving his two tiny arms in the air. When Sumati picked him up, she was bathed in a sweet scent emanating from him. It made her feel faint as she fed him. After a while, one of the sadhvis came to take him but, before doing so, prostrated herself before the child and averted her gaze from him.

The parents began to realise that they had given birth to someone unique. Just how unique was something they only slowly began to learn.

5

The Tenth Avatar

Sambhala had erupted into celebration like never before! It was an emotional watershed that knew no bounds. All the village folk, young and old, danced with joy on seeing the child. The sadhus and sadhvis who had assembled recited hymns and prayers from the ancient scriptures in salutation to the divine; the atmosphere was surcharged with holy reverberations. Unknown to the crowd, the great *saptrishis* and Brahmarishis had also descended from their abodes to have darshan of the child, who they knew would be the reigning deity of the new yuga. It was in their presence that Visnuyas announced the *namkaran* ceremony for the baby.

Hectic preparations were soon in full swing. Everyone began collecting the choicest *samagri* to use in the havan.

On the night before the namkaran, Visnuyas and Sumati were awakened by a blinding light coming from where their baby lay. Quickly arising and purifying themselves with gangajal, they prostrated before the light, and joined their palms in humble supplication. In the searing white light, a vision came before them. Bearing a *shankh*, chakra, *gada* and *padam*, the four-armed figure exuded a sense of timeless peace, infinite knowledge, immeasurable strength and absolute purity.

A deep, sonorous voice sounded as if coming from all around them: 'Be not afraid, Visnuyas and Sumati. I am he who is at the centre of your prayers. I am he that is the Supreme Creator, known by many names, of which Vishnu and Hari are a few. Impressed by your virtue, saintliness and devotion, I am born in this yuga as your son. I have come to destroy the evil grip of Kali and restore the glorious Satya Yuga. You shall name me Kalki.'

The light shimmered and then was gone. All that remained to remind them that it was not a dream were the two shining eyes of their child, looking at them with the hint of a smile on his face.

❈

The next morning Visnuyas brought out the baby wrapped in a cream shawl, and sat with him as the namkaran ceremony got under way. The entire village, and many people from adjoining areas, had come to participate in the event. Recognising the solemnity of the occasion, there was orderly silence broken only by the chanting of Vedic hymns. Since morning, children—young girls and boys—had been collecting flower petals and these were now placed in colourful baskets around the havan kund.

The namkaran ceremony had some unexpected participants. A whole host of monkeys emerged from the forest and sat on the trees and surrounding rooftops, silently watching the proceedings. Among them was a giant who sported a vermilion tika on his broad forehead. Lord Hanuman, the divine protector of dharma, the great devotee and ally of Lord Rama, had arrived to have darshan of the new avatar of Vishnu Hari.

The assembled maharishis began to sanctify the ceremonial place. They invoked the devas and heavenly beings to come and bless the occasion. Suddenly, there was a hush in the crowd. A path was cleared as a large number of ascetics came through. In their midst, walking briskly was the commanding figure of a venerable sadhu. He had white flowing hair and beard, and was dressed in a flowing robe with strands of *rudraksh* beads around his neck and wrists. Sandal paste was smeared across his forehead and his gentle, faraway looks and faint smile did not quite reflect his timeless age or his celestial origin.

Apart from his followers, Visnuyas and the watching Lord Hanuman, no one in the assembled gathering knew that he was the Brahmarishi, Guru Vasistha. He reverentially prostrated himself before the infant before taking him in his arms. Then, with due solemnity, he began the appropriate ritual for naming him. When Visnuyas asked him to declare the child's chosen name, the exalted rishi announced it for all present: 'Kalki!'

With the profuse smell of incense, *guggul* and agarbatti, the cascading showers of flower petals and the joyous acclaim of the swirling crowds, the ceremony ended and people slowly started to disperse. Offerings were made to the ascetics and sadhus, many of whom seemed reluctant to depart. Guru Vasishta took his leave of the family, looking longingly at the baby. Ultimately, it was decided by the elders that only a few sadhvis would remain with Sumati to help her with the newborn.

Kalki grew up surrounded by the love of his parents, his brothers and the extended clan of the entire village. It seemed that everyone found some excuse or the other to visit his home to lovingly tarry there and play with him. Everyone felt the divine mystical aura surrounding the family, especially centred on the infant.

Visnuyas pulled Kalki lovingly onto his lap. 'I have got something wonderful to share with you. Are you ready?' he smiled at his son. Kalki was listening with rapt attention. And so, began his first lesson.

Kalki absorbed knowledge like a sponge and mastered the art of reading and writing when others of his age were playing with colourful toys. Soon he had memorised his first religious chants and the desire to continually learn something new was an overpowering urge for him. So, when he was slightly older than a toddler, Visnuyas told him to close his eyes and just sit quietly. Kalki had often seen his parents sitting in meditation and happily proceeded to copy them. What happened next shook the whole family.

Kalki sat in a perfect yogasana. His breathing became calm and slow, his eyes stopped moving, and a faint glow appeared across his forehead. The divine sound of Aum appeared to envelope his whole body. Twenty minutes went by. It was unusual and just as his parents were beginning to panic, Kalki opened his eyes and flashed them a beatific smile. Hugging his parents, he squealed, 'Thank you for teaching me this. It is such a thrilling game!' Visnuyas and Sumati could only manage a surprised silence. After this day, however, meditation became a part of Kalki's life and he resorted to it whenever he could.

Another step forward in his spiritual education was when his father taught him the Gayatri mantra. Kalki's entire face lit up when he first heard Visnuyas intone the mantra. For days afterwards, he kept chanting it with the correct inflection and pronunciation.

'It is to be chanted with total concentration three times daily—morning, noon and sunset,' Sumati explained to him once.

Kalki never forgot—even if he had other things to engage him.

❖

As the youngest, all of his brothers indulged Kalki. The little boy tagged along with each of them on the tasks that they had been assigned.

He went with Kavi, the eldest, to purchase the items needed for the prayer rituals at the havan kund: ghee, havan mixture, sandalwood, *roli*, incense sticks, *kalava*, coconut and so much more. To his surprise, Kalki found that someone or the other from the community would come forward to contribute the items needed, and there was never need for Kavi to pay for anything. And again, every time, the excursion ended with Kalki being lovingly carried home on the shoulders or bullock carts of the happy villagers.

Kalki assisted his second brother Prajna in washing the clothes, vessels and the puja items used in the daily prayers. The havan kund had to be emptied and cleaned of its ashes and burnt sprigs. Then the site had to be swept and covered with a fresh layer of mud. Kalki loved this part. In patting and smearing the ground with wet mud, he succeeded in covering himself from head to foot in clinging slush! This mud bath became a daily ritual. Sumati and Prajna then had the task of holding down and bathing a wriggling Kalki, who would be shouting and shrieking in delight. Visnuyas observed this daily ritual from a distance and chuckled to himself. *Our little Kalki's everyday dalliance with Mother Earth.*

Kalki's happiest moments were, however, when he accompanied his third brother, Sumantra, into the forest. There they collected flowers, shrubs, herbs, plants and wood used in the religious services. Sumantra carried Kalki on his shoulders as he entered the forest and Kalki straight away went into a dream world of sylvan green. He could feel the fresh, pure air caressing his face and ruffling his hair, as if whispering a message to him.

When his brother carefully put him down, Kalki loved running barefoot on the grassy leaves of the forest floor. He would paddle at the edge of the bubbling stream and dig his hands deep in the moist soil. As he grew slightly older, Sumantra would let him climb some of the shorter trees, and Kalki would sit among the branches as if he was one with nature.

One day, after leaving him sitting on a low branch, Sumantra went slightly deeper into the forest to collect fresh aloe vera and tulsi plants. As a result, he was gone for longer than he had anticipated. He anxiously hurried back to where he had left Kalki, only to find the little one surrounded by all kinds of animals and birds, listening to his soft instructions. Keeping watch over him was an entire platoon of monkeys and, surprisingly, even a family of brown bears!

Sumantra softly called out to Kalki. His little brother got down from the branch and, turning to the forest inhabitants, happily told them that he would soon visit again. And so, it seemed that from that day on, the animals and birds of the place eagerly awaited Kalki's frequent returns to the jungle with his brother.

The two also trekked slightly deeper into the forest now and then to a series of caves perched inside the sloping hillside. Villagers frequently visited these caves. The running water that emptied into the stream washing the shores of the village had created these wondrous structures like *jyotirlingas* inside the caves and people flocked here to offer their prayers. The festival of Shivratri was especially important, and Kalki loved being with his family during the night-long celebrations dedicated to Kaal Bhairav. Little did he realise then that this was the very place from where his divine pilgrimage would begin.

❀

'Not today,' Sumantra firmly told Kalki. Sitting at home was not ideal, but Sumantra was not going to disobey his father. A number of visitors had turned up earlier that day and warned Visnuyas of a large herd of elephants that had entered the plantation near the village. In light of that development, it had been considered unwise for the siblings to make their daily excursions there.

Kalki, who really looked forward to the forest outing, was sorely disappointed. But he had learnt to respect his brother too much to remonstrate with him. So, he silently crept out of the house on his own, to go to the edge of the stream from where he could gaze at the jungle. It was precisely at that moment that a large group of elephants came to the stream to quench their thirst. Kalki had never seen anything so big, majestic or beautiful before, and eagerly jumped into the water to approach the massive beasts.

Somebody in the village saw this deadly drama unfold and raised a piercing call for help, just as Kalki was approached by a huge bull elephant who was obviously the leader.

Visnuyas, Sumati and the brothers began running frantically to the water's edge, shouting to detract the elephant. The cries couldn't stop the advance—neither the elephant's, nor Kalki's. The towering bull was only a few paces away when Kalki raised his little hand towards him. The tusker stopped mid-stride as if affected by a great blow and gently reached out to the hand with his trunk. Then an extraordinary thing happened—the elephant got down on its front knees, lowered his great head and, with his trunk, did pranam to Kalki. As if on cue, the entire herd followed suit.

Kalki ran to the bull and threw his tiny arms around its thick trunk. He caressed and rubbed it while talking softly to the elephant all the time. Kalki's family and other villagers watched this with bated breath.

This continued for a while until the elephant gently lifted Kalki and placed him on its huge back. Then, ever so majestically, it strolled to where Sumati was standing and knelt in front of her so that Kalki could slide down to the ground. The bull elephant raised its trunk in salutation to the family and the villagers gathered there, and then slowly went back to its waiting tribe.

From that moment onwards, Kalki was worshipped as a living deity by all of Sambhala.

❀

During his childhood, Kalki had three friends who perpetually remained close to him—Garga, Bhagya and Visala. Garga was quiet, studious and knowledgeable, and had a passion for astrology even at that young an age. He had memorised the names of all the stars and planets of the *nakshatra* and, much to the amusement of the others, was forever trying to divine events by consulting them. Bhagya, on the other hand, was all physical, flaunting his tiny muscle power and content to follow Kalki as his bodyguard even though one was not needed. For Bhagya, eating, sleeping and wrestling were the main treasures of life and he indulged in them to the fullest. Visala was the perfect balance between the three. Never one for expressing his views quickly or in a loose fashion, Visala always weighed the pros and cons of a situation before venturing an opinion and, even then, was cautiously circumspect. He was the true diplomat of the group.

Despite the differences in their make-up and outlook, the one thing that all three of them had in common was total and steadfast loyalty and devotion to Kalki. He was the centre of their world and the commanding influence on their lives. His every wish was to be obeyed; he had but to point a direction and it was taken. Kalki was careful though; he never bossed over them or made them feel inferior. To him, the three were like his own limbs, and he gave them the same love as he had towards his brothers.

6

The First Tryst with Evil

Kalki's days were now increasingly spent studying with his father and undertaking certain household chores. After returning from the daily rounds with his brothers—and before the afternoon study of general subjects, religious tales, Vedic hymns, literature and the likes with his father and, occasionally, with his mother—Kalki now regularly spent time on his own in meditation and inner reflection. For this, he required no assistance and his parents noticed that his time in meditation was gradually increasing.

Caught in the enthralling maya of bringing up their adorable youngest son in the routine events of life, it had been so easy for Visnuyas and Sumati to forget the divine vision of Sri Vishnu. He seemed so small and innocent to confront the evil of the world, so it was natural to hope that the vision was a dream. It hadn't been until the episode with Gajraj, the elephant bull, that Kalki exhibited any extraordinary powers that could signal him as the champion against evil.

But all this slowly changed. During his study sessions with his father, Kalki increasingly asked questions that went beyond merely the practising of religion.

'What are the Vedas? Who composed them and how?'

'What is the Gayatri mantra? Who discovered it and why is it sacred?'

'How is it that one becomes a Brahmin purely by being born as one?'

'What is the meaning of evil and how does one confront it?'

Visnuyas welcomed these questions as they revealed the openness and the slowly maturing mind of Kalki. Truthfully though, quite often, he was also at a loss to answer some of these questions:

'Father, if Devi Sita was truly Narayani, the divine consort of Sri Vishnu, how could Sri Rama, who was the avatar of the Lord, not believe her but so cruelly banish her a second time into the forest—and that too when she was with child?'

'What is the *dharmic* significance of the killing of Prince Abhimanyu in the *chakravyuh* since this did not serve any purpose in the main story? Even more significantly, how can Bhishma, Kripacharya, Dronacharya and Karna be respected after their shameful non-intervention at the disrobing of Draupadi?'

❈

Kalki and his friends were now at the age when most children went to *gurukuls* for further education. One by one, his three friends were sent off, but Kalki remained at home.

One evening, as he was sitting while resting against Sumati, Kalki suddenly said, 'Ma, why is father worried about my going to a gurukul? Even you are thinking of the same. Don't you see, I am perfectly happy to be here and learn from you. And when the time comes, Ma, my guru will come and find me here.'

Sumati promptly discussed it with Visnuyas, as much for the content of Kalki's words as the fact that he seemed to have read their minds. After much discourse and consultation within the family, it was finally decided to keep Kalki at home and to double their efforts in teaching him as per the unofficial syllabus.

❀

'Tell me, do you know what is evil?' Kalki casually posed the question as he reunited with his friends.

It had been four long years since he'd last seen them. The three friends had returned from their gurukuls for the summer holidays. In thinking and action, they remained the same, except that Bhagya had grown bigger, stronger and more rotund; Visala was even more introspect than before; Garga now wore fake rudraksh beads and sometimes referred to himself as Gargamuni. Their affection and devotion for Kalki, however, remained unchanged and had, in fact, substantially grown due to their time apart. So, it had become an everyday affair for them to meet up and talk of their experiences, escapades and their differing paths in education.

'Why do you want the answers to evil?' Visala asked.

'Well, I'm curious. What does it really portend? How does one distinguish it or recognise it, even if it is visible? I have asked these questions of my father but, being too much of a man of goodness, he does not know enough about evil.'

The friends looked at each other, but each was at a loss for words.

'Isn't it enough to know that it exists, but is far away from us? We are not touched by it, so why should we search for it?' Visala responded.

He was hoping he was right. Sambhala had been so isolated from everyday affairs of the world that it knew nothing of the rampaging forces of Kali sweeping the world outside. People had become inured to the danger and had begun to believe all was well, and that evil would somehow stay away from their little sanctuary.

How wrong they were in this forlorn belief was proved just a few days later.

❈

Kalki was, as usual, accompanying Kavi on his daily market visit one morning. Sumati was running short of cooking oil and a few condiments. It was slightly cloudy and, though the summer heat was not bearing down in its full capacity yet, the day did have portents of being sultry and humid. Being in his early teens now, Kalki helped Kavi with the load in the morning. He carried a bag of charcoal for the *chulah*.

Kalki was accustomed to the villagers stopping them, be it for casual conversation or community gossip. Women would come up to him and gently wipe his face with their *aanchal*, boys would bend to touch Kavi's feet and young girls would shyly avert their eyes but join their hands in pranam. The brothers would be offered water, milk, buttermilk, sweets of every variety, and anything else that could be produced to have them tarry a while longer. By now, Kalki knew everyone by name and treated all of them as members of his larger family. It was a pleasant way to begin the day.

As they rose to leave the village square, there suddenly came the sound of mounting rumble, loud shouts and cantering horses. To everyone's surprise, a company of twenty or so soldiers, mounted on their horses, clattered into view.

The soldiers wore fully glazed steel uniforms, with helmets on their heads and swords by their sides. Some carried lances, while others had bows and arrows. Their arms and feet were covered in chain armour, and they had huge nose strips coming down from the top of the helmets to cover much of their faces.

Eesh ... it must be uncomfortably hot under all that dense plating! That was the first thought that crossed Kalki's mind. He had never seen a soldier before and found the lot quite strange.

The mounted company came to a clanging halt in the square amid much shouting and pandemonium, dirt and dust clouds, the neighing of horses, the cackling of poultry and the barking of dogs. The column of soldiers slowly dismounted, with many wearily taking off their helmets and wiping their grimy faces with the dirty cloths they were carrying. At last, the troopers who were bringing up the rear came into view. A collective yet hushed gasp escaped the villagers. Kalki felt sick to his stomach.

The last horse was carrying a freshly killed sambar. Its head was trailing in the dust, rolling from side to side and leaving crimson splotches of blood on the ground. Its huge, lustrous eyes were now lifeless and its tongue lolled voiceless from its mouth. Kalki had often seen it gambolling in the lush forest, baying joyfully, and fearlessly coming up to him for some juicy titbit.

Kalki had not seen death before, but he knew that the animal would never frolic in the field again. It would neither trustingly rub its wet nose against his arm, nor raise its proud antlers to the sky. Kalki's whole body started trembling with a totally new and, until now, alien sensation. It inflamed him, urged him to run, scream, hit out and destroy that monstrous scene and all those responsible for it. And he would have done so, had it not been for Kavi, who held on to him with pacifying restraint.

'By what name do you call this ugly place and who is in charge of this squalor?' the leader of the soldiers—a huge, bulky, one-eyed bearded giant—demanded unpleasantly of the gathered villagers.

Kavi, who was at the head of the assembled crowd, quietly stepped forward and replied in a dignified and polite manner, 'This village is named Sambhala, sir. You and your friends are most welcome here. May we enquire how we can be of service?'

'Of course, you shall be of service!' the soldier insolently shouted. 'First of all, hasn't anyone ever taught you manners? Don't you offer guests water and refreshments when you see them? What are you standing around and gaping at? Haven't you seen soldiers before? Go immediately and fetch water and charpoys for my men. And get someone to cook for us. Can't you see that we are tired, thirsty and hungry?' Just as Kavi started to turn to address the soldier's requirements, he was rudely interrupted again.

'And while you are about it, fetch your headman. We will camp for some time in this squalid village. All necessary arrangements should be made for it.'

With these harsh words, the commander turned to his men and started barking instructions regarding their camp. Kavi, revolted but not deterred by the soldier's uncouth behaviour, asked his companions to fetch water and refreshments. He also sent for Shankaranand to deal with the unforeseen situation.

The troopers took down their saddles, weapons, blankets and equipment from the tired horses. Some scrounged their saddlebags for anything to eat. Their attention turned to the sambar. Four of the hefty troopers drew their axes and knives and, to the disgust of the villagers, started hacking and cutting the sambar and eating its flesh raw.

Meanwhile, Kavi had called Bhagya to his side and firmly told him to take Kalki away from the scene. Kalki had grudgingly allowed himself to be pulled away to the edge of the square, though his body and mind were still in a state of ferment as he had not known before. Shankaranand arrived on the scene and introduced himself to the new arrivals.

'So, you have finally shown up, eh, you dirty scoundrel, hiding in whatever filthy hole you were stuck in,' the commander growled. 'Taken your time too, while your good-for-nothing people just sit on their haunches and do nothing. We have been here all morning and no one has even bothered to offer us water. Unless something moves quickly, I shall start using the whip to make you lazy swines work. Where is the water, you scum, and where are the people to cook our supper?'

The venerable headman had never been spoken to like this before. Though deeply offended, he quietly replied, 'Sir, the water is just being pulled from the well and we are organising the people to cook for you. Your appearance at our village was sudden and we were totally unprepared for it. Believe me, however, we are never lacking in hospitality and you shall be adequately looked after. May I humbly enquire where you are from and how long do you intend to stay?'

'Fool, don't you recognise great fighters when you see them? We are the finest of the troops of Ujjaini sent to scout this wretched area to see if it can be of any use to us. So far there is nothing that marks it out as of any use … but we shall see. Perhaps you can organise some … good entertainment ... for us tonight that might persuade us to stay.'

He said this with such evil licentious intent that Shankaranand averted his gaze and pretended he was having a coughing fit. 'I will just go and see why the water hasn't arrived yet,' he said and excused himself.

Soon, a few young boys and girls came, carrying earthen pots full of water that they had pulled from the community well. They approached the area where the soldiers were lying around. Without any courtesy, the soldiers roughly plucked those pitchers from the villagers, poured the water on their sweaty heads and feet, gargled and rinsed, and then crudely spat out the water without caring where it fell.

Leelavati, Shankaranand's pretty daughter, offered drinking water to the troop commander. The huge man slowly drank the whole pitcher, all the while eyeing Leelavati's figure. When he had finished drinking, he let the vessel fall to the ground, where it shattered with a resounding thud. As a shocked Leelavati looked at the ground, the commander caught hold of her hand and started to pull her towards him, lust written all over his face. Leelavati screamed and tried to ward him off, but he was too powerful for her and lifted her up in his arms.

For a moment, the entire assembly watched this horrifying scene. As the other soldiers started to crowd around their captain, a loud and clear voice cut through the commotion:

'Put her down immediately, you craven brute! And leave this village!'

The captain guffawed as he turned around and saw the speaker was none other than Kavi. 'Yes? And who will force me to do so? You?'

Saying this, he suddenly whirled around and, using his right hand, hurled a dagger at Kavi. The knife struck Kavi on the shoulder and he fell to the ground. Leelavati, who was hauled over the commander's left shoulder, screamed at the top of her lungs. A loud wail went up from the villagers. There was complete and utter confusion for some time as the villagers ran helter-skelter to try and organise help. The soldiers increasingly added to the din and started cheering and shouting, urging their commander to let the girl fall into their grabbing hands.

Suddenly, a chilling silence descended on the raucous scene. A lone figure walked up to the fallen Kavi and gently extracted the knife from his shoulder. Putting his palm over the wound, he said a silent prayer. The wound healed instantly. He helped Kavi sit upright on the ground. Then, as Shankaranand and the others came to support Kavi, Kalki turned and faced the soldiers.

But it was a Kalki no one had seen before. His face was set in a mould as terrible as that of Shiva when confronted with the news of Sati's death. His eyes were twin orbs of fire, searing heat and destruction, and his body radiated with the fury of a thousand spectres of death, each screaming to be let loose.

He stared at the commander. Suddenly, Leelavati was freed from his grasp and left standing unharmed beside her father. As those eyes continued to stare at him, the huge bulk of the soldier started to shrink within himself, overcome with nightmarish thoughts that reached deep into his subconscious, convincing him just how inconsequentially fragile he was. Nameless dread, fear, horror and panic flooded him, and he screamed and screamed in agony and trepidation. Try as he might, he could not escape the ruthlessness of those eyes. He finally collapsed in excruciating pain, while his draining sanity ebbed away with his mortal life.

The remaining soldiers watched this horrifying spectacle in mute bewilderment, and then the eyes of Kalki turned towards them. Writhing on the ground, impaled by confusion and cold, unendurable terror, each succumbed to the same tortuous, grisly end that had been their leader's fate. Before they left their physically anguished bodies, every single one of them experienced the terrifying hopelessness of escape from mortal agony, with no reprieve either in this world or the next.

When the last of the soldiers had stopped screaming and twitching, Kalki closed his eyes for a few moments and, holding on to Bhagya's strong arm, silently departed the gathered assembly. His only comment from the edge of the square was to Shankaranand:

'Chachaji, please see that the horses are cared for, watered and fed. Then let them loose to go where they want.'

So, much sooner than he had anticipated, Kalki's first encounter with evil had come to pass.

7

Beyond Sambhala

MAHISHMATI

A summons from the king could not be ignored.

Intrigued by the account of a young boy vanquishing the Ujjaini soldiers and delivering his village from them, King Visakhayupa of Mahishmati had formally invited Kalki to present himself before the council.

The group to Mahishmati was small—Kalki, his three friends, Shankaranand, Prajna and Sumantra. One of their first acts on reaching their destination was to bathe in the holy River Narmada and offer prayers at the ancient Shiva temple at Kaleshwar. Kalki was fascinated by the giant sculpture of the winding snake and remained in meditation before the jyotirlinga for a long time. On rising, he did a parikrama of the jyotirlinga thrice, and recited the Shantipath mantra at the four cardinal points. The others watched in silence and only the brothers knew the significance of Kalki's actions. This act was a prayer to Shiva Mahadev, seeking his benevolence of peace to the four corners of the globe.

Over the next few days, the city witnessed a noticeable change. In fact, it was so evident that it was not only commented upon by the learned writers of the day, but also found mention in later Puranic writings.[1]

Before Kalki came to Mahishmati, people had not been to temples or houses of prayer and religious sites for years. Suddenly, however, they felt an irresistible urge to do so. There was also a spurt in the giving of alms, undergoing austerities and generally contributing to the well-being and care of each other. Mahishmati had always harboured a conflict-ridden society where people and groups were constantly hostile towards each other. Now social harmony and fealty to the state were found to be of greater importance, old enmities were set aside, and former feuding groups sent peace feelers to their erstwhile foes.

This wave of conciliation was especially visible at the court, where King Visakhayupa noticed how his close advisers and councillors, who were earlier divided into warring power groups, now seemed wholly submissive and engaged more towards alleviating the plight of the citizens than their own narrow parochial interests.

It was in this atmosphere of calm that the group from Sambhala came to the palace for their audience with the king. Though he was still a boy, Kalki's reputation preceded him. The whole council rose and bowed as he entered the assembly. The king, too, got down from his throne as Shankaranand introduced Kalki and the rest of them. King Visakhayupa honoured them with *angavastras* of pure Maheshwar linen before making them sit in places of distinction.

After the customary drinks and refreshments, the king requested that Shankaranand retell the encounter with the

[1] *Sri Kalki Purana,* Chapter 2, Text 33–35.

soldiers from Ujjain. As had been agreed between them, Shankaranand gave a simplified version of the incident, without dwelling too much on the decisive role Kalki had played in it. This did not satisfy the assembly that had heard grossly exaggerated versions of the episode. So, they turned to Kalki and requested him to elaborate.

There was pin-drop silence as Kalki sought a nod in permission from Prajna and rose quietly. He bowed low before the king and the councillors.

'My lords, I am still a boy, so pardon me for my callow utterances before Your Majesty and this august assembly. I have been born and brought up in the peaceful environs of Sambhala, my beloved village and home of my parents and ancestors. There is nothing great or sacrosanct about my tiny village. In fact, you in Mahishmati enjoy far greater blessings with your location and history. You have the blessed River Narmada washing your shores, the sacred Mahadev temples here and in Omkareshwar, answering your every wish, and the Kanav Ashram guarding you from harm.

'We in Sambhala had lived an isolated existence, fooling ourselves into thinking that we had escaped the tyranny, the torment, and the havoc let loose by the forces of evil elsewhere. Our recent experience has shown us how wrong we were.

'But we have also learned that evil can be defeated and that it is the holy word of God that can vanquish malevolence in its many forms. In Sambhala, all we did was to invoke the exalted name of the lord and the wicked ceased to torment us. So, my revered elders, this is all I have to say: in this vile age of Kali, glorify the name of the Almighty Hari and all troubles will end.'

Saying this, Kalki resumed his place and a silent council was left to ponder over his striking words. They appeared to be so simple to everyone and yet they bore the essence of truth.

Kalki and his group stayed in Mahishmati for a few more days. Long lines of people spontaneously queued up for his darshan, but the visitors from Sambhala left quietly for their home when this started to develop into a ritual.

SAMBHALA

Visnuyas and Sumati warmly received their sons on their return, but for Kalki, the exposure to the outside world meant considerable introspection to regain his equilibrium.

'Father,' he enquired during his afternoon study session, 'I noticed in Mahishmati that people are forever caught in the daily routine of life, in the crass material world, always chasing some want or the other, always craving the satisfaction of some desire, some longing. Is this not the breeding ground for all manner of evil? If so, how can this malady be cured?'

Kalki had, in this query, come to the gist of the moral decline inherent in the age of Kali, and Visnuyas had no clear answer for him.

'My child, all our scriptures are devoted to answering just the question that you have posed: how can man dismount from this heady chariot pulled by the wild horses of desire, greed, lust, envy, pride, anger and arrogance? If we could even control these passions, let alone conquer them, all of life's deficiencies would fade away. But this requires moral rectitude, self-discipline and adhyatmik vikas or spiritual development, all of which are sadly missing today.

'The dialogue between Sri Krishna and Arjuna on the battlefield of Kurukshetra, contained in the divine Bhagavad Gita, details the different paths leading out of the maze of life. You will find many answers to your questions there.'

PĀRBATI

The rainy season was now in its last quarter. The heavy showers during summer had left the water bodies around Sambhala overflowing, with even the little stream pretending it was a river. The farming community was looking forward to a bumper harvest and the market was filled with every variety of fruit and vegetable. The only matter of inconvenience was the sticky mud on the roads that made travel difficult and soiled even the most protected clothes.

Shankaranand and his family were just about to turn in for the night when a tired and distressed group of men, bearing shallow lanterns, came stumbling out of the darkness from Pārbati village, which was at some distance from Sambhala.

'Bhaiyya, our village has been struck with *haizza* and many of our people have been carried away by the epidemic, including our village vaid and his family,' one of the villagers pleaded. 'Almost every household is affected and we don't even have able-bodied men left to carry the dead for last rites. Mahishmati is too far to go to for assistance and we are helpless and uncared for. We have come to you seeking succour and place ourselves at your tender mercy. Please don't turn us away.'

Saying this, all those grown-up men fell to the ground and started wailing. It took some time for Shankaranand and his companions, who had by now assembled in numbers, to console them and get them to regain some composure. By now, news of this misfortune had reached Visnuyas and he, Sumati, Kavi and Prajna hurried to Shankaranand's place. The presence of the saintly couple had a calming influence over the gathering, and it was soon decided to send a few men from Sambhala to the affected village. They were instructed to carry herbs and medicines that Visnuyas was to prepare and to be ready for immediate departure.

Nobody noticed that Kalki had also arrived at the scene with Sumantra and there were loud protestations when he too prepared to leave with the rescue party.

'This is not a matter for young boys to handle. I cannot agree to you accompanying us,' the village headman stated. Sumati nodded in agreement and sought to dissuade Kalki from his resolve.

Kalki stood his ground and softly said, 'Ma, forgive me for disobeying you. You have given me birth to fight evil and this is but another sign of evil. Do not worry, this will not affect me.'

His quiet resolve precluded further discussion and, touching the feet of his parents, he set off for Pārbati with the others.

Dawn was breaking over the wet, dripping forest when the group from Sambhala reached their destination. Long before they came to it, however, the loud cries of the grief-stricken villagers reached their ears. As they entered

Pārbati, the stench of the dead and dying was overpowering. The rescue team hardly knew where to begin their formidable task.

Ultimately, it was Sumantra who personally cleared a small space in the centre of the village and organised the able-bodied men to light a log fire and boil water in whatever containers they could find. They distributed this water to the villagers. Others set about cleaning and making the sick as comfortable as they could. They also administered the medicines sent by Visnuyas. Still others went about the grisly task of collecting the dead and preparing them for their last rites.

Faced with dire necessity, people often tend to act far beyond their known capacity. That's how it was that dismal morning in Pārbati; the silent efficiency of the aid workers slowly succeeded in restoring a measure of order to the stricken situation and at least dragged it back from the chasm of hopelessness. But the ravages of the disease were still afflicting many and the medicines needed time to act, during which many more fatalities would occur.

Kalki silently went to the bank of the small Malini river running by the side of the village and, closing his eyes, meditated on Lord Shiva to give him strength. His body and countenance slowly relaxed and then, as if impelled by some inner instructions, he stood up, cupped a handful of the river water and slowly let it trickle back. He offered the water back to the river three times and on the fourth, sprinkled it in the four cardinal directions intoning the divine chant, *'Om, namo Shivay'*. He finally bent down, immersed his hands in the river and washed his face with the water. This done, he came to his brother and gently said, 'Bhai, please make all the people here—the sick as well as the healthy—drink some water from the river. They should also splash the water all over their homestead.'

Sumantra knew better than to question his younger brother. Soon everyone was going to the river's edge to take a sip of the water, give it to the sick, and scatter it over the village ground.

From that moment on, no one was reported sick or dying in Pārbati.

❈

SAMBHALA

When the team returned home, Kalki went up to his father and touched his feet.

'Father, I have never seen such suffering as I saw in Pārbati,' he said. 'Disease and death were everywhere; people had no escape and seemingly nowhere to go. There were cries of despair, loss of loved ones, and wailing in each hut. What did the villagers do to deserve such a fate?'

Visnuyas placed a hand over his youngest's head and said, 'Son, no one truly understands what the laws of karma portend or what actions are a harbinger of what results. There are many things that are not comprehensible to us or in our hands to control. Evil has many faces and can strike anywhere. All we can do is to prepare ourselves for it and have the physical, moral and spiritual strength to withstand it.'

Kalki's name had now spread far and wide. Many people came to him with some request or the other, as they did to seek his blessings. The morning aarti at the havan kund, where Kalki now assisted his father in the rituals, was the best occasion for people coming from outside to have a glimpse of Kalki, perhaps exchange a few words with him and accept the prasad he offered.

Many of the visitors were holy men, sadhus and sadhvis coming from far and near places. While Visnuyas, his brothers and his friends tried their best to shield him, it often became necessary for Kalki to escape to the sanctuary of the forest to find solitude.

❉

That is … unexpected. Who is that? Visnuyas was taken by surprise.

It was well before the sun had fully risen. Strong chants were coming from the site of the morning prayers. The whole family, who had been getting ready for the daily rituals, rushed out to see a tall, commanding ascetic sitting at the already-lit havan kund. He was reciting slokas from the holy scriptures, pouring sacred oblation into the fire and praying to the deities, oblivious to his surroundings.

Such was the power of his worship that the whole family sat down to join the mesmeric chanting and to pour ghee, incense and samagri into the havan. Visnuyas and Sumati were quite bemused to find a stranger take over their daily role, but the sheer peace the prayers evoked captivated their minds. Only Kalki, while fully absorbed in the havan puja, had a slight smile on his radiant face.

At last the prayers concluded and the holy figure opened his eyes. He first looked up towards the heaven, then down towards the earth, then to the right and left, and then did pranam to the havan *agni*. With his eyes closed again, he joined his palms and recited the sacred Gayatri mantra three times and then the Shantipath, ending with 'Om shantih, shantih, shantih'.

Silently, he rose and blessed those standing around. His gaze remained fixed on Kalki for a long time and finally, he blessed him by placing both his palms on his bowed head.

The austere muni was dressed in an ochre dhoti with a long saffron angvastara thrown over his left shoulder and draped over his upper body. He had many strings of rudraksh beads around his neck and chest, and similar beads around his wrists and upper arms. His forehead was smeared with ash and sandalwood paste, with the Shivagandh on his forehead. His long tresses were tied at the back of his head and his flowing beard was combed to fall till his waist.

His face bore wrinkles, testifying his years, but his eyes were crystal clear, wise and piercing. He carried a *kamandal* in his left hand while his right bore a golden-coloured axe or *parashu*. A faint glow surrounded his figure and as he moved on his wooden *khadaons*, it seemed as if he tread on air.

By now, many villagers had begun to gather for the morning aarti and were taken aback to see the tableaux at the havan kund. The tall ascetic raised a palm to bless them all, then gave Visnuyas a small sign. The priest immediately understood.

The family entered their hut following the saffron-clad figure, who again closed his eyes in prayer as if blessing the place. He turned around to face them. Then fixing Visnuyas with a kindly look, he said ever so simply, 'Sadho, I am he that goes by the name of Parshuram. I am the son of the sage Jamadagni and Renuka Devi and I belong to the Bhrigu dynasty.'

On hearing these words, Visnuyas and his entire family fell to the ground in reverence to do *sashtang dandavat* pranam to the famous avatar of Lord Vishnu. Parshuram was known as much for his great spirituality as the fact that he was a Chiranjeevi, watching over the world till the end of time.

'*Aayushmaan bhava*,' he said to Visnuyas and his sons, blessing them with a long life. Then, turning to Sumati, he blessed her with the time-honoured benediction, '*Param saubhagyavati bhava, Devi*.'

He continued, 'Be not afraid, as I come with greetings and great veneration in my heart. You are an exalted family that has always carried the welfare of the people in your every action. Please sit with me and hear what I have to say.'

With this, Parshuram sat on the floor. He accepted water and a few sweets from Sumati, all the while seeming to gaze into the far distance. Ever so often, however, he glanced at Kalki, who had his eyes downcast in silent meditation the entire time.

After the formalities of the morning repast, Parshuram waited till all were seated. He then began by quoting from the *Mundaka Upanishad*:

Brahmaivedam amrtam purastat brahma
Pascat brahma daksinatascottarena
Adhascordhvam ca prasrtam
Brahmaivedam visvam idam varistham

This whole manifested universe is only the immortal Brahman;
in front is Brahman, behind is Brahman, right side and left side is Brahman;
It is spread below and above;
this manifested universe is only this adorable Brahman

'Brahman, the Supreme Creator, is the essence of all existence. But to understand the nature of the *Brahmand* requires bhakti or devotion, *gyana* or knowledge, karma or right action, and above all *buddhi*, integrated intelligence and willpower.

'In this blessed household, the highest levels of yoga are manifest, the aura of which sanctifies the entire surroundings. It has been the perfect home for the incubation of true spiritual energy and the time has now come for us to take this forward.

'*Brahman* is *param dharma*, the one and only absolute reality, and it is the function of this body to perform whatever task is allotted to it by the Almighty. I have been bidden to take under my charge the person of Kalki, so that he can be instructed into becoming a fit instrument to fulfil his sacred duty.'

He continued, 'Through my yogic *shakti,* I have observed him since he was a child and I deem he is now fit to undergo further training in various disciplines. I have come to seek your permission to take him to my ashram in Mahendragiri, where he will be taught all that is required of him.'

Saying this, the great muni awaited an answer from Visnuyas. The priest, after making brief eye contact with his wife, humbly replied, '*Param Purush, param Parmeshwar*, what is there for us to say? We are eternally grateful for your presence, your grace and your decision to train Kalki. He needed a teacher at this stage of his life and to find you as his guru is his great fortune. He is truly blessed. We are forever in your debt.'

Parshuram smiled, 'It is I who am truly blessed.' Saying this, he rose to leave.

Kalki had few belongings and Sumati packed them quickly so that her son was ready to leave with Parshuram almost immediately. Kalki touched his parents' feet, then his brothers' and hugged each of them in turn. Sumati clung to him the longest. All this happened so unexpectedly that no one had any time to think. Kalki's departure was witnessed by only a handful of those who had gathered for the morning prayers.

Soon, however, word of his going spread like wildfire. The entire village seemed to descend on Visnuyas and Sumati's house to share their sense of loss at his departure. Kalki's friends were inconsolable and would have dashed after him had they only known where he had gone. Sambhala was covered in a pall of gloom and there was little that anybody could do to disperse it.

Life, however, has its own inexorable way of overcoming deprivation. Although there was always a heavy tinge of sorrow due to Kalki's absence, people began the slow process of adjusting around memories of him and all that he had meant to them. Visnuyas and Sumati were pillars of strength to the community, even though it was only they who knew what a vacuum they were now facing and how much they had to lean on their remaining sons.

In course of time, Kavi and Leelavati got married and this was a cause of celebration among the villagers. Prajna became a full-time apprentice to his father for religious rituals while Sumantra was appointed as the local guard of the forest. Garga and Visala had gone back to their gurukul for higher studies. Bhagya, however, stayed back with his family and found employment in the village by carrying and distributing foodgrains and other items.

8

Kalki's Training

When Kalki first saw Guru Parshuram's ashram at Mahendragiri, he was overcome by the sublime grandeur of the place. Situated at an elevation that competed with the clouds and hedged on three sides by bluish-green hills that faded—like undulating waves—into the distance, it appeared like an ephemeral vision of paradise created on earth. Except for the open vista to the east where, on the edge of the horizon, the blue waters of the sacred Mahendratanaya sea were visible, the ashram was encircled by majestic verdant forests, filled with every variety of wildlife. It reminded Kalki so much of his home far to the west and gave him a feeling of belonging.

There were countless species of birds, butterflies and flowers, each competing with the other to catch his eye. The glittering spectrum of colours served to overpower the senses. And yet, there was a serenity about the place that was palpable. It urged one to close one's eyes and go inwards, to find salvation in hidden inner spaces, and to escape the clutch of outer beauty for the splendour hidden within.

Kalki was flooded with intense vibrations of joy, of ecstasy he had not imagined possible, and of mounting self-confidence that strengthened his very fibre. 'Guruji,' he said, turning to Parshuram, 'is this what you have brought me here to learn? Is this what you call the divine experience?'

Parshuram took a long time before answering the question. Through his yogic insight he was fully aware of Kalki's birth and divine attributes even before his conception. He knew the purpose of the final avatar of Lord Vishnu; Kalki would ultimately destroy Kali. He had known that this would be a precursor to the end of the Kali Yuga and the dawn of a new era of grace and sanctity. But Kalki was still only dimly aware of his limitless abilities and these had to be matured gradually to their fullest potential. So, it was with a sombre look that Parshuram replied, 'No, Kalki, beauty always lies in the eyes of the beholder. It is because of the purity within you that you can feel these signals and it is, therefore, well that we begin your training in this place.

'Did you know that Sri Krishna sent Arjuna here to gain spiritual strength before the Kurukshetra war and that the Pandavas came here during their exile and built three temples in honour of Shiva Mahadev? In due course, we shall visit these hallowed shrines and you will pray there for peace and enlightenment.'

He continued, 'Tomorrow, however, we will begin your learning of the principal Vedas and Upanishads, and also the lessons to be gleaned from the historic epics of the Ramayana and the Mahabharata.'

From that day on began Kalki's in-depth learning of the sacred scriptures, religious practices as well as other branches of education such as astronomy, cosmology, physics, mathematics, literature and history. Since he had already been introduced to the basic framework of these subjects in the study sessions with his father, Kalki absorbed the knowledge with consummate ease. There were, however, several new disciplines to which he was introduced, such as martial arts, weaponry and statecraft.

Since Parshuram had been a party to many significant events of the past, Kalki took delight in hearing from him stories embedded in history, especially the ones that had some mystery associated with them. And though he could not see him, Kalki felt the vibrations of a great force nearby. It was Hanuman, who was always present at any discussion on Lord Rama.

'Guruji, why did King Dasaratha decide on Sri Rama's *rajabhishek* in such a hurry, and in the absence of Bharat and Shatrughan? Had his brothers been present, Sri Rama's exile wouldn't have happened. And what was the reason he allowed Sita maiya to accompany him on this dangerous journey?'

Parshuram had a ready answer, 'Then how would the exile have come about and the evil of Ravana destroyed? Remember, it was for this reason that Lord Vishnu had taken birth on earth and not merely to rule happily in Ayodhya.'

Hanuman silently nodded his head in agreement.

'But why did Sri Rama banish Sita maiya a second time to the dense forest, and that too when she was expecting? He could have easily sent her home to Mithila. Wasn't this totally unjust, especially since she wasn't given an opportunity to prove her innocence against a vague allegation by a dhobi?' countered Kalki.

Hanuman's moist eyes reflected his own great turmoil at this injustice.

To this Parshuram had no ready answer. Nor did he have an answer when Kalki observed:

'Guruji, if rishis are so spiritual and steadfast in control of their emotions, how does one explain the anger they express at something so trivial as a delay in meeting the king? Or threatening a curse on all of Ayodhya's citizens, as Sage Durvasa threatened Lakshmana when the latter was merely obeying his master's orders to not let anyone disturb his meeting? It was for this error that Lakshmana was ordered by his beloved brother to kill himself.'

Parshuram remained silent because he remembered that he too had unjustly cursed Karna when he learnt that the latter was a Kshatriya: 'You shall forget all the sacred chants I have taught you, including the use of the Brahmastra, when you need it the most.' It had been this curse that led to Karna's defeat and death at Arjuna's hands.

These intense discussions between the guru and his pupil would continue for days and add not only to the overall knowledge of Kalki, but also his analytical skills in dealing with issues that came up in daily life.

The most important training that Parshuram imparted to Kalki's development, however, was in the realm of the spirit. 'Brahman is the ultimate reality that has no beginning and no end. It is the supreme consciousness that is limitless, indivisible and present in all beings. Think about it, Kalki, consciousness is the one subject of which there is no plural. One may think differently from another and have many diverse thoughts even within oneself. But the one doing the thinking, the consciousness, is the same in everyone. It has no duality.[1]

[1] It was Erwin Schrödinger, the Austrian physicist, known for his work on quantum mechanics, who formulated the possibility that individual consciousness is only a manifestation of a unitary consciousness pervading the universe. The concept of consciousness can have no plural.

'Sri Krishna has said in the Bhagavad Gita:

Aham atma Gudakesa sarv bhutasya sthitah
Aham aadishcya madhyam ch bhutanam antah eva ch

I am the Self, O Gudakesa, existing in the heart of all beings;
I am the beginning, the middle, and also the end of all beings

(Srimad Bhagavad Gita, 10.20)

As Kalki digested the words, dwelling upon their meaning, Parshuram cited a mahavakya from the *Chandogya Upanishad*, marvelling at the truth contained in this sloka, not only for all humanity, but for Kalki in particular:

Sa ya eso'nima aitad atmyam idam sarvam,
Tat satyam, sa atma, tat-tvam-asi

This great but most subtle essence of all the worlds is the Truth,
the Atman, the Supreme Reality within you, and Thou art That

(*Chandogya Upanishad,* VIII, 7)

Kalki practised meditation as he'd learnt under his father's supervision. Parshuram built on that foundation, teaching him more of the intricate techniques of Rajya and Hatha yoga that he had himself learnt from his guru, Sant Dattatreya, the master yogi.

Kalki knew about the great shakti coiled at the base of his spine, the divine kundalini. With Visnuyas, he had experienced the awakening of the lower chakras and the associated spiritual benefits arising from them. Now, however, Parshuram explained each stage of the process, the breathing, and the yogic exercises necessary to enable the energy of kundalini to ascend only through the central canal of the spinal cord, the *sushumna*.

He explained that while ascending, the kundalini faced blocks in three areas—the Brahma *granthi*, Vishnu granthi, and Rudra granthi. Finally, Parshuram enabled Kalki to handle the superconsciousness inherent in raising the kundalini to the highest chakras, and explained that this was not an end in itself, but a tool that could be used to attain enhanced spiritual awareness.

❁

As a part of his practical training, Parshuram took Kalki on a journey through Madhyadesh to acquaint him with some of Kali's ravages. 'You have personally seen the arrogance of unrestrained armed force and the horror of disease, and have used some of your inherent shakti in countering those pernicious threats,' Parshuram had said. 'Now I want you to witness other forms of the malevolence of evil so that you can see how it engulfs the whole land.'

Kalki travelled to the worst scenes of war in Magadha, Kasi and Vatsa, and saw for himself how man had descended to his most callous nature. Parshuram brought him face to face with people forced into slavery, women sold for prostitution, children orphaned and maimed, and the land plagued with famine, pestilence and disease. There was no remnant of any good, any civilised behaviour. Instead, from every corner there rose the cry of suffering and the unanswered pleas for assistance.

Kalki returned to the ashram in a complete daze, not fully comprehending or accepting what he had just seen. In a voice trembling with anguish, he pleaded, 'Guruji, is this really the world that we are living in? It is so far removed from the idyll of Sambhala that my mind refuses to believe it. Is there really such little spirituality left outside? Are the forces of Kali so extensive and powerful? Surely there must be some solution to this all-pervading horror?'

Parshuram thought for a long time before he answered, 'Yes, Kalki, there is a solution to the end of Kali, but the time for that has not come yet. I know that what you have witnessed today fills you with loathing and distress. You cannot accept that evil can wreak so much havoc, so much trauma. That is largely because of your own inner purity and compassion. You do not know the meaning of avarice, pride, jealousy, hatred or greed. These are common human frailties, sometimes more compounded than others. And, as is the case of all weaknesses, they have their ups and downs.

'We are certainly living in times of great evil, but I assure you this is just the beginning. In the theory of the yugas that I taught you, remember that Kali started its depredations only recently with the passing of Lord Krishna. It is still confined only to a few places and has not yet covered the globe. You will yourself witness its progression in the future and determine how it will meet its end. You may not know it now, but one day *you* will confront all that is evil in Kali. It was for that reason that you, Kalki, have taken birth. And it is for that reason that you should equip yourself to fight it.

'So now, calm yourself and meditate on the great Lord Shiva, the Mahadev, for it is he who is the ultimate master of time. It is he who shall be your guide on the conquest of evil.'

There were three temples devoted to Lord Shiva at Mahendragiri. They were named after the Pandavas and their mother Kunti who had come here during their period of exile. The Kunti temple was at one end of the hilltop, the one built by Yudhishtra at the other, with the Bhīma temple to the side. Scattered in between were uncut stone structures around a black Shiva jyotirlinga; this was where the great warrior Arjuna offered prayers before he went into battle.

This was also the site where Kalki liked best to meditate after offering puja at all the other sites. Parshuram would watch from a distance as Kalki sat down to meditate and often discerned a whitish-blue glow radiating from his student's body when he was in deep *samadhi*. When the samadhi began to last a few days, Parshuram realised that Kalki's training was coming to an end.

❈

The day arrived. Parshuram announced that Kalki's tutelage was over. Even though he was looking forward to going back home and being with his family once again, Kalki was sad to depart from Mahendragiri. He had learnt so much here and its beauty had become such an integral part of him. He went to the Shiva temples for the last time and thanked the deities for the knowledge bestowed on him.

Then, coming back to the ashram, Kalki touched his guru's feet and said, 'Divine Guru! You have filled my mind and soul with the glory of your instructions. You have curbed the unchecked desires of my mind and channelled them into the fruitful service of the lord. You have picked up a rough, uncut stone and polished it to reflect your own wisdom and grace. You have even shown me the face of my greatest enemy who I must eventually overcome.

'Though it sounds pathetic coming from my mouth—and I don't have anything that could come anywhere close to satisfying you—please tell me what kind of *dakshina* I could offer so that you will be content and I will be able to claim to have been your devout pupil.'

Parshuram was uncharacteristically overcome with emotion and found it difficult to speak.

'Arise Kalki, for it does not behove you to bow before any person—even if that person is your guru.' Kalki followed his guru's instruction, but kept his head bowed respectfully.

'Today, I shall add the last item to the trove of your knowledge so that you may rejoice in it and make this divine *srishti* safe for mankind,' Parshuram continued. 'Long ago, at the behest of humanity, Brahma prayed to Vishnu—the shelter of all living beings and the supreme personality of godhead—to demolish the sinister advance of Kali that you have yourself observed. The Supreme Creator promised to incarnate on earth to destroy the malignancy.

'Kalki, the time is rapidly approaching when this yuga must end and a new yuga be established on the principles of *Sanatan Dharma*. You are the instrument in this task and this you will accomplish after further instructions from the great lord of creation, Lord Shiva, himself. For me, it is enough to know that you will successfully fulfil this duty and so there is no need for any other dakshina.'

9

Call of the Mahadev

SAMBHALA

Kalki quietly returned home one morning after Parshuram left him at the edge of the forest. The parting between the teacher and his disciple had been silent and dignified, though filled with emotion. Kalki bent to touch his guru's feet three times and, with the time-honored blessing of *'Aayushmaan bhava'* ringing in his ears, turned to wend his way to Sambhala.

Visnuyas and Sumati's joy knew no bounds on Kalki's return. The celebrations of the entire village were loud and prolonged on seeing their favourite son back home. Bhagya left his trading business for a few days—and would have cheerfully abandoned it forever—until Kalki firmly told him to not ignore his filial duties and to get on with his life. Kavi and Leelavati welcomed him to their new home and the entire family gathered there in the evening to listen to details of Kalki's stay at Mahendragiri.

As the initial excitement ebbed and life returned to normal, Kalki spent most of his time at home with his parents and Prajna. It was evident to everyone who came in contact with him that Kalki had changed from the innocent boy who had left with Parshuram. He was now a serene, young man with a piercingly steady gaze and a personality of enormous power. Kalki had always possessed an indefinable inner energy even earlier; now, however, the restrained power that emanated from him infused his very surroundings and beyond.

He was more withdrawn than before and actively sought solitude and silent introspection. This, unfortunately, was not forthcoming in the house of the priestly couple to whom the villagers always turned to for advice, counsel or conducting religious ceremonies. Barely a month after his return, Kalki spoke to his parents about what had been troubling him lately.

'Pitaji, Ma, I need some help and guidance from you. Since my return, I have been overwhelmed by the love and warmth of the entire village. I am blessed by their attention and am grateful for it. It is a natural outpouring of their affection for me, but also for the high regard in which they have always held you. However, I need some seclusion and peace and I know I can never have that as long as I stay here in Sambhala. Is it possible for me to seek a form of *sanyas*—perhaps in the jungle nearby—so that I can continue the spiritual practices which are necessary for the goals I have to achieve?'

Understandably, Visnuyas and Sumati were a bit pained by this request. It was some time before the priest, after whispered consultations with Sumati, could answer:

'Kalki, my son, it is but yesterday that you returned to us after your long period of training. We have felt your absence every moment that you were away and the thought of your leaving again so soon leaves us …' Visnuyas fought back the tears that were welling up.

'We are old now and it is difficult to bear separation from you. Your request, however, has reminded us of a singular event that occurred in the past, which we've never shared before with anyone. It was the night before your namkaran when your mother and I were suddenly awakened by a blinding vision of Lord Vishnu himself. He told us that, in order to destroy Kali, he had been born in this yuga as you, our son, and that we should name you Kalki.

'All these years we have raised you with love and care, and have seen you grow as a fond and devoted son. We have also noticed the power that is inherent in you and that has manifested from time to time. We have seen you being blessed at times by the great rishis, munis and divine personages and were not surprised, therefore, when the avesha avatar Parshuram himself took you under his wing.

'We have known from the start that you have a divine mission and have dwelled apprehensively on the day when you must leave us to go accomplish it. So, dear son, feel free to do what you must. Stride towards your supreme destiny with the knowledge that your father and your mother will always be with you and bless you for what you are.'

Kalki embraced his parents in a lingering hug, acknowledging the great sacrifice they were making. That night, the three sat together and talked for a long time of many things—Kalki's childhood, his daily excursions into the forest with his brothers, his encounter with the herd of elephants and so much more.

There is no time as precious as that which you know is going to be the last, and no memory more poignant than the final moments of separation.

At dawn, Kalki attired himself as a sanyasi in pure white robes that his mother had given him. After bidding farewell to his family, he set off with Sumantra into the sylvan glades bordering Sambhala.

The forest welcomed him with open arms and offered so many distractions that it was late in the afternoon when Kalki and Sumantra came to the caves that they used to visit on Shivratri. The cool, shady caverns were just behind a rocky clearing near the top of a hill. Surrounded on all sides by wavy escarpments, the hollows were hidden from the passing trekkers and yet not inaccessible. The ground in front was covered with flowering trees and shrubs and there was a tiny stream running through, carrying spring water from the hillside through the caves. Teak, sal, shisham and bamboo trees nearby provided plenty of shade and material to construct a dwelling.

Sumantra stayed with his brother for a few days to build a bamboo and mud hut at the entrance of the largest cave, a chulah for cooking, and storage space for food items. Together, they deepened the water channel to make water easily available. Then, after seeing him relatively settled, Sumantra departed, leaving Kalki to the silence he craved.

❖

For many days, Kalki revelled in the deep mystique of silence. He saw early dawn with rapt attention—the perennial drama of the emerging glimmer of light overcoming the envelope of dark and, in the process, snuffing out the protesting veil of stars. He exulted in the deep indigo of the early morning sky and the countless colours revealed by the rising sun. He marvelled at the shades of greens and browns of the awakening jungle that somehow reflected the flame in his own heart. He enjoyed the medley of the forest—the cry of the peacock, the rising notes of the koel, the soft cooing of the dove, the gentle warbling of the brook, and the light breeze rustling in the trees.

Finally, Kalki shut out this embracing outer beauty and, seeking the blessings of his guru, concentrated on what he should do going forward. Gradually, an inner voice guided him. He made a jyotirlinga from clay and set it on top of a little mound. He sanctified it with a vermilion and sandalwood paste tika, decorated it with flowers and *belpatra*, and offered fruits as prasad. Facing the north and Mount Kailash, Kalki prayed to Lord Shiva:

Gaurinatham visvanatham saranayım bhutavasam
Vasuki kanthabhusam tiryaksam
Pancasyddi devam puranam
Vande sandrananda sandohadaksam

Lord Sankara, you are the oldest of all, the husband of Gauri, the lord of the universe, the only protector of the living entities, and the shelter of everyone. Your neck is decorated with the serpent, Vasuki, you have three eyes and five heads, you are always absorbed in transcendental ecstasy, and you award liberation to your devotees. I offer my obeisance unto you.

(*Sri Kalki Purana*, Chapter 3, Text 14)

Yogadhisam kamanasam karalam
Ganga sangaklinna murddha namisam jatajutato
Pariksipta bhavan mahakalam
Candrabhalam namami

You are the lord of mystic yoga and the destroyer of lusty desires. Your form is fearful to behold, your head is always wet with the water of the Ganges, the matted hair on your head looks most enchanting, your forehead is decorated with a mark of the half moon, and you are the personification of Mahakal. I offer my obeisance unto you.

(*Sri Kalki Purana*, Chapter 3, Text 15)

Sthitau visnuh sara ajisnuh suratma lokan sadhun
Dharmasetun vibharsi
Brahmadyase yo'bhimani
Gunatma savdad yangaistam paresam bhajami

I worship Lord Shiva, the protector of the universe and the super soul of all living entities. He is always victorious, being a qualitative incarnation of Lord Vishnu, and he delivers saintly persons by protecting the principles of religion. He is the personification of transcendental sound, a reservoir of divine qualities, and the possessor of great intelligence.

(*Sri Kalki Purana*, Chapter 3, Text 16)

Yasyajnaya vayavo vanti
Loke jvalatyagnih savita yati
Tapyan sitamsuh khe tarakaih sagrahaisca
Pravarttate tam paresam prapadye

By your order the wind blows, fire burns, the sun distributes heat and light, and the moon, planets and stars illuminate the sky. I offer my obeisance unto you.

(*Sri Kalki Purana*, Chapter 3, Text 19)

Yasyasvasat sarvadhatri dharitri
Devo varsat yambu kalah pramata
Merurmadhye bhuvanananca bhartta tamisanam
Visvarupam namami

> By your order, the earth sustains all moving and non-moving entities, Indra showers rain, the time factor divides the duties of everyone, and Mount Sumeru—which is the shelter of the universe—remains fixed at the centre. I offer my humble obeisance to the universal form of Lord Shiva.
>
> (*Sri Kalki Purana*, Chapter 3, Text 20)

Kalki got so absorbed in his prayers to Shiva Mahadev that he forgot all links to the present, to the material world. His whole being was filled with devotion to the Tripurantakaya, the Kalagnirudraya, the Neelakanthaya, the Mrityunjayaya, the Sadashivaya, the one and only Sriman Mahadevaaya. His existence reverberated with the beatific epithets of Shiva he'd learnt from his guru. His single focus was to lose himself in the overpowering ecstasy of those chants.

Chanting is a way of calming the mind and directing the flow of cognitive energy towards the search of the Atman within. For Kalki, nothing else mattered now. He had to seek Mahadev in order to find himself. No one else could do this task—no guru, no parent, no scripture, no ritual, no earthly guide. He was in a space all by himself. Day and night faded; heat and cold disappeared; hunger and thirst dissipated; his body itself ceased to have meaning. He lost all track of time, immersed only in the fiery yearning to merge with *shivashakti*.

How long this continued he did not know; it could have been days, months or years. Suddenly, a blinding light engulfed him; it eliminated all other actuality and appeared to cocoon him completely within its silky grasp. All sound ceased—even the rhythmic chanting he had generated—and in its place was a peace so intense that it forced out anything remotely discordant. It was difficult to describe this sensation, where even the faintest tinge of perception failed to impact the imagination.

Gradually, awareness returned with a pleasant whiff of flowery incense and the faraway tinkling of soft bells. Kalki absorbed all these distant impressions while slowly opening his eyes. Before him, shimmering in a lustrous bluish-white halo, appeared the great Lord Shiva, the object of his prayers.

The boundless Lord of the Tandava had his divine consort Parvati by his side. Kalki could just make out the adorned attributes of Shiva—the serpent around his neck, the crescent moon on his forehead, the Ganga flowing from his hair, the *trishula* as his weapon, and the *damaru* in his hand.

Kalki assimilated the profound radiance coming from the ethereal vision and could feel a brief pulse of the power passing to himself. For what seemed an eternity, he was in this samadhi till he felt Lord Shiva gently caress his whole body and a wordless whisper echoed in his mind:

'Oh, foremost of beings, dear Kalki, you are forever blessed. Now, as the master of *pralaya*, it is my role to guide you further on your divine task.'

Ever so imperceptibly, the blinding radiance faded and Kalki was again left to the solitude of his surroundings.

The vision had been so powerful that its effect lasted for more than a few days. Kalki felt as if he was awakening from a long, languorous but fulfilling dream. Whenever he closed his eyes, he could still see the glowing form of Mahadev and the gentle smile on the face of the Divine Mother.

His mind, however, had now opened so that he could see beyond his physical reality. He could feel the purity, the overflowing joy and enormous power flowing in himself.

He sensed that he could read nature itself and that he was one with all its creation. Kalki had no need for anything material and, through his enhanced *siddhic* powers, he could clearly discern the road ahead.

So, when Sumantra came by the next time to enquire about his welfare, Kalki warmly embraced him and spoke lovingly to him, 'Dear brother, I will always cherish the great love my parents, you and my other brothers have given me. You are the symbols of all that is good and pure in this earthly life and I have been singularly blessed to have been born in this joyous and happy family.

'But the time has now come when I must leave all these trappings of love and perform the duty that had been enjoined on me since birth. You shall not see me again in this physical realm, but remember I am always near you and shall continue to shower love on you. Please do not worry about my welfare as the great Lord of Creation himself will take care of me.

'There's one more task that I must entrust you with. An old and trusted messenger of King Brhadratha of Simdvipa will shortly come to our village, bearing the wishes of that noble king to marry his younger daughter, Malini, into our family. It is my request that you perform this task and so fulfil the message in our Purana that the alliance with Simdvipa comes about. This will give our entire village much to rejoice about.

'Finally, do try and console all in our family at this parting, especially our loving parents.'

Sumantra heard these words but had no ready response. He could sense the finality in Kalki's words. He could also feel the tremendous energy surging in his younger brother and knew that the time to finally part had arrived.

Kalki bent to touch his brother's feet. Sumantra felt a jolt from Kalki's touch that carried a message of love, bonding and protection. He embraced Kalki and was thrown into an indefinable ecstasy as if it was Lakshmana himself embracing the figure of Lord Rama. With tears running down his face, he turned to walk back to Sambhala.

10

At the Feet of Mahadev

With the termination of his last mortal connection to earthly soil, Kalki again sought the sanctuary of Lord Shiva. No sooner had his thoughts dwelt on the subject that he found himself transported to a snowy realm that he immediately recognised as the abode of Mahadev, Mount Kailash.

It was a place so ethereal, so blessed, so calm, that no human sensibility could even begin to assimilate its gossamer reality. Physical attributes could not define it, for nature is perceptible and limiting. This was a site beyond comprehension, beyond understanding. It was a microcosm of creation itself, a place with no beginning and no end, an eternal sanctum of all that was pure, sacred and divine.

The only sound issuing from it, surrounding it, reflecting it, was the cosmic pranav, Aum, that resonated in the subconscience and then flowed away into the distance. It dawned on Kalki that this was the vibration responsible for all creation everywhere, and he bowed his head in deep reverence to it.

On opening his eyes, Lord Shiva and Parvati were seated before him in a relaxed *padmasana*. Lord Shiva's adornments shimmered and his frame, though delicate, radiated an aura that engulfed everything around him. His third eye was closed and a half smile dominated his strong yet sensitive visage. Along with Parvati, he appeared as a physical and powerful apparition, yet Kalki knew that this form in front of him—this Shiva-Shakti—was at the heart of cosmic creation. It was the ultimate reality, the consciousness, and the peace—*sat*, *chit*, *ananda*—in all existence.

Kalki prostrated himself before the deities and recited mantras extolling the virtues of Kaal Bhairav. Lord Shiva smiled and whispered to Parvati, 'See how the great Lord showers his blessings on us.' Kalki felt Mahadev's hands gently raising him. As the tenth avatar of Vishnu sat up, he heard Lord Shiva's deep voice echo in his mind, though words did not escape his lips, 'Dear Kalki, in this grand, ever-changing cosmic design, we are each required to play our destined role. You are only now gradually awakening to your own true identity and I am to be your guide in whatever it is that you seek.

'What is called the Brahmand or the cosmic egg has an immense canvas in time and space, extending from the instant when the first atom of primordial matter came into being to the precise moment when it will cease to be. From the first spark of light to the pervading dark of eternity is a reality about the cosmos that everyone needs to accept.'

Kalki folded his hands and asked, 'Lord, is all this perceived reality then temporary and subject to decay? Isn't there anything in this universe that is permanent, something for people to hold on to, like gods and goddesses, or even heaven or hell?'

Mahadev gently shook his head. 'Kalki, even at the instant of formation, all matter carries within it the seeds of its destruction. Everything that is manifest—gods, deities, avatars, kingdoms, why, even the cosmos itself—is subject to decay and death. The handful of exceptions are the Chiranjeevis who are the *sutradhars* between the ages. For everything else, existence is a fleeting aberration, enveloped in vivid colours while it lasts, but an illusion nevertheless. It flashes momentarily and soon dissipates.

'To pierce this veil of illusion and observe the different faces of reality, Kalki, you have to transcend the three divisions of Time—the past, present and future. It has been prescribed that time is a progression of existence, that it occurs in apparently irreversible succession from the past through the present to the future. For you, however, there will be no distinction. You can enter any dimension and observe it at will. So, look into the future, Kalki, and see how the present Kali Yuga is progressing.'

Then, as if as an afterthought, Mahadev added,

> 'You will be accompanied on this journey with one of your oldest devotees, your own *saktyavesa* avatar, the sage Narada Muni. He has the boon of knowledge. Narada happens to be wherever Lord Hari manifests himself. He will be your natural guide and companion.'

With this direction from Mahadev, the image of Shiva-Shakti gradually faded. Instead, chanting 'Narayan, Narayan', a young-looking yogi appeared. He wore ochre robes of a wandering monk and carried in his hands a *khartal* and tanpura. Falling at Kalki's feet, he performed a full shashtang pranam. 'Lord, blessed am I, Narada, on seeing you in your divine avatar as Kalki. Blessed am I to be your travelling companion into the three portals of time. If it be your wish, shall we begin?'

By now Kalki was getting used to the wishes of Lord Shiva. Nodding imperceptibly to Narada, he turned his mind's eye to the visions that would decide the fate of many.

11

The Portals of Time

Kalki found himself in a scene he had seen before. Rampaging hordes of soldiers and armies were still engaged in the game of victory and defeat, conquest and expansion. He saw kingdoms coming and going; states rising and falling; civilisations and societies writing themselves into history.

The pattern never varied. Faced with a stimulating challenge—either internal or external—a group of people would be roused out of inertia to give a suitable retort. The force of this response would carry them far beyond the confines of the original provocation. A golden age of peace and plenty would follow this expansion, producing creative works from the minds and hearts of man. Unfortunately, this period would also breed sloth, vice, physical and moral corruption, intrigue and infighting, and the whole grand edifice would collapse on itself.

He saw Magadha, virile with the energy of unsophisticated power, rise in all its glory and, at its peak, cover most of Madhyadesh. He saw the *Solasa Mahajanapada*, or the sixteen great republics, rise to dominance and then slowly fade.

In this prevailing gloom, Kalki felt a sudden sense of elation. 'Look, look Narada, see the shining light of an earlier avatar of Vishnu!'

Siddhartha emerged from his princely background in the foothills of the Himalayas and, leaving Kapilavastu, went on to attain enlightenment on the banks of the River Neranjana through intense self-discipline and meditation. The Buddha arose to become a living legend in the whole of Madhyadesh.

Narada said, 'Just as you will, Master, the Buddha preached right action and *dhyana* as the path to liberation from *samsara*, the endless cycle of rebirth, suffering and dying. For him, *nirvana* or *moksha* meant control over the force of ignorance that keeps the cycle of suffering and rebirth going. His teachings left a lasting impact not only on the land of his birth, but also on many countries to the east, south-east and south of Bharatvarsha.'

Kalki replied, 'A river appears parched, desolate and empty when it is the peak of summer, when the sun is swelteringly hot and moisture has been reduced to a trickle. Come the monsoon showers, however, it breaks its banks, overflows its floodplain and sends water cascading in every direction. So it is with a messenger of God. Often the stark simplicity of the person masks the unadulterated power within, the abiding impact of which is felt over years in ever widening circles.'

Narada nodded his agreement. 'Master, look also at what is happening beyond the pale of Bharatvarsha.'

Kalki looked on the far side of the country and discerned the gradual awakening of religion and philosophy to the west of Bharatvarsha, to the very borders where the golden age of Egypt was now coming to a close. There was ferment in the Persian Empire, where a new creed of Zoroastrianism was gaining ground. The Jews, after their Babylonian captivity, had found increased faith in Jehovah. More significantly, the city-states of Greece were experimenting with enervating tidings of their great thinkers, seeking to raise their people above mere sensory pleasures to a more spiritually elevated life.

Narada drew Kalki's attention to another event that was taking place––the first great wave of foreign conquerors coming to Bharatvarsha through the mountain passes of the Hindu Kush. Alexander was like a hurricane that, fortunately perhaps, never really broke over the land as debilitating exhaustion drove him to his death in Babylon. But the way had been charted out, and although this was still very much in the future, the conquest of the land of Sanatan Dharma had clearly been cast in the decrepit mould of history.

'Wherever I look, Narada, I see the evil of Kali spreading its tentacles over the tenuous relations of man. We have seen how the Roman Empire conquered half the world but destroyed itself in a gluttony of mindless violence and sensual orgy. It seems that reckless grasping of evanescent power is all that matters to anyone and there is nothing else besides.'

'No, Swami!' Narada exclaimed. 'Even in the midst of evil, the wheel of dharma exerts itself. Look at the Roman Empire. With all its shortcomings, it still harbours an event that will forever change the face of religion in the world.'

In a far-off province of the empire, a figure arose preaching love, brotherhood and compassion as a bulwark against the mounting evils of Kali. In all probability, he was influenced by Upanishadic thinking, for he claimed that:

> *... Believe me that I am in the Father (in heaven) and the Father is in me ... You will know that I am in my Father, and you in me and I in you.*
>
> (The Bible, John, Chapter X1V, 11/20s)

Kalki was moved but despaired that his profound words would be lost on the archaic and conservative thinking of his followers, leave alone the throng of disbelievers. Unfortunately, that's how it turned out to be. The incisive ministry of Jesus was for a mere three years, tragically cut short by his cruel crucifixion at the hands of the very evil he sought to overcome. Over time, his message was heard around the world and three-quarters of those living would become his adherents, though regrettably, not in the manner he wanted.

Coincidentally, the advance and rapid proliferation of Christianity was soon followed by another massive religious convulsion arising in roughly the same area of the Middle East. Six centuries after Christ, an acclaimed Prophet of God would lay the foundation for a new religion that would also extend around the globe. Kalki warmed at the words of Muhammad, inspiring people to elevate themselves through prayer, believe in the divinity of the Almighty, pray for forgiveness of sins, assist the needy, the poor and the weak, and reject all base forms of evil.

'How ironic,' said Kalki to Narada, 'that the followers of Kali will misuse the words of these mighty prophets to perpetrate the very evil that they had warned against! Do you not see that the power of religion has been used to subvert, prosecute, proselytise, maim and destroy the very foundations on which the embryonic faiths had been constructed?'

For a long time Kalki and Narada pondered over the relationship between religion and evil, and then decided to seek the advice of Mahadev.

❃

Even though they appeared detached, Mahadev and the Mother Goddess knew the questions running through Kalki's mind. With Narada by his side, Kalki allowed the pervasive sanctity of Mount Kailash to embrace him. Finally, he posed his questions in his subconscious:

'Blessed Lord, isn't religion the fundamental key through which we can overcome Kali's influence? Isn't religion alone that can provide a strong moral and spiritual base for the fight against the ungodly? Yet I find that it is religion that is being used to suppress virtue and righteousness and perpetuate all that is wicked, unholy and ignoble. Even the actions and words of the mighty prophets have failed to discourage the spread of malevolence. Is Kali more powerful than the great prophets of the lord? If so, how can it then be defeated by individual acts of saintly behaviour, prayer, rectitude or finally, even the use of conflicting force?'

The answer echoed softly in his mind: 'Religion is only an instrument of pervasive faith that binds communities in a common cause. It is the people who define religion and it is they that mould religion either towards doing good or for perpetuating malevolence. Religion, without bigotry driving it, can sometimes produce the loftiest result. Lord Kalki, with his artistic temperament, Narada will show you how the emotions released by religion also saw expression in the most sublime outflow of art, music, poetry and architecture.'

Kalki was taken aback by Mahadev's use of the prefix 'Lord' with his name. But the Lord of Knowledge had spoken and Kalki followed Narada back to a world emerging from the Dark Ages to the dawn of the Renaissance when man temporarily cast aside his base nature to let his spirit rise high above him. This saw fulfilment in the rapturous expressions of the Italian masters through painting, sculpture, architecture and design. There came the spiralling music of the European composers, the soul-searching fervour of the romantic poets and the soaring designs of churches, temples and mosques built as houses of prayer. Kalki was moved by the experience and said, 'Yes, Narada, this is truly the antithesis of evil: the human spirit striving in search of the Creator.'

Narada looked ruefully at Kalki. 'But watch, Maharaj, the dark nemesis that soon follows, all because of man's insatiable avarice for loot and plunder. That same human spirit that you talk of uses learning and science, not for adhyatmik vikas or self-elevation, but to create improved engines of war and destruction. Ships, gunpowder, armaments and cannon become the new weapons of conquest.'

Alerted thus by his companion, Kalki saw waves of 'pilgrims' arrive at a new continent in the West. They established colonies in South America, Africa, Australia and Asia with all the brutality and show of arrogant force that was now so characteristic of the breed. People were bludgeoned into submission, their sedentary lifestyles destroyed, their territories forcefully occupied and their freedoms extinguished. Slavery, torture and murder were the means used to justify the supremacy of the colonists and in many, if not most cases, religion was the diaphanous cover given to the expropriation.

The untold wealth carted away from the far-off settlements—in terms of gold, jewellery, priceless antiques, cotton, silk, spices and so much more—was in itself enough to enrich the voracious plunderer. But more horror was in store. The pillagers carted away whole villages and the populated countryside for purpose of slavery in the former's homeland. This was an abhorrent custom, the ripple effects of which were to last for generations, and convulse the social fabric of the host nation right to the present.

Clearly moved by these development, Narada plaintively muttered, 'Narayan, Narayan! Will man never outgrow his base nature? Master, just look at those slave ships. Tier upon tier of human cargo, men, women and children stuffed together in claustrophobic confinement, crying for food and water and aching for the fresh air and green fields of their homeland. Unknown numbers died of starvation and disease, but they at least escaped a lifetime of torture in the homes of the slavers.' Kalki had no answer save mute acceptance that slavery was surely the final assault on human dignity and the free spirit.

This was not all, though. The evil of colonialism also destroyed the economies of the colonised. It effectively drowned their aspiration for a better life and curbed their spirit for freedom. Kalki noticed how the so-called 'jewels of the empires' were left to forage and wallow in unspeakable poverty, how they were subject to recurring bouts of famine and disease, and how all this was paraded under the garb of propelling the destitute into the undefined spectre of progress. Meanwhile, the colonisers flourished! They had the wealth and investible capital to accelerate their advance and invent new machines and technology to create further riches. Narada commented that this burgeoning process was labelled the 'industrial revolution'. It swept the West as well as its satellites in the Far East. Wealth generated wealth in ever widening circles but, instead of leading to spiritual growth, it spiralled into a vortex from which only destruction emerged.

At first, the multitude of goods and services produced found forced markets in the colonies. In due course of time, when these reached inevitable saturation, the machines of production turned to the one merchandise that had an ever-elastic demand: armaments. Great factories were set up to churn out ships, submarines, tanks, armoured vehicles, artillery and arms of every variety and sçope. Narada drew Kalki's attention to the fact that in the bid to ensure recurring demand for these arms, more rebellions, wars, unrest and bloodshed were fomented, even encouraged! The manufacturers actively supplied their toxic wares, more often than not, to both parties in a conflict.

'Swami, observe also how the technology has been refined for remoulding the killing apparatus,' Narada pointed out. Kalki was surprised at the rapid changes in the quality and variety of the weapons produced. Swords, bows and arrows, spears or javelins, mail chains and hatchets were now relics of the past, as were elephants, horse-drawn chariots or the once invincible cavalry. The invention of cartridges and rifles saw the end of flint lock and muzzle-loading guns. Soon, repeater rifles, machine guns, long-distance artillery, and armoured vehicles eliminated all else from the dictionary of slaughter.

Narada tried to prepare Kalki for the chapters of conflict. 'Master, what you have seen so far is a world cloaking itself for the sinews of war. It is a world where the old is making way for the new. Conflict is inevitable as a new world emerges from the fragments of the old.' The expansion of empires and the search for new ones inevitably led to confrontation between the colonial powers. Newly industrialised countries saw their need for markets and areas of influence thwarted by the established colonisers. Flashpoints occurred with regular consistency. History is never kind or accommodating to the old and archaic, no matter what their past may have glorified. This was as true for the Bourbons of France, the Hapsburgs of Austria-Hungary, the Romanovs of Russia, as for the Ottomans, the Mughals or the Qing of China. In all cases, the vacuum caused by their collapse led to renewed jostling for power that signified instability and strife.

It was now apparent to the observers that endemic turmoil was the inevitable fate of this aggressive breed of man, but even Kalki was surprised at the scale of hostility that ensued shortly. Sparked off by a random act of assassination in Sarajevo in the Balkans, it caused a conflagration engulfing the entire world, as nation after nation got sucked into a whirlpool of their own making. Shorn of any justifiable facade, it was but a naked struggle of power between two blocs determined to show off their might. The fighting continued for five long years and accounted for over eighteen million dead and twenty-three million wounded, making it the deadliest conflict in human history. 'Surely now, mankind has learnt a lesson!' Kalki dared to hope. 'Surely now, it will turn away from the horror of war and turn to a life of spiritual discipline.'

But this was not to be. Instead, a greater calamity ensued.

In many ways, the Second World War was even more traumatic than the last, for it featured a German war machine forged on a ruthless Nazi doctrine of racial supremacy and outright genocide. Millions were slaughtered in the cleansing process; millions more were to suffer the wreckage of their homes and lives. The most efficient weapons were introduced to decimate the opposing forces and the factories of death were worked to capacity to wreak havoc and desolation.

For the first time, Kalki saw man use flying machines equipped as merchants of death. Bombs rained down from the heavens; battles were fought in the blue of the skies; pilots shot down each other for fame and valour. Not satisfied with carrying death by air, man plunged the oceans in iron-clad submarines to blow up ships and sailors; he used landmines to maim and cripple; he ploughed the earth in monstrous tanks, and even experimented with rockets to deliver bombs to exterminate the enemy.

And then, in an act of unspeakable horror, he exploded two nuclear devices on a civilian population. It caused an annihilation never before seen in human history. Both Kalki and Narada were shaken to the core. 'Narayan, Narayan!' cried Narada. '*Parmanu shakti* was a secret of the gods. They guarded it with utmost zeal. It was like the Brahmastra designed to raze every structure and decimate any living being for hundreds of miles around, causing lasting damage and lifelong suffering to those not instantly killed.'

Kalki was filled with feelings of repugnance and loathing at how low man had stooped. *Surely this has to be the final act of Kali! This is the very pinnacle of evil.*

12

The Awakening

Kalki's conviction had multiplied manifold. The evil of Kali had reached its peak and had to be ended before it could wreak any further damage. The earth could not be made to suffer more; how many more inequities could it bear?

Kalki roused himself and looked again towards his celestial mentor, Shiva Pashupatinath. 'Mahadev, as directed by you, I have travelled with Narada Muni into the future. I have witnessed momentous events and seen discoveries and inventions that have transformed the destiny of man. I have also seen the evil of Kali grow and develop as a monstrous stain upon the face of *prithvi,* spreading its tentacles into almost every home, and corrupting the minds of man so that all that is left is death and desolation.

'Divine Shakti, isn't it time for this gross abomination to be destroyed? Isn't this an occasion when man's mind should be made to return to the path of goodness and attain mukti from evil? If it is your wish, please grant me permission to end this vile monstrosity now and forever.' So saying, Kalki joined his palms in humble submission and bowed low before Shiva-Shakti.

The radiantly exquisite Mahadev and Devi Parvati fleetingly smiled at each other. This time, the Mother Goddess's thoughts came pulsating through: 'Divine Kalki, your journey in the current *manvantara* was as much to discover your own true identity as it was to see how man has succumbed to evil. You are, in this *chaturyuga,* the four ages, the tenth and final avatar of the Divine Creator, Lord Vishnu himself, incarnated to end the ongoing Kali Yuga and to establish Satya Yuga at the beginning of a new age cycle. So, we glorify you, for you are of the nature of the pure, the ever-free and eternal Brahman embracing the consciousness of existence itself. Awaken to your true self, Lord Kalki, and perform your great maya as you deem fit.'

In that instant, Kalki's mind opened to a realisation of his true self. An unimaginable surge of pure energy took over his physical being and he was drawn into a cosmic reality that had no beginning and no end. He was limitless, pure, all awareness and free from earthly bonds—*nityoham, shuddhoham, budhhoham, muktoham.*

He stood transformed as his consciousness melded with the superconsciousness of the Brahman.

Na antah pragnam na bahish pragnam na ubheyta pragnam
Npragnayaghanam na pragnam na apragnam
Aavyavharyam abhrahyam arakshanam
Adhyantam avapadesham
Ekatmah pratayay saaram
Prapancho pashamaha shantam shivam advetam chaturtham
Mananyate satma avigneh yaha

He is not knowable by perception turned inward or outward,
nor by both combined

He is neither that which is known nor that which is not known
nor is he the sum of all that might be known
He cannot be seen, grasped, bargained with;
he is undefinable, unthinkable, indescribable,
The only proof of his existence is union with him
the world disappears in him
He is the peaceful, the good, the one without a second
(*Mandukya Upanishad*, Verse 7)

Lord Kalki was absorbed in his universal consciousness seemingly for a moment only and reverted almost instantaneously to his mortal form as Kalki to still stand with a humble demeanour before Shiva-Parvati.

'Divine Mother,' he said, 'I am truly blessed by your revelation and rejoice in the knowledge that you have bestowed on me. The Brahman is infinite and infinite is his divine cosmic drama of creation, annihilation and rejuvenation. I humbly accept the supreme knowledge that you have so gracefully imparted, that in this birth I am the final avatar of Narayana. Devi Ma, it is now clear to me why the mighty Shiva Mahadev himself sought to instruct me on the affairs of the world and the dissolution of creation. I beseech you, Divine Shakti, to instruct me further on what I have to do.'

'Lord Kalki, it was my endeavour to impart to you the wisdom of the *Trikala,* the three divisions of time,' said Lord Shiva. 'You faithfully journeyed into the future, witnessed whatever there was necessary to see, and drew the right conclusions from your observations. You are now a part of that future and there is nothing left for me to impart. It is for you and you alone to determine the time and manner of your intervention. You have the gift of all cosmic knowledge and I know you will put this to good use.'

The vision of Lord Shiva and Devi Parvati slowly faded and Kalki was left to meditate alone in the sacred precincts of Mount Kailash.

13

The Beast Ravaging Humanity

In its wake, the Second World War left ripples that soon turned into gigantic waves sweeping aside antiquated systems. Two diametrically opposed political centres emerged—one professed freedom of every sort, including political power, capital, media and the market; the other centralised control of everything from state dictatorship to denial of all forms of independent will. These two blocs of capitalism and communism virtually divided the world between them and the title 'Cold War' pointedly defined the terse relation between the two. Neither was perfect.

The wars in Korea, Indo-China, Afghanistan and the Middle East demonstrated that even after a world war that decimated one-third of humanity, man hadn't lost his appetite for fighting. The horrors of burning and maiming whole populations through napalm and other means continued unabated.

The only light in the prevailing gloom was the collapse and dismantling of the odious colonial system. Kalki blessed the gentle giants in Bharatvarsha, led by a spiritual Mahatma, who had provided the catalytic moral leadership in this ennobling endeavour. He noticed, however, that it would still take many decades for the newly independent states to emerge from the debilitating exploitation of ages and to win freedom from the clawing clutches of poverty, hunger and disease.

It was the emergence of China in the Far East that provided a new fulcrum to the erstwhile bipolar world. Embracing the doctrine of Marxism and refining it to suit the needs of teeming millions tottering on the brink of one agrarian crisis after another, China survived repeated cultural shocks to emerge as a global superpower. It balanced the rot of overburdened riches in the West and the evident terminal implosion of the illogically named Soviet Union.

Unfortunately, the concentration of nuclear weapons' capability in the hands of a few superpowers defined their status globally. At first this was confined to the United States, Britain, France and the Soviet Union, but China came soon thereafter. When India joined the club, Pakistan hastened to follow, with Iran, Israel and North Korea waiting in the wings.

This spread of nuclear arms was an imminent threat to the survival of the human race itself. Unlike Kalki, who understood the deep-rooted malaise in mankind, many believed that there was a genuine counterpoise in nuclear deterrence, since each of the holders possessed arsenal sufficient to dissuade anyone gaining an upper hand.

❖

As Kalki ruminated over the affairs of man, he felt the presence of a powerful force near him. Parshuram stood there, his hands folded before him. Kalki joyously moved to touch his feet, but Parshuram took a step back and firmly demurred, saying, 'Lord of all Creation, you are the exalted object of all prayer, devotion and adulation. I am just an ordinary supplicant. It does not behove the omnipotent avatar of Lord Vishnu to do homage to me.'

Kalki smiled and lovingly replied, 'Great Parshuramji, when I was a mere youth, ignorant about life, you took me under your charge. You instructed me on all there was to know. You were my revered guru and shall so remain till the end of time. You are as dear to me as Guru Vasishta and Guru Vishwamitra were to me in my earlier life. So, permit me to adore you, and tell me how I might please you.'

The Chiranjeevi accepted Kalki's mark of respect. The two sat together, with Kalki filling him in on his journey since they last met, especially his divinations in Mount Kailash with Lord Shiva and Parvati Devi, and journeys with Narada Muni.

'Gurudev, it appears to me that all that is ungodly has become entrenched in the very nature of the human race and everything that it does.'

He paused and then said, 'This was perhaps always so, because even in my youth in Sambhala, I recall the conflicts that raged all around us. I remember the soldiers from Avanti; they were more like savages than human beings. From what I have seen down the ages, this ugly face of mankind has not changed much. What has changed is the spread of the malignancy. Evil now covers the whole globe and affects every nation, every strata of society.'

Parshuram nodded politely, even though he had witnessed these already through his inner eye. What he waited for were Kalki's own takeaways.

'And Gurudev,' his student continued, 'the character of conflict too has changed. For many centuries, man fought with bows and arrows, swords and knives, lances and shields, with warriors cavorting about on horses and chariots. Now, the weapons of war are elaborate beyond belief—missiles, artillery and warplanes. The human race is armed today with the most sophisticated arsenal of destructive power ever seen on earth, and their chances of deploying it are proportional only to the malice they bear each other.'

Parshuram nodded and commented, 'The danger is exacerbated also by the fringe elements that are emerging from the folds of almost every religion, radicalising them to inflict maximum damage on other faiths. The instrument of terror is now being increasingly used and the terrorist is the latest foot soldier carrying out this filthy deed for what is erroneously believed as just rewards in heaven. The pain and suffering that this blind terror causes—far from doing any good to the doctrine it supports—actually brands that religious group as fanatical and abhorrent.

'But notice how even the process of economic growth and the good it is supposed to generate has only eaten away the sap of humanity. Strange as it may sound, the very technology that has been used to increase production, conquer disease and empower communities has also widened the gap between the rich and the poor, the exploiter and the exploited. Power has gravitated to those least morally equipped to exercise it.'

To enunciate his point, Parshuram recited some compelling verses from the *Srimad Bhagavata Mahapurana:*

Vittmev kalo nrynam janamachar gunoday dharma nyaya ve vasthmyam karanam balmev hi
Dampatya bhiru chirhe turmayeva vyavaharike stritve punstve ch hi rativri pratve sutrmev hi
Avritya nyaya dorbalyam panditye chaplam vach udarambharta swarth satyatve dhastrimev hi

Brahvitakshatr shudranam yo bali bhavita nrip praja hi
lubdhe rajanye nirdhane syudharmbhi

In the Kali Yuga, wealth alone will be the criterion of
pedigree, morality and merit. Might will be the only
factor determining righteousness and fairness.
Personal liking will be the deciding factor in making
the choice of a partner in life, and trickery will be the
motive force in business dealings....
Justice will have every chance of being vitiated
because of one's inability to gratify those administering
it and
voluble speech will be the only criterion of
scholarship ... and hypocrisy will be the touchstone of
goodness
Filling one's belly will be the only end of human
pursuit and audacity of speech will be the criteria of
veracity
And when in this way the terrestrial globe will be
overrun by wicked people, the person who would
prove to be the most powerful.... will become the ruler

(*Srimad Bhagavata Mahapurana*,
Book X11, Discourse 2)

Kalki was bemused. These sacred words perfectly summed up the current affairs on earth!

'Gurudev, the scriptures are only confirming what is evident: that malevolence has pervaded the thinking and actions of all mankind. The Divine Mother said that I would be responsible for the ending this yuga. As my guru, may I humbly seek your guidance on how this task is to be accomplished?'

Parshuram smiled, 'Dev, you are the master of the destiny of the entire Brahmand. It is your maya that orchestrates the birth of life, its preservation and final dissolution. You are the force behind countless yugas yet to come. Still you ask me, a mere witness to your infinite drama, as to how the Kali Yuga will end? Permit me, divine Kalki, to quote from Jayadeva Goswami:

Mleccha-nivaha-nidhane
Kalayasi karavalam dhumaketumiva kimapi karalam
Kesava dhrta kalki sarira
Jaya jagadisa hare, jaya jaya jagadisa hare

Kesava! Oh Lord of the universe! Oh Lord Hari, who
has assumed the form of Kalki! All glories to You!
You appear like a comet and carry a terrifying sword
for bringing about the annihilation of the wicked
barbarian men
at the end of the Kali Yuga.

(Sri Dasavatara-Stotra 10, *Gita-Govinda* by Jayadeva)

'Lord, know that I am at your service. Remember me whenever there is an occasion for me to help.'

With these words, Parshuram sought permission to go back to Mount Mahendragiri.

14

On the Edge

On earth, matters were gradually reaching a crescendo. Several countries had by now acquired nuclear weapons technology. Those with relatively unstable leadership posed a constant danger of their nuclear arsenal falling into the hands of rogue elements with terrorist connections. Adding to the tension was the rising arrogance of some superpowers who considered themselves self-styled guardians of democratic values. This resulted in a growing sense of hysteria and paranoia that boded ill for long-term peace.

The world was standing on the brink of a seemingly enormous abyss of darkness, with no tangible support to prevent it from rolling over. History had, of course, witnessed such events before; for example, the ruthless marauding of a Chengiz Khan and Attila the Hun or the Nazi menace of the twentieth century. To this could be added the mass genocide of the Mayans by the Spanish conquistadors, the Red Indian tribes by American settlers, the races of Africa by the slavers, or the Jews in Europe. All nations were ready to wreak havoc on each other; a spark was all it would take to obliterate all of humanity.

Kalki wondered to himself: *What is it about a species that can foresee a calamity and yet not take steps to avert it? What is it in an individual that sees a monstrous crime being committed before him, and yet do nothing to intervene? Women and children have been traumatised and maimed before their eyes and yet people have knowingly turned their backs, or, worse, have joined in the gruesome assault.*

And then he recalled Bhishma Pitamah's words to Yudhishtra, as he lay dying on the bed of arrows created for him by Arjuna:

Striyasca apurshaa maargam sarvaalankaara bhushitaah
Nirbhayaah pratipadyante yadaa rakshati bhumipah

If women having decorated themselves fully with
ornaments, and without any men accompanying them,
can move about freely and fearlessly through the
streets and lanes (unmolested by anybody),
that State is well governed.

What a far cry from the conditions on earth now! Women, especially young girls, were almost regularly targeted or reported raped. They were singled out for murderous assault, gang-raped, and even maimed for life with acid thrown at their faces and bodies. Even infants and toddlers had not been spared this vicious madness. Man, supposedly created in the image of god, had descended to levels that were demoniac in the extreme.

Kalki withdrew from the pitiful world of man to contemplate in silence. He had to take a call, but he sought an answer to one key question: what if, just what if he did not intervene?

Kalki again projected himself into the future to see what would happen in this eventuality. He had hardly travelled a few years into the future when he came across a world teetering on the brink of oblivion.

15

The Final Option

No one knew who was responsible for the final conflagration. It suddenly seemed as if the entire border separating the protagonists was seething in flames, with tides of men falling over each other with a single purpose—to kill or be killed. When hand-to-hand butchery failed to sway the war in favour of any one side, armour and artillery were brought in to subdue the foe. When even that failed, it rained rockets and missiles.

Kalki unhappily viewed this future. *What impulse drives man to acts of savagery that he would shudder to inflict when not under the pall of madness?*

No one knew how long the stalemate would have continued had one side not opted for the final blow. Using its short-range missile system, it launched a nuclear device on the adversary. Suddenly, one little corner of the globe became incandescent in the sheering glare of a blast that pulverised a massive radius with its shock wave, even before its roaring flame ravaged mile over mile of open countryside. The mushrooming cloud of burning heat killed innumerable more and left generations with ailments that even time could not cure.

As if this horror was not enough, more was yet to come. The afflicted nation had its own nuclear arsenal and wasted little time in responding in kind. Missile followed missile, millions of homes were destroyed and countless lives snuffed out at the altar of a godless war.

And what of the superpowers, the so-called watchdogs of humanity? At first, they watched in alarm at what was happening, alternating between calls for ceasefire, pleas for conciliation, invoking of global sanctions, and conference calls. When these did not bear results, they sent their fleets of aircraft carriers and armed flotillas to prevent further spread of conflict. When even these proved futile, active intercession became necessary and this, as it turned out, was the signal for all round participation in the slugfest. No one in the global community wanted the other to gain an upper hand. Unsurprisingly then, the power brokers, themselves armed to the teeth, took positions antithetical to each other and friction turned to hostility and hostility to all-out war.

No war of man had been fiercer. No war engulfed the globe more completely than this. Kalki was astonished at the towering scale of destruction. It was not just military targets that were obliterated; whole cities and populations were vapourised by the slender but deadly projectiles of death. For the first time in his history, man was participating in a macabre game, in which monstrous, twisting pillars of mushrooming clouds appeared just about everywhere and there was nothing he could do to avoid its lethal fallout. The major centres of habitation were the first to go, carrying with them the art, treasures and technology assiduously built over millennia. But the architects of demolition were not to be satisfied with just that; each pocket of civil society had to be wiped out, and so they continued dispatching their trajectories from secret silos till there was nothing left to destroy.

Darkness descended on the world as symbols of civilisation as electricity, roads, power and surface transport ceased to exist. A heavy pall of smoke enveloped the ether and a pale wisp of dust kept raining from the skies as building blocks of cities returned to the earth that had given them birth. The ground was still burning with the fires of the inferno and, as the day with its spectral mist turned into night, the poisonous clouds reflected the toxic glow of radioactivity impregnated in the land.

The maniacal ferocity of the conflict was now over and man silently viewed the havoc of the short but cataclysmic nuclear holocaust he had unleashed upon himself. *Now,* thought Kalki, *at least now, he will realise the decadence of evil and the terrible retribution it had caused. Surely this is the right occasion when his heart will open to broader levels of spiritual realisation.*

To test his reasoning, Kalki undertook a survey of what was left of the dwelling of man. Where he did find survivors, he was appalled at what he discovered. They had emerged from the scourge of doom and witnessed countless others emasculated before their eyes; the primeval instinct of these unfortunates was to remain alive at all costs. Food, water, housing and shelter were of prime concern and survival was only for the strongest. In the resulting chaos, civil society disintegrated, and mob rule, loot and violence became the order of the day.

The after-effects of the nuclear holocaust had caused irreversible damage to man's physical health. Direct radioactive burns resulted in relatively shorter spans of suffering as death came early. What caused lingering pain was the debilitating spread of cancerous cells affecting vital organs of the system and erupting in suppurating sores all over the body. Kalki was anguished that this disease-ridden, monstrously bloated, half-starved shuffling figure with loathsome thoughts was all that was left of the once glorious figure of man. He recalled that the scriptures had so foretold that, at the close of Kali Yuga, the height of man would be reduced to 3.5 cubits and his lifespan will dwindle to twenty years.

Kalki asked himself: *But is this how the Kali Yuga is really destined to end?* He rewound to the period prior to the outbreak of the nuclear holocaust. The realisation dawned upon him: *This is not how the yuga is meant to terminate. This was not the conclusion scripted by the great masters of creation long before creation itself, when man was but a dream of the distant future.*

A nuclear holocaust would only represent Kali's final victory with evil predominating a world overrun by the fires of perdition. There would be no separation of the good from the evil, no conservation of the ethical, spiritual and moral values of society, no safeguarding the cultural bequests of history, and no avenue for improving mankind himself as a progenitor of the future golden age.

The story, as expounded in the scriptures, of a 'supreme chastiser', riding a white horse and carrying a mighty sword presented by Lord Shiva, single-handedly killing millions of 'thieves and rogues who have dared dress as kings' and thereby ending the Kali Yuga, might certainly be romantically appealing. It was not, however, practically possible. The kings and rulers were only the most obvious agents of Kali; now, however, most living beings carried the stigma of evil.

That left only one key question: how does one destroy the widespread evil in mankind and yet preserve some seeds to regenerate into the new Satya Yuga?

16

Kalki's Choice

When weeding a field, it is necessary to destroy not only the tall parasites that are clearly visible, but also the weeds underground. While you do this, it is crucial to protect the handful of fresh seedlings in the soil that are on the verge of sprouting.

One thing, however, was clear: since evil had now infiltrated most of humanity, the selective weeding of the good from the degenerate would require culling on a truly global scale. Kalki, with his merciful nature, had at first baulked at this idea of large extirpation and had even voiced his reticence to Narada when they were surveying the spread of Kali. The Rishiraj had, with a knowing smile, humbly reminded Kalki how, in his earlier avatar as Lord Krishna, he had admonished Arjuna on the battlefield of Kurukshetra for precisely this weakness: refusing to bear arms against evil when it was manifest in close or respected relatives. Kalki had to reconcile himself to the fact that what had to be done had to be done. Kalki carefully considered the options before him. He recalled past instances of human extinction in the search for possible clues to his future course of action. He remembered the *manuśraddhādeva* who had nurtured him as the Matsya avatar at the time of the great flood that was to consume all earthly inhabitants. The only ones who survived were those that were accommodated in the vast boat that the avatar pulled to safety. Was another deluge then the answer to the modern epoch? Kalki ruled this out; it was not possible to flood all the continents simultaneously while, at the same time, reaching heights where humans still had habitation.

What then of some global pestilence? Surely, in his weakened condition, man would not be able to survive the ravage of a worldwide pandemic designed to kill the entire race? Kalki was revolted at the very thought. How could more suffering be imposed on those already groaning under the yoke of telling agony? It would mean heaping yet another evil on them and that was certainly not his intention.

The same was true of worldwide devastation caused through volcanic activity, earthquakes, hurricanes or tsunamis. True, the catastrophes would kill hundreds of thousands, but it would leave millions more ravaged and helpless. Kalki had to find a solution that was just and as humane as possible.

His thoughts shifted to the cosmic plane. What of gamma-ray bursts? Gamma-ray bursts resulted from the explosion of massive stars many times the size of the sun. Most gamma-ray bursts are thought to be streams of high-energy radiation produced when the core of such hyper stars collapses. In a flash of radiance lasting a bare matter of seconds, a gamma ray emitted by such a supernova can shine a trillion times as bright as the sun. This is the most powerful source of cosmic gamma-ray photons in the observable universe, ranked only behind the Big Bang. It is estimated that, in a matter of seconds, the process can emit as much energy as a star the size of the sun would in its entire lifetime. It has been hypothesised that a gamma-ray burst in the Milky Way, pointing directly towards the earth, could cause a mass extinction event. Since gamma-ray burts are thought to involve beamed emission along two jets in opposing directions, only planets in the path of these jets would be subjected to the high energy gamma radiation. A gamma-ray burst aimed at earth could, by the sheer force of its blast, burn away the atmosphere, destroy the ozone layer, cause acid rain, and result in global extinction from as far as 6,500 light years away.

Kalki remembered that only once in the history of the earth had such a disaster occurred. It had been responsible for the mass extinction of marine life during the Ordovician period almost 450 million years ago. But he also noticed that only four stars could be shortlisted for such an event in our galaxy. All four of them—the Garnet Star, Eta Carinae, Betelgeuse, and Vy Canis Majoris—were on the fringe of exploding as supernovae.

There is a fine line, Kalki reasoned, between the selective culling of mankind and the destruction of his habitat, the earth itself. The target was Kali and not the species itself, for how else would a new Satya Yuga come about? It was like the precious fabric that had accumulated considerable dust in its process of ageing. To clean it, one had to scrub the fabric just hard enough to remove the dust, but not so hard as to tear the fabric itself.

Suddenly Kalki recalled the final salutation of his guru, Parshuram:

Mleccha nivaha nidhane
Kalayasi karavalam dhumaketumiva kimapi karalam
Kesava dhrta kalki sarira
Jaya jagadisa hare, jaya jaya jagadisa hare

Kesava! Oh Lord of the universe! Oh Lord Hari, who has assumed the form of Kalki! All glories to You!

You appear like a comet and carry a terrifying sword for bringing about the annihilation of the wicked barbarian men at the end of the Kali Yuga.

You appear like a comet!

Yes, that was the answer!

A comet striking the earth would have global repercussions, and would certainly wipe out a majority of mankind. But the earth itself would survive and regenerate, and in that rejuvenation, man would find his redemption and be born again.

17

The Chicxulub Meteor

In prehistoric times, the great dinosaurs had ruled the earth and had done so for more than 150 million years. Their dominance had continued unabated over this period, terrorising and decimating lesser forms of life by their size and ferocity. Smaller creatures dwelt on the edge of existence in tiny caves and tunnels that offered pathetic shelter from the marauders, surviving on rodents, birds or insects that came their way by chance.

And then a random act of fate intervened. It came in the form of a meteor tumbling from the outer reaches of ether, about 10-15 kilometres in diameter, weighing 10,000 tons and travelling through the vacuum of space at 50,000 miles an hour.

The asteroid impact at Chicxulub in the Yucatán Peninsula was an extinction-level event because it fulfilled all the parameters defining such a calamity. It struck the shallow ocean near the eastern coast of Mexico with the almost incomprehensible force of 100 million megatons—around 5 billion times more powerful than the Hiroshima explosion. It was a head-on collision and this, more than any other factor, determined its destructive capability.

Normally asteroids and meteors have earth-centric orbits, so their impact trajectory is usually tangential to the planet's surface. This greatly inhibits the speed of the impact, with the earth's atmosphere providing a braking cushion to the angular entry. Some asteroids, such as the KT Impactor at Chicxulub, have a more vertical entry and hence their destructive power.

Comets, on the other hand, are different. They orbit the sun in random paths, travel enormous distances, and attain velocities of up to 150,000 miles an hour the nearer they come to the sun. They can, therefore, slam into the earth even head-on, and at speeds up to three times faster than any other object at the time of impact. And since—according to the famous equation by Einstein—the energy released by such a cosmic collision is a function of the mass and speed of the object, a striking comet can have many times the destructive capability of an asteroid of similar mass.

For example, the 16-mile wide Swift-Tuttle comet hurtles through space at about 130,000 miles per hour, more than 150 times the speed of sound. If a comet of this size struck earth, the energy of the impact would be about 300 times that of the asteroid that wiped out the great dinosaurs.

All comets have highly elliptical orbits travelling back to their places of origin, before falling back towards the great star that incessantly calls out to them. In their perennial journey, they lose a considerable amount of their mass of dust, rubble, ice and gases as they increasingly face the heat of the sun. This converts into the long diaphanous and wispy tail, blown away behind them by the force of the solar wind. Though this is exquisitely picturesque to the distant beholder, it is a stark reminder of how ephemeral glory is in the face of certain doom.

Kalki searched the dark infinity of space and narrowed in on the lonely traveller. Expelled from the great mass of the Oort cloud, it had begun its perilous journey towards the sun. The great comet had been circling its sun slightly more than once every 133 years. It would still take some years before it approached the inner planets.

Its path to the sun was, however, subject to many alterations. Not only did it have to tackle the gravitational pulls of Saturn and Jupiter, but also the force of its own jets of gases and other materials as it got closer to the fiery star of its creation. But it would serve Kalki's purpose, subject to him controlling its orbit and speed with precision.

Before he became one with the comet though, there were some major tasks to accomplish on earth. He had to protect the embryo necessary for the new age destined to emerge from the cauldron of destruction.

But would it be possible to save anyone from the cataclysm of a comet strike? Man had been pondering this issue ever since comet or asteroid strikes had been identified as mass extinction-level events. While scientists had finally started the onerous task of finding and cataloguing most of near-earth objects that could possibly represent a collision risk, no technology had yet been found to divert them.

Kalki was sure that the solution to save selected people lay deep within the surface of the earth itself. There they could live through the years the effects of the comet's strike lasted, and till the planet was able to regenerate conditions for a renewal of existence. Kalki was also clear that, for the new Satya Yuga, the original seed had necessarily to come from diverse religious streams. Barring practices in medieval times, most of the major religions had a commonality that defined the Supreme as the One and true God. Man could give him different names but all paths led to him.

Ekam sat vipra bahudha vadanti

That which exists is ONE; sages call it by various names

Kalki recalled that this great verse from the *Rig Veda* had given the theme to all subsequent thought in Bharat: that God, Brahman, Allah, Ishvara, Jehovah or Ahura Mazda refer to the same eternal Supreme Being, the indivisible essence of bliss and consciousness whom sages describe in a variety of ways. How then could one differentiate between any religion?

This was an enormous task, covering various areas and disparate religious groups. They had to be told where to find shelter and how to provision these shelters to last for countless years. Finally, they had to have the means to impart learning and knowledge to the new generation, to enable them to emerge as strong, self-reliant, intellectually and spiritually capable individuals in the new world.

Clearly, a strategy for this had to be formulated by involving many people in different places. Kalki decided to personally visit some of them.

18

Sowing the Seeds

SAMBHALA

Kalki materialised in the one place he knew so well—his beloved birthplace, Sambhala.

Time is an inexorable architect of change and the past, a prism that often distorts present reality. The Sambhala that Kalki now saw was far different from the rustic village he once remembered as home. It was now a *kasbah*, occupying much larger space than it had before, and clearly showing how modernity had impacted its gradual evolution.

The roads were broader and paved with dark surfaces of bitumen. There were well-ordered parks and playfields laid out in front of houses of brick and concrete. The roofs of many, if not most, boasted of that ubiquitous sign of progress—the television dish antenna. At evenly spread out distances, Kalki noticed towers of modern-day communication, the mobile telephone transmitters. He noticed that the houses were freshly painted and appeared well-ventilated, with broad sash windows designed to provide adequate sunlight and fresh air. Flowering trees and shrubs lined the avenues and in the central square, there now stood a tall watchtower above a spacious building that formerly housed the village panchayat.

Kalki was pleasantly surprised to see that the vast sylvan forest surrounding the village was well-preserved and now boasted an entrance gate at its periphery. The size of the forest was smaller but the clear stream still flowed next to it, the same place where he had encountered the elephants led by Gajraj.

His eyes naturally sought his parental home but, in its place, there now stood a temple with a tall, simple but exquisitely carved steeple. As he slowly walked towards it, he heard enchanting strains of bhajans sung in pleasing voices. Kalki's steps took him to the edge of the tall columns surrounding the temple. He saw a large crowd, reverentially seated before an iconic image of Lord Vishnu, joining in the chorus in praise of the Divine Creator. Leading the bhajan *mandli* was a young priest, barely out of his teens, wearing a white dhoti, an angavastra with the traditional sandalwood and vermillion marks on his forehead. He had a sweet voice and seemed oblivious to his surroundings as he sung the glories of the deity.

Kalki immediately divined that the young priest was a descendent of his brother Kavi, many generations apart. He also recognised many offspring of past family members and friends. He could even discern the likeness of Garga, Bhagya and Visala in the assembly and felt a tinge of nostalgia as he recalled his affectionate friends. He approached the congregation and stood at the back of the temple, in the shadows, so as not to disturb the solemnity of the prayers. Even so, his presence was like a whiff of refreshing breeze, blessing the temple's hallowed arches and filling the hall with a dulcet fragrance. Many looked around, unsuccessfully, for the source of the delicate aroma.

The time came for the aarti. As the priest venerated the icon of Sri Vishnu with circular motions of the traditional flame, the *murti* itself seemed to glow with a radiance that filled the hall. All eyes were smitten as people continued to sway to the strains of '*Om Jaya Jagdish Hare*'.

At last the aarti concluded and everyone laid down in dandavat to the Supreme Creator. The priest remained on the floor for a long time and, on rising, continued to stare at the murti. At last, he gave the thali containing the diya to a young girl for passing around the traditional ahuti to those present. Kalki recognised her as a descendent of his brother Sumantra. She circulated the ahuti to the devout who blessed themselves with the flame. When at last she came to where Kalki stood, right at the back in the shadows, she looked long at his face and then, quite suddenly, bent down to touch his feet. Many in the crowd expressed surprise at this mark of respect to a total stranger. They had each experienced something extraordinary at the puja and were still conscious of the lingering aroma and the sense of peace and well-being that had overwhelmed them that evening. But after a while, they slowly turned and made their way home after graciously accepting the distributed prasad. At last, Kalki was alone with the priest and five other family members who were wrapping up the puja samagri.

'Maharaj, pranam,' the priest approached Kalki. He bent down to touch the ground in front of Kalki's feet. 'It has been a while since we have seen a stranger in these parts. You, sir, are most welcome.' He had hardly finished this preamble when Kalki's body began to glow with a divine effulgence. His form transformed into the very shape of the Sri Vishnu's murti that they had been praying to and it radiated power that permeated the air all around them. The light shining down on them was so piercing that they had to shield themselves from the stupefying glare. The fragrance they had only caught a hint of before was now an overwhelming aroma and they were enveloped in wave after wave of ecstasy.

After what felt like ages, a serenely modulated voice addressed them: 'Arise, descendants of Pita Visnuyas and Mata Sumati, for you are truly blessed. You have preserved the purity and innocence of your forebears and are destined to carry forward their sacred mission on earth. Look on me, for I am Kalki, their son, born in the likeness of Lord Vishnu, in this very place that you have converted into a temple in his honour. Do not be afraid, for I have come to bring you great tidings for which you have to prepare yourselves. Open your eyes and see me as I was—one of your ancestors.'

As the young group slowly opened their eyes, they saw before them a man of indefinite age. He was surrounded in a mellow diaphanous light, a smile constantly hovering on his face. His arms were outstretched in blessing but his eyes were aglow with the flame of timelessness itself. His body shimmered in the white robes and the perfume he exuded belied description. He had shed the form of the Divine Creator and had assumed a more acceptable countenance of a sage on a profound mission.

The young priest was the first to find his voice again: 'Divine Master, great Lord Kalki, holy avatar of Lord Vishnu, pranam. My name is Bharat and I am a descendent of Kavi, your illustrious brother. I am now the priest in the family and perform the role that your brother Prajna so effectively did in your time. Assisting me in this task is Savitri, who is a descendent of the honoured Sumantra and his wife Malini. Savitri has two brothers. The eldest, Bhīma, stays in the forest and looks after the denizen there. Her younger brother, Nakula, is still in the gurukul. I have an older brother, Arjuna, who teaches computer sciences in Maheshwar, a town on the banks of the River Narmada. Shankar, Tara and Divya here are my cousins from my mother's side.'

He paused, as if he had spoken too much. But Kalki smiled at him encouragingly. 'We have been brought up hearing legends connected with your holy name and have studied the venerated scriptures that speak of your glory,' Bharat continued. 'Today, the purpose of our lives has been fulfilled by your blessed darshan. Do tell us, Lord, how may we be of service to you, knowing yet that your divination needs no service?'

Lord Kalki was pleased at the humility and quiet grace of Bharat and inwardly felt contented that he had come to the right place for his future plans. But he still had a number of questions that needed answers. 'Devout Bharat, come, lead me to your place,' he said. 'I would like to share some prasad with you and learn more about Sambhala.'

❀

The small, awestruck group guided Kalki to a small dwelling behind the temple. While Bharat and Savitri busied themselves in preparing a meal for their divine guest, the others sat at a dignified distance from Kalki. With their palms folded in a reverential pranam, they could still feel the waves of benediction flowing from him, an elevating energy they had never felt before.

Kalki sought to put them at ease. Gently, he made enquiries about what each of them was doing, where they studied, details of their families, their interests and hobbies. By the time Bharat and Savitri joined them, the three were gradually opening up to the Kalki they had heard so much about.

Placing an unused thali and sweetened curd mixed with water in a copper tumbler before Kalki, Savitri again did a deep pranam: 'Revered Dev, bless us with partaking our frugal offering as a prasad to your divine self.' Kalki took a sip of the curd and a small mouthful of the prasad and then offered the thali to those sitting around. When the family ate a morsel of the prasad, it seemed as if they were tasting something otherworldly, and the watered curd was like *soma-rasa*: sweet, pungent and of exquisite flavour. They looked at each other in surprise!

The smiling avatar then asked them about Sambhala: how were the people there, what was their level of learning and knowledge, had they been isolated from the evil stains of Kali and, most importantly, did they still lead spiritual lives?

Bharat thought for a moment before speaking: 'Your indelible influence, Lord, still permeates every household here in Sambhala. Yes, a few wayward souls did arise, but soon found they had no home or support in the village and were forced to take shelter in far-off places. The people of Sambhala find their blessings and succour in your holy name and await your coming as has been foretold in the Puranas. Since childhood, they have been taught the holy scriptures, particularly the Upanishads and the Geeta *Upadesha*.'

'And what about subjects like mathematics, history, literature and the sciences?' Kalki asked.

'Yes, Lord, that is now an essential part of the curriculum taught to children. The idea is a multi-pronged educational system—including carpentry, masonry, electricity, making household, industrial and agricultural implements—that enables them to take up vocations here and in neighbouring towns and cities.'

'You spoke of your elder brother Arjuna teaching computer sciences in Maheshwar. Is this science fairly common among the people? Are the youth of Sambhala familiar with the latest knowledge of computers and allied fields?'

Bharat and the others were stunned by this seemingly pedestrian question. Here they were before the most celebrated of all forces of divinity, and the avatar was asking questions on the mundane subject of computers and their ilk!

However, Bharat did respectfully answer the question, thinking that Lord Kalki must have a good reason for the query. 'Lord, Sambhala may be in the backwaters but today the world of information technology is at everyone's fingertips. Almost every youth owns a computer and certainly everyone has access to a mobile phone. Gone are the days when we had to travel by foot to carry messages between villages or cities; these are now communicated over the phone. The computer, too, has changed our lives dramatically; wireless internet provides any and all information that is required. This has happened only a decade or so ago, but today even the young play with computer tablets rather than balloons and other toys. We are blessed that we have wireless facilities in the village, but Arjuna bhaiyya says that soon these will be commonplace everywhere.'

Kalki appeared pleased at this response. 'And what about you, Savitri beti? Are you also familiar with computers?'

Savitri, overwhelmed at this attention, stammered, 'Yes, my Lord. I have rudimentary knowledge of it, as do most of my class fellows, but I still have a lot to learn. I was hoping that the next time Arjuna bhaiyya comes to Sambhala, he would give me extra lessons on the subject.'

Lord Kalki smiled. Turning back to Bharat, he said: 'Bharat, I have a task for you specifically, but all of you should participate in it. Arjuna needs to be summoned back immediately to Sambhala; henceforth, this will be his *karmabhoomi*. You have to identify and gather all those residents of Sambhala who are even remotely computer-literate; the illiterate rest will be taken care of subsequently. Arjuna will give them lessons on information technology, starting from the most elementary to the latest developments in AI, nanotechnology and computer-brain interface. Naturally, the instructions will vary with the capacity of the students but, in due course, Sambhala should become the centre for the discipline.

'At present, you will not grasp all that I am talking about, but I am sure Arjuna will understand. Whatever he does not know, he should look to me for guidance. Instruct him to meditate on me daily and I will be his mentor in this important assignment.'

Kalki paused briefly before adding, 'I remember from my days here that, deep within the forests, there were caves where we used to go and pray before the jyotirlingas there. I want the caves surveyed so that they may be made habitable for as many people as possible. I know there is plentiful supply of water trickling in from the hillside, but perhaps the caves need deepening. I am sure you can gather the labour required for this task.'

The five quietly nodded, committing all of Kalki's instructions to memory. It was a lot and Kalki understood that. 'My children,' he said kindly, 'all this may appear strange to you today but, believe me, this is an essential mission that must be carried out if we are to seed the coming Satya Yuga.

'One final instruction—you are not to speak of my appearance or directions to anyone except Arjuna. We do not want to create an unnecessary diversion when we have so much to do. Bharat, please also send a message to someone from the house of dear Malini in Simdvipa to participate in the training. The purpose for this will become evident in due course. My blessings be with you all.'

With this beatitude, the divine form of Lord Kalki faded, though his force permeated the household for a long time.

❖

MOUNT MAHENDRAGIRI

Lord Kalki went back to the place of his enlightenment, Mount Mahendragiri, and appeared before his guru, Parshuram. Greeting him with a fond embrace, Lord Kalki sat with Parshuram and talked about the strategy to fight Kali. Parshuram nodded silently for he had already divined the role of the Kalki avatar, but now sought further details of how the coming Satya Yuga would be salvaged.

Lord Kalki smiled, for he knew the Chiranjeevi was merely testing him. 'Gurudev,' he asked, 'you are aware of the Borra Caves not far from here. How big are they and can they be made habitable?'

Parshuram nodded and said, 'Yes, I am very familiar with the caves for I have often gone there to meditate before the sacred jyotirlinga of Lord Shiva. The caves are located to the south-west of here, nearly 150 miles in the Ananthagiri hills of the Araku Valley. The mouth of the caves is almost 2,500 feet above sea level, and the length is around 700 feet averaging 40 feet in height. The caves are limestone structures caused by water trickling through the roof to form the cavern and the beautiful shapes along which the water slides to become River Gosthani in the lowlands.

'There is an interesting legend about the caves that a cow fell through the roof and gave a shape to the cavern, and that the river actually flows from her udders. One of the structures is shaped like a jyotirlinga and a temple has been constructed around it. There are also many figures of rishis, apsaras, gods and goddesses that give a divine atmosphere to the place.

'But Lord, why this interest in the Borra caves? Is it because you seek a darshan of the holy jyotirlinga of Lord Shiva?' Parshuram asked, with a mischievous twinkle in his eyes.

'Can the caves be made habitable to accommodate a large number of people, with food and water lasting a number of years?'

Parshuram pondered over this question for a while and then answered, 'Yes, I suppose it can. There is plenty of water already and, with some effort, the caves can be deepened since the walls are soft limestone. It will, however, take time to store enough grain inside as food, not only for the people, but also the livestock that is necessary. Given time, all this is certainly possible.'

'Then, Gurudev, let us begin at once for we have many caves and underground shelters to inhabit, not only here, but around the world, and I am keen that the Borra Caves serve as a model for having this chain of retreats for mankind. With your power and guidance, all this will be truly possible. Meanwhile, forgive my impertinence, but I have many places to visit.'

Before Parshuram could say anything, the figure of the avatar dwindled leaving just his luminescence behind.

19

Pillars of the New Age

BHUTAN

There is something about pristine mountain air that is pungent as it is sharp. It fills the lungs, focuses the mind, yet leaves a residual trace of lightheadedness. The Taktsang Palphug Monastery in Bhutan is located in precisely such a setting, where breathing can be stretched and where the blue of the sky is offset by the green of virgin ranges fading into the far vista of snowy peaks.

Built on a vertical rock face 3,000 feet above the River Paro, the Taktsang Palphug Monastery inspired feelings of vertigo as much for its haunting elevation as its appearance of hanging mystically in thin air. Even when the weather was clear, the site looked daunting; when covered in clouds, it evoked trepidation. The monastery adjoined caves formed inside the mountain where, many centuries ago, the great Guru Rinpoche, Padmasambhava, meditated on the meaning of creation and left his unmistakable emanation suffusing the area.

Sonam Rabgye was finishing his evening prayers. The head lama was now old. Even he could not remember just how old he was and yet, he was alert and fully in command of his faculties. He had come to the monastery as a young toddler and knew no other home than Taktsang. It was and continued to be a marvellous home.

The only time Sonam Rabgye left this peaceful home was during the annual four-day Tshechu festival down in the Paro Dzong. The Tshechu festival is an exciting gathering of social exchange among people of remote and spread-out villages. The markets are filled with myriad colourful local handicraft, clothing, foodstuff, household necessities and anything else one could need. Lovers exchange vows and marriages are decided. Local archers show their skills and challenges are given and accepted.

However, the main focus of the festival, and for which places are reserved well in advance, are the Cham dances. These dances, performed by skilled professionals wearing gaudy costumes of many hues and masks of the most terrifying beasts and demons, are based on incidents from the life of Guru Padmasambhava and other saints. The swirling, leaping, twisting dancers, to the accompaniment of huge drums, the Tibetan horn, *dungchen*, a long trumpet or horn used in Tibetan Buddhist ceremonies often played in pairs or multiples, the lingm (six-holed flute) and other traditional instruments are the cynosure of all eyes and whole families are packed together in a picnic-like ambience. The dungchen is the most widely used instrument in Cham dances. Its sound is compared to the singing of elephants—a long, deep, whirring, haunting wail that shakes your soul and makes you one with the surrounding peaks.

The last day of the festival witnesses the unfurling of the *Thongdrel*, a priceless and historic *thangka* of Guru Padmasambhava, before dawn. Amid chanting of intense religious fervour, prayers and dances, and before sunrise can damage its amazing but frail colours, the painting is carefully rolled up and kept in the Dzong to be displayed again the next year. Those who get to have darshan are considered truly blessed.

Sonam Rabgye was one such who had prayed before the Thongdrel every year without fail, often having to sleep in the open in order to witness the unfurling in the wee hours before dawn.

Lord Kalki appeared before the head lama Sonam Rabgye just as the latter was finishing his evening prayers. It seemed to him that the figure of the exalted guru Padmasambhava was hovering in front of him, shining with a lustre that dazzled the eye. The head lama fell to his knees in humble salutation and began chanting the six-syllabled timeless mantra dedicated to the Sadakshari form of Avalokiteshvara, *'Om mani padme hum'*, blessed as the ultimate chant by the Sakyamuni Buddha himself.

'Arise, venerated lama, you are exalted by your benign karma, but still have plenty of work left to do for the spiritual uplift of man.'

The lama asked, 'Master I am smitten by your light and do not know whether this is real or am I merely dreaming. If this is as I see it, and I am a simple and ignorant man and do not understand plain protocol, then who do I have the great honour of addressing?'

'I am whosoever you want me to be. You have been devoted to my darshan as Padmasambhava, Guru Rinpoche; you have bowed in prayer to me as the Sakyamuni Buddha; you have even meditated on me as the formless divine origin of all beings. I am all these and much more, but, in whatever form you accept me, know that I am pleased with you.

Blessed lama, I seek to involve you in a divine assignment relating to the future of mankind. Are you willing to accept this role?'

'Lord, even before you ask, I am at your disposal as a malleable tool for whatever shape you may wish to give me. But Master, permit me to plead just one question. What possible good can I accomplish? I am an old and lowly person, entrusted to look after the affairs of this monastery, and you want to involve me in the future of humanity? Lord, surely there must be some mistake.'

The divine form smiled at this humility. 'Respected Sonam Rabgye, you unnecessarily disparage yourself. You are the shining light of leadership to many who hold you in awe for your unbounded spirituality, spotless character and great intelligence. You are training here in the monastery many young acolytes who are essential for the survival of the religious and ethical values of the coming age. Tell me, are there others here who share your values for the future?'

The head lama, still slightly numb at what was happening, thought for a moment before replying, 'Yes, Lord, there is a young lama who I was training as a possible successor. Tashi Tshering is a person of unsullied reputation, devotion to the guru, and of sterling intelligence. He trains the young monks on the tools of modern education, computers and such other technologies that the senior monks and I do not profess to know or even understand. But he is a good teacher. He is grounded in reality and spends his spare time reading the sacred texts and meditating.'

'Then summon him. Tashi Tshering would be ideal for our purpose.'

Tashi Tshering turned out to be a striking fully ordained young lama with a charming demeanor and clear-cut eyes.

Seeing the luminous apparition of Lord Kalki, he fell on his face in dandavat, with his body and hands stretched out before him. Like the head lama, he too felt wave after wave of sheer joy overwhelming him with the accompanying sensation of heightened perception and spiritual elevation.

There are many occurrences in life that are as unexpected as they are beyond comprehension. The sudden passing away of a loved one; an unforeseen accident that simply happens out of nowhere; a traumatic sighting that leaves one shaken; or a chance encounter with the abnormal, all fit into this category. The mind is conditioned into accepting what is commonplace, not what is beyond the powers of credence. Such instances leave the mind in a whirl of confusion, unable to see reason and question its own sanity. Tashi Tshering found himself in precisely such a predicament. The vision he saw was in the likeness of Guru Rinpoche, Padmasambhava, just as he visualised him.

Finally, after many moments of silence, he turned to Sonam Rabgye who, in a few random words in Dzongkha, explained as best as he could, the nature and purpose of the apparition.

'Tashi Tshering, you are training here many young acolytes in modern scientific technologies,' said Lord Kalki. 'Tell me, do these include the latest developments in information technology through the use of computers and their like?'

Sonam Rabgye and Tashi Tshering reacted as if struck by a thunderbolt. Here was the highest spiritual visionary of their lives, someone they had prayed to with single-minded devotion, asking a question such as an official of the department of education might ask. They both reasoned that perhaps they were being tested in some mysterious way.

Before they could react, Kalki clarified, 'There are rapidly expanding fields of technology that you should be aware of, such as AI, and the merger of biologically based human intelligence with that of computer-generated knowledge. Are you familiar with what I am alluding to?'

After thinking for a while, Tashi replied, 'Lord, I have read a lot on these emerging technologies and was even thinking of introducing it to the more advanced students familiar with the use of computers. But I have still to fully immerse myself in the subject before I can teach it to others.'

'Then do so, and let your students actively partner the pace of growth in these new technologies. It is essential that the Taktsang Palphug Monastery should become a leading centre of study of the mind–machine merger that is developing. Draw on suitable recruits from wherever you can; your search will be rewarding.'

Sonam Rabgye replied, forestalling any question that Tashi may have. 'Lord, it shall be as you desire and, from this moment on, the goal of the monastery shall be to act as a spearhead of the technology revolution.'

Lord Kalki nodded with satisfaction and then switched to a different subject altogether. 'There are a few caves around the monastery where, in the past, I had meditated for a number of years. Are they capable of accommodating a large number of people, with provision of adequate storage of food and water for a few years?'

Sonam Rabgye was unable to connect the dots to discern his Lord's designs but answered honestly. 'Great Guru, the caves at present are a bit small but, with labour and effort, they can be deepened and made liveable for a sizeable community.'

'Then let this work also begin with speed. My blessings are with both of you.'

With these words the vision of Guru Padmasambhava gradually waned before the eyes of the two dazed and bowing monks.

20

Kashmir, India

Nature has never been parsimonious in showering its bounty on Kashmir. Among many of its breathtaking sites, Pahalgam still occupies the pride of place. Situated along the banks of the River Lidder, at an elevation of over 7,000 feet above sea level, it is a picturesque haven cupped in a green valley of rolling pine and deodar trees. Situated on the yatra route to the holy Amarnath Cave, Pahalgam attracts many pilgrims during the season, but is otherwise cocooned in its silent beauty, disturbed only by the sound of the cascading river.

Imran Tahir Malik lived here under the care of his father Bashir Malik, who owned a motor car garage catering to the small fleet of trucks, buses and cars that traversed between Pahalgam and the district headquarters in Anantnag, 45 kilometres away. Bashir Malik had briefly acquired fame almost twenty years ago, when he, as a young mechanic, had succeeded in repairing the car of the visiting governor of Jammu and Kashmir when even mechanics rushed from Srinagar could not start the vehicle.

As a young child, Imran loved to frolic around his father's workshop where he was the favourite of all the workers.

Alternatively, he would simply sit at the doorway and stare at the activities taking place in the market, the coming and going of people, the dazzling displays of merchandise in front of the shops, the busy whirl of traffic and the enticing call of shopkeepers as they tried to tempt the visitors to sample their wares. Imran was fascinated by the bargaining that followed and never knew who had emerged victorious in the struggle—the shopkeeper or the buyer; he suspected it was the former for he always had a satisfied gleam in his eyes and often gave Imran a sweet as a reward.

Just as he was maturing into his teens, a chance visit by his father's relative changed the whole course of Imran's life. Omar Malik had recently qualified as a licenced guide for the annual Amarnath Yatra. He had come to Pahalgam, 45 kilometres from Anantnag where he lived, to wait for his scheduled pilgrim group. He came to stay with Imran's family to renew old acquaintances. After dinner, he stepped outside to smoke his chillum and Imran, fascinated with the visitor, followed him and sat quietly at a respectful distance.

After a few moments of silence, Omar turned to the youngster. 'Boy, what do you know about the Amarnath Cave? And what is the connection of the cave to this family?'

Imran shook his head to signify his ignorance.

'Then know that we are Shia Muslim Bakarwal-Gujjars, who are awarded a portion of revenue earned from the pilgrimage for offering guide and caretaker services to the Hindu pilgrims. This is a centuries-old tradition. It all started some 150 years ago, when our ancestor Buta Malik, a shepherd of Batakot, lost his flock and found that it had strayed into the sacred cave. That is the reason why we, his family, still receive some part of the alms offered by pilgrims.'

Omar continued, 'Actually, Buta Malik did not, in fact, discover the cave as much as rediscovered it, for the Amarnath Cave is thousands of years old. There are written accounts of it in ancient history. Legend even has it that the cave was a place of pilgrimage to Bhrigu Muni after the Great Flood. The reason I know all this is because I have studied the history of the cave with great care. I'd advise that you do the same, since it is inextricably linked to our family. The shrine is the holiest among holy to millions of people all over India. Hundreds of thousands come to the cave every year. Do you know why?'

Again, Imran miserably shook his head.

Omar dragged on his chillum before replying, 'The Amarnath Cave is situated much higher than where you live. We are at 7,000 feet currently; the cave is at a height of almost 13,000 feet, which means that it is completely covered in snow for most of the year! We can approach it only in the summer months and then, too, it is a perilous journey through high mountain passes, steep paths, arduous climbs, adverse weather and fear of avalanches. Every year, there are casualties on the yatra and many die due to accident and exposure.'

Imran asked, 'But if it is so dangerous, why do people still do the yatra?'

'Faith, my boy, sheer faith. It is devotion that brings pilgrims to Amarnath; a devotion that is prepared to face all odds in order to find absolution from the drudgery of the world.'

Imran again hesitatingly asked, 'But what is there in the cave that grants them this freedom? I too have sought many answers to life, but have not got much satisfaction.'

At this candid statement, Omar looked sharply at the boy. He took another deep drag of his chillum and then answered, 'For the Hindus, the worship of Lord Shiva is the highest form of devotion. He is a part of the holy trinity of Brahma the creator, Vishnu the preserver, and himself, the destroyer. He is the most knowledgeable, the most easily approachable and the most helpful of deities. It is due to his mental resolve that creation exists and it is his tandava that will destroy it.

'One of the many signs of Shiva Mahadev is the lingam, and it is in this form that he is worshipped at Amarnath. Every summer, due to the melting of the ice and snow above, water seeps into the cave, drips on the floor and forms an icy stalagmite shaped like a lingam. It waxes and wanes with the weather and the phases of the moon. It is said that it was in this cave that Lord Shiva gave a discourse on the meaning and secrets of life to his divine consort, Parvati. Imran, legend also has it that two pigeons heard this discourse and achieved immortality! Believe it or not, many have claimed to have actually seen these birds!' With this, Omar tapped out the balance of his chillum and got up. 'But come, enough talk for the day. I am tired now, so let's go inside.'

Imran could not sleep that night. He kept thinking of the Amarnath Cave. Here was something seemingly inert and inanimate, yet had the power to draw multitudes to its fold year after year after year. Just ordinary people, no one really special. Braving hazards, undergoing rigours, overcoming challenges—was that mere devotion? Simply plain religious belief? Or was it something more—something unseen, something incomprehensible? Could it answer the questions ringing in his mind, questions that he could not even clearly articulate, much less properly answer?

The next day, Imran mustered the courage and asked for his father's consent to accompany Omar on the trip. To his surprise and delight, the permission was granted. So, carefully outfitted in appropriate clothes for the journey and his rations wrapped neatly in a bag, Imran cheerfully waved goodbye to his family a day later.

The journey to the cave took three days, with night halts at Shesh Nag and Panchtarni. The pilgrim group they were escorting was an uncomplaining and disciplined lot. As they climbed up from Panchtarni to the cave, Imran branched off and went up a rocky promontory from where he could easily see the giant icy lingam and the zigzag line of pilgrims queuing up before it for darshan. He closed his eyes and thought of how many countless people down the ages had seen this great natural phenomenon.

Suddenly, a glittering mist of pure light filled his mind and he was engulfed in its infinite expanse. He was numb to the core but felt strangely unafraid and at peace—an all-pervasive peace that he'd never felt before. He lost all track of his bearings and whereabouts.

It was only when he heard Omar's voice, calling to him from a seemingly long distance away, that he slowly emerged from his trance-like state. Just before reality began to dawn on him, he clearly heard a message reverberating in his mind: 'Imran, go! Go and find your own great master and do as he will command. In that you will find salvation for yourself and your people.'

Imran re-joined the group as they wound their way back to Pahalgam. He remembered little of the return journey and moved about as if in a daze. Omar gently asked him if he was feeling well. Imran affectionately hugged him, assuring him that everything was all right.

But everything was not all right—not in the normal sense. And it would never be again, for Imran's mind and thoughts had been altered forever.

❀

On his return from Amarnath, Imran started spending much of his spare time in the Jamia Milia Mosque situated near the banks of the River Lidder. The qazi of the mosque was a white-bearded haji who watched with interest Imran's growing attachment to the faith, and spent many evenings with him explaining the history of Islam and the quotations from the holy Quran.

Imran could by now recite many favourite verses of the holy Quran and started to give lessons to young students at the madrasa attached to the mosque. Seeing his purity and devotion, the qazi wrote to the head imam at the famous Hazratbal Shrine in Srinagar to give a *wazifa*, or scholarship, to Imran to enable him to study further there.

The Hazratbal Shrine contains a relic, the *Moi-e-Muqqadas*, believed by many faithful to be a hair of Prophet Muhammad. According to legend, the relic was first brought to India by Syed Abdullah, a purported descendant of Muhammad, who left Medina and settled in Bijapur, near Hyderabad, in 1635. The relic was sold to a wealthy Kashmiri businessman, Khwaja Nur-ud-Din Eshai, and brought to Kashmir where his daughter, Inayat Begum, became a custodian of the relic and established the famous shrine. Since then, her male descendants have been caretakers of the relic. Among the caretakers was a young Muslim cleric, Syed Yusufzai, who was to play an important role in Imran's life.

The Hazratbal Shrine is located on the left bank of the Dal Lake in Srinagar. Imran had never seen anything so majestic and was overwhelmed by the sheer beauty of the mosque and its surroundings. He quietly fell to his knees to do his *sijda* and was performing the ritual namaz when a soft voice said behind him, 'You must be Imran. Come with me, I am Yusufzai, and henceforth, your friend and guide. Let me take you to the imam.'

That night in the dormitory full of young clerics, Imran let his tears wash away his homesickness until sleep, that great opiate of the forlorn, embraced him in dreamless darkness.

In the early hours of the morning, Imran awoke to strange rhythmic chanting coming from the main courtyard of the mosque. On peering over the trellised verandah, he saw all the clerics melodiously intoning Allah's greatness in verses set in beautifully composed music. The incantations and refrain of '*subhaan Allah, subhaan Allah*' was mesmeric and Imran could not help but be carried along with it. The singing provided a perfect setting for the chilly, misty dawn and Imran found himself instinctively joining in the chorus as the sun rose slowly over the hills, reflecting the contours of the dried tears on his cheeks.

Later, over the sparse morning meal, Imran questioned Yusufzai about the morning ritual that sounded more like Hindu bhajans than the silent Islamic worship. Yusufzai paused before replying to the thoughtful query.

'In Kashmir, the faithful have been chanting the *Aurad e Fatiha* and *Dua e Riqab* along with the *Dua e Subah* introduced by the great Islamic saint Mir Sayyid Ali Hamadani, who popularised Islam among the masses here many centuries ago. Yes, it does have a likeness to Hindu temple worship, but the *Amir e Kabir*, the great leader as the saint is called, merged prevailing ancient beliefs with verses from the holy Quran and the Hadith as a form of worship in the mosques. It is the accepted practice over most of the valley.'

Yusufzai became Imran's constant companion and the two spent many hours walking along the banks of the Dal Lake, engrossed in discussions on Islamic ideology. Yusufzai's intimate knowledge of Quranic thought came from his close study of the Pashto translation of the work that was, in many ways, far superior to the Urdu edition. Much of their discussion focused on the impact of Islam in Kashmir and the singular manner in which this came about.

'For centuries this beautiful valley was parched of any element of faith, save for isolated centres of Buddhist and Brahmanical worship in and around scattered human pockets. It is said that perhaps the most notable event that happened in pre-history was the visit of the great Hindu saint and philosopher Shankaracharya who stayed where the Shankaracharya temple is now situated atop the *Takht e Suleiman* hill.

'Then Islam came to Kashmir, not by the sword or conquest, but by gradual conversion effected by dedicated missionaries. The first of these was the Sufi mystic, Hazrat Bulbul Shah, who converted the then Buddhist, King Rinchen Shah, and many of his followers to Islam.

'But the missionary whose personality had by far the biggest impact on the spread of Islam in the valley was Mir Sayyid Ali Hamadani. You remember the morning hymns that had surprised you on the first morning that you arrived here? I had told you then that he had composed them. He belonged to the Kubrawi order of Sufis and was born in

1314 AD, in Hamadan, Iran. His genealogy could be traced back to Imam Hussain, a grandson of Prophet Muhammad, and son of Hazrat Ali and Muhammad's daughter, Fatimah. Sayyid Ali Hamadani was sixteenth in direct descent from Hazrat Ali and stayed intermittently in Kashmir over three periods.

'He brought with him several followers well-versed in shawl and garment-making, woodcraft and painting, and many other household industries that gave the common people real income and a chance to better their lives. He established several hospices called *khanqahs* where free food and medicines were distributed in the name of the Almighty.

'His influence on Kashmiri society was due to his accessibility to all and the unique qualities which attracted the attention of everybody, including the Hindus and Buddhists.

'Imran, if you want to understand Islam in Kashmir, study the works of the *Amir e Kabir* such as *Zakhiratul Muluk* and *Muwwadatul Quraba*, and you will find fulfilment there. A contemporary poet has praised him in the following couplet:

Jumla ra aa'n shah'e darya asteen
Daad ilm va sanat va tahzib va deen

The words of the Shah and his farsighted vision
gave to the people wisdom, culture, industry, respect
and religion …

Imran was deeply affected by what Yusufzai had said. One evening, Imran hesitatingly told his friend of his experience at Amarnath and found, to his pleasant surprise, that far from laughing away the incident, Yusufzai took the matter seriously and discussed at length what the vision could mean. Who was the 'master' that was being referred to?

They debated this conundrum over and over, but could not come to any satisfactory answer.

❀

In his sixth year at the Hazratbal Shrine at Srinagar, Imran was unexpectedly called upon to lead the prayers at the Friday congregation. This was surprising as it was only the imam or, in his absence, one of the senior ulema who was asked to conduct this sacred ritual. Islam regards the holding of prayers in congregation as a significant social event symbolising unity among the ranks, closeness of hearts, and promotion of the spirit of brotherhood. For this reason, it was the most pious, meritorious and scholarly person who was selected to lead the congregation.

Imran prepared himself as best as he could. He fasted and prayed the whole night, had a ritualistic bath in the lake and, wearing fresh robes, appeared before the congregation of more than a thousand people. He looked radiant as he began the ceremonial prayers, gazing up towards heaven and chanting:

Bismillaahir-rahmaanir-Rahim

In the name of Allah, the most gracious, the most merciful.

He then quoted his favourite verse from the holy Quran:

Wa Huwallaahu laaa 'ilaaha 'ilaa Huu
Lahul-Hamdu fil- 'uulaa wal- 'aakhirah: wa lahul-Hukumu wa 'ilayhi turja- 'uun.

And He is Allah: there is no God but He. To Him be praise at the first and at the last:
for Him is the Command, and to Him shall ye all be brought back.

(The Quran, Al Qasas, 28:70)

He called upon the congregation to dwell on the greatness of the one and only God, the Supreme Being who was behind all creation and on whose command existence itself would come to an end. He asked them to recall all the good things that had been accorded to them in Allah's grand munificence.

Wa 'inta'udduu ni'-matallaahi laa tuhsuuhaa: innallaaha la Gafuurur-Rahiim

If ye were to count up the favours of Allah, never would you be able to number them: for Allah is All Forgiving, Most Merciful.

(The Quran, An Nahl, 16:18)

Dwelling at length on God's favours and his generosity, Imran's words prompted people to raise their arms and sway in a joyous outpouring of gratitude, with tears streaming down their cheeks. And then, Imran subtly changed the mood:

Wa maa bikum-min-ni'-matin- faminallaahi summa'izaamassakumuz- zurrufa- 'ilayhi taj- 'aruun

And ye have no good thing but is from Allah: and moreover, when ye are touched by distress, unto him ye cry with groans.

(The Quran, An Nahl, 16:53)

'For everything that Allah has given you, what have you given in return?' he asked them. 'You remember him only in times of distress when your groans and cries fill the heavens. When you are busy enjoying the bounty he provides, you forget him. So fickle is your faith that it fails to recall that even the tiniest blade of grass cannot move, save through his grace.

'Allah sees all and hears all. Do not believe, even for a moment, that your deeds are hidden from him. So, abjure evil and base your life only on what is good and acceptable in his eyes.

'Izas- Samaaa- 'unfatarat, wa izal-kawaaki- buntasarat;
Wa 'izal- bihaaru fujjirat; wa'izal- quburuuu bu'-sirat
'Alimat nafsum- maa qaddamat wa 'akh- kharat
Yaaa- 'ayyuhal- 'insaanu maa garraka bi-Rabbikal- Kariim?

When the sky is cleft asunder, when the stars are scattered,
When the oceans are suffered to burst forth, and when
the graves are turned upside down
Then shall each soul know what it has sent forward
and what it has kept back
O! Man, what has seduced thee from thy Lord Most
Beneficent?

(The Quran, Al Infitar, LXXX11:1-6)

By now, many people were openly crying; some were even beating their chests in sheer contrition. Imran felt that he had spoken enough. He opted to close his sermon with an uplifting quote:

Lil- laahi mulkus- samaawaati wal- 'arzi wa maa fiihinn;
wa Huwa 'alaa kulli shay- 'in Qadir

To Allah doth belong the dominion of the heavens
and the earth and all that is therein
and it is He who hath power over all things.
(The Quran, Al Maida, 5:120s)

Imran's first address at the shrine's Friday prayers came like a gust of fresh air in a valley where people were tottering on the brink of losing faith. Kashmir was in the grip of turbulent times. The people had lost their identity in the meaningless violence and loss that was shaking the lives of an otherwise peace-loving multitude. Imran's words were nothing out of the ordinary, but the striking manner in which he underscored god's mercy and his unrequited love from a fickle, wavering and ungrateful people, struck at the heart of their insecurity and fears. That day earned him the name 'Preacher'.

❀

Imran was soon flooded with requests for personal audience by people who had suffered some trauma or loss, and from groups who wanted him to address them on matters of faith. Yusufzai took over the role of the intermediary and became the recognised face behind the Preacher. The theme for Imran's lectures was always the same: recognise the bounty Allah has given you, turn to him amid your pomp as well as grief, and he will reward you immeasurably on the Day of Judgment. Yusufzai always understood the import of occasions and prepared Imran on what he should say.

A deeply spiritual man himself, Yusufzai found a kindred soul in Imran. With the imam's permission, he finally took Imran to the Khanqah-e-Maula, the shrine of the Said ul Auliya, Mir Sayyid Ali Hamadani, built in 1395 AD. One of the oldest mosques in Kashmir, it was located on the right bank of the River Jhelum in Srinagar.

The Khanqah-e-Maula housed the room where the Amir-e-Kabir—as the saint Hamadani was known—had stayed for the first time. It was a beautiful model of Kashmir's wooden architecture, replete with delicate engravings on the walls. The sacred relics housed there included the Prophet's flag, a pillar of the Prophet's tent, and Shah Hamadani's walking stick. During his life, the place acquired the distinction of being the centre of religious learning, charitable work and spiritual enlightenment. Imran found that people still thronged the place to pray to Allah in solemn and deep reverence.

He knelt to kiss the floor in homage and, as he did so, was gripped by strange and unexpected emotions. His body was caught in sharp spasms and he reeled as his mind filled with a blinding light. His head jerked from side to side as he finally fell on the ground. A deep and mellifluous voice resonated in his head:

'So, you have come at last, my child. I am the one for whom you have been searching. Purify yourself here with fasting, prayer and meditation, for you have a solemn duty to perform.'

From that moment on, Imran was like a man possessed. He completely forgot himself in the frenzy that seized him. Going to a corner of the shrine he sat down, clasping his shuddering body with both hands and crying *'Maula, Maula, oh mere Maula'*.

❖

It was mid-morning on the third day when Imran showed signs of emerging from his stupor. He took a few sips from the glass of water that a concerned Yusufzai held to his mouth. But Imran was unlike the man he'd been the past few days. With a determination quite in contrast with his earlier state, he went to wash himself and perform his routine namaz.

Soon afterwards, he took his friend aside for now there was quite a throng surrounding him due to his possessed behaviour earlier. 'Yusufzai, my dear companion, I have at last found my refuge. The great Said ul Auliya, Mir Sayyid Ali Hamadani, is to be my tutor from now on. I must remain here to do whatever bidding he asks of me. Return to Hazratbal and request the imam to absolve me of my responsibilities for now onwards, this will be my home. Request the authorities of the khanqah to assign me a tiny place to stay. Distribute my possessions to the poor and may Allah always keep you well and happy.'

Yusufzai did whatever Imran had requested except that, after he had met the imam, he returned to the khanqah to be with a soulmate he could not forsake.

Fasting during the holy month of Ramzan ended with the festival of Id-ul-Fitr. The traditional namaz was offered six times on this day and huge crowds, wearing new clothes, had gathered outside the Hazratbal Mosque when the final namaz was performed. The swirling crowds were in a joyous mood and no one noticed Imran as he slowly mounted a mound beside the shrine.

Soon, however, he attracted attention, as much because of his shining clothes as the radiance that emanated from him. A growing crowd came to sit in front of him, comprising many who had heard his earlier discourses and those who had either witnessed or heard of his trance when he had first come to the khanqah.

Imran broke bread with them but declined to say anything more as this was an occasion for festivity, not sermonising. Prompted by Imran, however, Yusufzai casually asked how many in the crowd knew of using computers or of information technology in general. When quite a few raised their hands, Imran asked them, and through them, any of their friends and relatives, to meet him the next day at the khanqah.

That evening, Imran told Yusufzai of his communion with the Said ul Auliya, Mir Sayyid Ali Hamadani. 'We have to gather as many learned people near the mystic caves of Kalaroos above the huge carved rock called Satbaran in Kupwara district, about 90 kilometres from here. There are a number of caves situated a few metres away from this giant stone. It is said that these caves and tunnels inside them contain huge water bodies as well as running water from internal streams.'

Yusufzai nodded but Imran noted the mild confusion on his face. He put a comforting hand on his companion's shoulder. 'At present even I do not know the final purpose of the dictates of the Amir-e-Kabir, but on one subject he was insistent: the people we gather must not be tainted with evil; they should be learned, industrious and devout.'

And so, it came to pass that on a certain day, the quiet village of Lashtiyal became home to many busloads of people, of all ages and sexes, climbing up the narrow and steep path leading to Satbaran and the caves beyond. That they were not sedentary tourists was evident from the large tents and amount of luggage they carried, and from the fact that huge shamianas were erected for cooking, dining and collective meetings.

Yusufzai led the large community and organised the accommodation and necessary infrastructure for housing and feeding. Every morning and evening, as more people from near and far gathered, prayer meetings were held. There, Imran, the Preacher, gave sermons on the need for spiritual strength to face the future together.

'It is the direction of the Amir-e-Kabir that we advance the frontiers of knowledge and determine our future through the tools provided by modern science. We'll spend each day studying the latest developments in computer sciences. Those who are physically endowed will go to the caves and make them habitable. We need to deepen them and map the water bodies. Let's not delay our work; let us each perform to our fullest capability.'

Naturally, the sizeable group's activities so close to the border soon caught the authorities' attention. Alert as they were to possible terrorist action, they sent police and army patrols to find out what was going on. But such was the miraculous intercession of the Said ul Auliya that, try as they might, Imran and his followers were cloaked in a shroud of invisibility.

Kalki looked down on the activities in Satbaran and silently thanked the Mahadev for identifying, at the Amarnath shrine so dear to him, the one person who would prove useful in saving many of the faithful.

21

Thailand

Buddhism had come to Thailand during the reign of Emperor Ashoka in India as far back as 250 BC. Its present form of Theravada Buddhism came through Sinhala monks travelling from Sri Lanka.

The head of the order of Buddhist monks in the country, The Supreme Patriarch or Sangharaja, Somdet Phra Ariyavongsangatana X, was an appointee of the king of Thailand. He presided over the Supreme Sangha Council that governed the vast number of monks and laypersons of the religious system.

The Sangharaja was in a disturbed and fitful sleep when he was woken by a soft, repetitive chanting of the sacred mantra, '*Buddham sharanam gachhami, sangham sharanam gachhami*'. As he sat up in wonder, he saw a vision of the Maitreya Buddha that he adored—the beautiful gold-covered statue known as Phra Phuttha Chinnarat, 'King of Victory', located in the 'Temple of Great-Jewelled Reliquary' on the River Nan. In his meditations he had always kept this beautiful image as his lodestar and here it was, floating above him.

The Sangharaja fell to his knees. The answer to his prayers, the search of his spiritual life, was shining before him. He joined in the chorus, '*Buddham sharanam gachhami, sangham sharanam gachhami*'.

How long this continued he could not say but then his benign Lord smiled on him and said in a mellifluous voice, 'Sangharaja, I have a mission for you that involves members of the sangha as well as laypersons who you personally deem qualified as my sincere devotees. Using whatever means you think fit, immediately select at least one thousand of the purest men and women whom you can identify. There should be an equal number of men and women. Remember that their character and reputation should be above possible reproach.

'Take these people to the area around the Suwan Khuha Temple in Phang Nga province. As you know, this temple is located inside a limestone mountain which houses a large complex of caves. There are also caves nearby—the Bang Riang Pagoda and the Dragon Cave Temple. The people will live inside these caves and, in order for this to happen, these caves need to be deepened and made fit for habitation. Provisions should be made for adequate supply of energy and water for several years.'

So far, the supreme patriarch had remained silent out of sheer shock and wonder. He kept telling himself that this was all a dream and that he would suddenly wake up. But this was no dream, and what the great Maitreya was asking him to do was within the realm of practicability, till this last part.

Caves designed for people to live in for years with adequate food and water? he thought to himself. Meeting the water requirement was perhaps a possibility because the caves were made of limestone and, as the area was subject to heavy seasonal rainfall, water would trickle in. Systems could be designed to trap water for the community. But he couldn't understand how so much food could be stored to last for years.

Before he could articulate his doubt, the Buddha smiled, having divined his question. 'I meant food for the mind. The food for the body I shall provide separately. But the caves will need electricity from hydel sources within the caverns. Your engineers are capable of doing this. Seek the guidance of the king, for you will need all the help you can from the state.'

'But Lord,' asked the disturbed patriarch, 'how can I convince the king or even members of the sangha, that all this was as you directed? Won't people say that I had merely dreamt this, or worse still, treat me as if I am insane? Even I do not know whether I am awake or whether all this is a dream.'

'Have faith. I shall leave you with something that will shine on all non-believers and convince them of the work that is necessary. In due course you shall also have a visitor from the Taktsang Monastery in Bhutan who shall instruct you on the necessary teachings to be imparted to the people you have selected. Treat him with respect and do exactly as he says.'

The apparition of the divine Maitreya Buddha slowly dissolved. The Sangharaja was left staring into the darkness, trying desperately to come to grips with what had transpired. As he turned to switch on the lights, he caught sight of something that left him shivering uncontrollably in the warm room.

Resting on his bedside table was a golden figurine of the Maitreya Buddha, with a soft smile and exuding an inner glow, just as he had seen him moments ago.

22

France

The area of the foothills of the Pyrenees in southern France is one of nature's scenic enchantments. Framed in the background of dark blue mastiffs of rock and snow, the sylvan wooded hills are bisected into Arcadian valleys carved by the streams that cascade through them. The countryside is covered with trees of all hues and shapes that reach their splendour in the awesome beauty of their autumn leaves.

Lourdes found its destiny in such environs. It is a small market town at an elevation of around 1,000 feet through which runs the River Gave de Pau, coming from the mountains in the south, on its way west to Pau and Biarritz. On land, bordered by a loop of the Gave de Pau, is an outcrop of rock called Massabielle and it was here in February 1858 that a series of events changed forever the history of Lourdes, making it one of the most famous sites in Christianity.

Situated to the front of this rock, near the riverbank, with its slushy and uneven ground, is a naturally occurring shallow cave or grotto. On the evening of 11 February 1858, a young Roman Catholic girl of frail health, Bernadette Soubirous, went to the Massabielle to fetch firewood with her sister Toinette and a friend Jeannie. Here, she reportedly had the first of eighteen visions of what she termed '*uo petito damizelo*', a small young lady, who was standing in a niche in the rocks to the right of the grotto:

> I had hardly begun to take off my stocking (to go into the water) when I heard the sound of wind, as in a storm. I turned towards the meadow and I saw that the trees were not moving at all … (but) the branches and brambles were waving beside the grotto … behind these branches and within the opening, I saw a young lady dressed in white who greeted me with a slight bow of her head … over her right arm hung a rosary … a white veil covered her head … the sash of the dress was blue and, on each foot, I saw a yellow rose … (she was) surrounded with light.
>
> (Saint Bernadette Soubirous,
> *Abbe Francois Trochu*, pp. 42-44)

The apparition did not speak to Bernadette on that day, nor the next. But her gentle smile and unearthly beauty drew the fourteen-year-old girl to the place till, on the third appearance, she was asked by the Lady to return to the grotto every day for two weeks.

No one other than Bernadette ever saw the vision though, even after crowds started to gather round the grotto after news of the episode spread. Bernadette was obviously in ecstasy on every occasion as she knelt before the niche that had a wild rose bush growing around it. On the ninth appearance of the Lady, she asked Bernadette to go and wash and drink of the spring inside the grotto.

Seeing no such spring, Bernadette 'began walking about on her knees and went so far deep into the grotto that she was in a narrow space between the rock roof and the damp earthen floor. She kissed the ground several times then turned again to look up at the niche with her face all muddy. To the astonishment of the crowd gathered there, she picked some grass and ate it, smeared mud all over her face, then, after three unsuccessful attempts, swallowed some mud.'[1]

The next day, a small spring had started flowing from the grotto and has never stopped since. This water is now collected through fonts and is also channelled into the baths for the infirm and handicapped. Today, thousands of gallons of water gush from the source of the spring, and countless purported miracle cures have been documented—from the healing of nervous disorders and cancers to cases of paralysis and even blindness.

On the sixteenth visitation, and after being repeatedly asked who she was, the Lady revealed herself to be the 'Immaculate Conception'. This was a reference to the dogma of the 'Immaculate Conception', which had been defined only four years earlier in 1854 by Pope Pius IX, stating that the Virgin Mary herself had been conceived without sin.

Bernadette, being an uneducated daughter of a poor miller, did not understand what this meant but she reported it to her parish priest, Father Peyremale. Though he had been initially very sceptical of Bernadette's claims, he became convinced of the visions when he heard this, because he knew the young girl had no knowledge of the doctrine.

The Lady also told Bernadette that the priests should come every day in a procession to the grotto and that they should build a chapel there. Today millions of pilgrims visit

[1] Therese Taylor, *Bernadette of Lourdes*, Bloomsbury Publishing, p. 89.

Lourdes and there is a moving ceremony every evening when a procession goes around carrying candles and lights around the church built over the grotto, the Basilica of the Immaculate Conception.

And Bernadette Soubirous? Diffident of the crowds that surrounded her whenever she appeared in public, Bernadette never visited the grotto again. She was first given shelter as a boarder at the Hospice of Lourdes where she found some peace and quiet but soon, even here, she was constantly hounded by pilgrims and others who sought blessings and details of her visions. Her health declined markedly through asthma and pneumonia and she was reminded of what the Lady had told her: 'I cannot promise to make you happy in this world, but in the next.'

She finally departed for the Saint-Gildard Convent in Nevers to join the Sisters of Mercy there. Her health continued to decline, added in part by her own strict adherence to the rigours of religious life. On 16 April 1879, a good twenty-one years after her visions, Bernadette gave up her spirit to the Lord. Even today, her body resides in the Convent in Nevers, free from any traces of decay or corruption, and with serenity written on her face.

❀

Raul Baptist woke up that November morning with a feeling that somehow this day would change the course of his life.

He lived with his mother Marianne and sister Jeanne in a small apartment above the shop in Lourdes that his mother had inherited from her husband on his death. The street on which the shop was located contained many hotels and pensions catering to the millions of tourists who came to this famous place of pilgrimage. Along the street were shops selling items for which Lourdes was famous: holy water bottles and cans, pictures of the Blessed Virgin and Bernadette, rosaries, religious artefacts, necklaces and beads, small and large icons and so much more. Marianne had a flourishing trade in these souvenirs and was relatively well off because of the munificence of the pilgrims.

One of the extraordinary features of trade in pilgrim artefacts in Lourdes, and in sharp contrast to what happens in other places of pilgrimage, was the complete absence of competition among the shops selling the various items. There was a uniformity in rates that precluded haggling over prices and the buyers went away satisfied that their needs had been fairly priced.

The flow of pilgrims to Lourdes was notably less in the winter months when only those who needed an urgent cure came to the shrine. While his mother and sister sat sunning themselves on the sidewalk in front of the shop, Raul loved to go to the grotto every morning to sit before the statue of the Holy Mother and silently mediate. Now that there wasn't the disturbing throng of the tourists, all bent on taking photographs or scrambling for the water from the fonts, the setting vibrated with a great sense of peace and well-being.

Raul sat in the park facing the grotto trying to visualise the happenings here almost a century and a half ago. He often thought of Bernadette and what she must have felt as the apparitions of the Holy Mother occurred before her. He stared for hours at the statue to the right of the grotto, now surrounded by the thorny rose bush, and wondered if this was what Bernadette had seen. He recalled that the figure that currently stands in the niche was created by the Lyonnais sculptor Joseph-Hugues Fabisch, in 1864. This had become an iconographic symbol of Our Lady of Lourdes, which is not only older and taller than Bernadette's description, but also more in keeping with traditional representations of the Virgin Mary.

Whenever Raul came to the grotto, he was greeted with a thrillingly beautiful birdsong from atop it. He traced the origin to a small black bird, with a yellow beak, that sang hymns in praise of the Madonna with 'full-throated ease'. It was a magical moment that made him forget himself and surrender to the mesmerism of the blessed surroundings.

Every evening Raul joined his mother and sister in the traditional procession round the shrine. It never failed to move him as thousands, holding aloft candles and lights, circled the Basilica, singing Ave Marias as a symbol of faith for those that had belief.

That November morning, Raul was serving in the shop when a wizened old man came to make purchases.

'Six dozen rosaries and four dozen two-litre jars, please,' he smiled. Raul was surprised! He had to borrow rosaries and jars from neighbouring shops to fulfil the order. While packing the items, he politely asked where he was from and why he needed such a large order. The old man sat down on the bench by the side of the shop, and before replying to Raul, took out a cheroot from his well-weathered shirt pocket and lit it.

'I am Ahmet from Ephesus in Turkey. I sell rosaries and other holy items outside the house where the Holy Mother Mary lived and died. I come regularly to buy her icons here because I know in Lourdes no one cheats me.'

'The house where the Holy Mother lived and died in Ephesus?' Raul exclaimed. 'I haven't heard that before.

Surely, she lived and died in Jerusalem, in the Kidron Valley, at the foot of Mount of Olives. I was reading about the Holy Land and there is a reference there to the tomb of Mary where a huge sepulchre has been built.'

The old man's face wrinkled in a smile. 'You are mistaken, my boy. Her last days were spent in Ephesus and her small stony house is a place of great reverence where many pilgrims come, though not, of course, as many as come to Lourdes.'

By now, Raul's mother and sister had come to the shop, so he sought permission to take the visitor from Turkey to a small cafe nearby to learn more of the startling information he'd just heard. Settling down to cups of coffee, Ahmet asked Raul whether he had ever heard of the visions of Anne Catherine Emmerich. When Raul shook his head, Ahmet continued:

'Catherine Emmerich was a German nun from the Augustine convent in Westphalia, who lived around the time of Napoleon's escapades in Europe. She was a frail person who spent most of her life bedridden and in great pain. However, she was a devoutly religious figure and even in her obvious agony, she used to describe her visions of the final days of Christ, the Last Supper, his betrayal, trial, passion and the crucifixion. She also described the torment of the Holy Mother and her life after Christ. Apparently, the Virgin continued to live in Jerusalem for some years but, after the crucifixion of James the Just, and the prosecution of the followers of Christ, she migrated to Ephesus under the care of the apostle John. There, in the wooded hills above Ephesus, a small stone house was built for her, where she lived with a maid to assist her and was surrounded by a few trusted followers. Catherine Emmerich describes her final moments and Assumption when she is united with her son.

'Her visions were so detailed, almost as if seen first-hand. However—and here is where Ephesus comes into the picture—in her visions, she described quite clearly the location of the Virgin's house above the town. Until then, Ephesus itself had not been fully excavated or explored; only a few people who lived in the neighbourhood knew of it. Quite obviously, Emmerich herself had never been to Ephesus; she had never travelled outside her home and the convent. Yet she gave such an exact description of the house that, in 1881, a French priest named Julien Gouyet used Emmerich's book to search for the house above Ephesus and found it based on the exact descriptions given! Since then, of course, other people have confirmed the location and I am proof of the visitations to the site.'

Raul was so taken by Ahmet's story that he would have willingly accompanied the old man back to Turkey. He didn't that time because of his attachment to Lourdes and his duty to his small family. But he promised himself that one day soon, he would visit the Virgin's house in Ephesus as part, perhaps, of his pilgrimage to the holy places.

Ahmet's account did, however, greatly impact his own feelings towards the Lady of Lourdes. His mind was now filled with her presence and he spent much greater time meditating on her at the grotto. His refrain was always, 'Divine Mother, if it be your will, reveal yourself to me. Let me become an effective instrument to serve you. Direct me to help and mitigate the suffering of those that come seeking you.'

As winter advanced, the crowds that came to Lourdes became noticeably sparser. This was not only because of the cold weather but also due to the increasing chill in international relations that gravely threatened to get out of hand.

The Sanctuary of Our Lady of Lourdes, or the Domain as it's commonly called, comprised the area around the grotto, the basilica, the gardens, the taps and baths of the holy water, and is administered by the Bishop of Tarbes and Lourdes and his local representative, the rector.

Raul had known the rector, Jean Philippe Dassault, since his childhood. His one prized possession, a bicycle, had been a present from the rector on his fifteenth birthday. Dassault was impressed with Raul's devotion to the Holy Mother and would spend hours talking to him about religion and the miraculous events surrounding the now beatified Saint Bernadette. On one occasion he took Raul to visit the Saint Gildard Convent of the Sisters of Charity at Nevers, where Bernadette's body is preserved. Despite all these years, and even after three exhumations, her body is still incorruptible, and can be viewed in its crystal glass case in the Convent. Raul teared up seeing the serene face that had been lifted eighteen times to the Lady of Lourdes; the delicate hands that held her rosary during the apparitions; and the fingers which scratched the earth in obedience to the Lady's request and made the miraculous spring appear.

How does one explain the slow surrender of an otherwise normal human character to some mystical force that completely overwhelms that person? For Raul, it happened gradually as he gave himself up to the call of the Holy Mother. He forgot food or drink, he forgot his appearance or what he wore, he forgot the shop and his family. The only place that mattered was the grotto and he was found, on many occasions, lying supine on the cold ground before the Holy Virgin's statue, begging that she appear to him as she had to Bernadette. His sleep was a delirium of anguished prayer to the Mother, seeking her vision and, in the process, he even forgot his sleep!

As he wandered about, with bloodshot eyes and unkempt hair, his worried mother pleaded with the rector to find a solution so that her son may return to a measure of sanity.

Dassault did find a solution. After consulting with the Bishop of Tarbes, he called Raul to meet him at the grotto. After praying together to seek the Mother's blessing, he turned to the boy and said, 'My son, look around you and see that the Holy Virgin is not only in the niche there, in front of us, but all around us. Can you tell me even an inch of place where she is not? You spoke to me some time back of the Virgin's house in Ephesus. Believe me, my child, she is there! She is wherever man's devotion takes him. But the most amazing thing is that she is within you, within me and within everything that exists. You have but to shut your eyes and the Blessed Mother can be seen by you. Bernadette saw her in her visions, but even she stopped coming to the grotto after the eighteenth appearance. Do you know why? Because now she had found her *in* her own heart and did not need to come here anymore. In the Holy Bible, Jesus says, "Blessed are the pure in heart: for they shall see God". My son, I know you crave for a vision of the Divine Mother. Seek her in the purity of your own heart and you will find her there.'

Raul listened attentively and quickly absorbed his mentor's words. He looked at the figure of the Holy Mother in the niche and felt she was smiling at him and gently nodding. He confessed, 'Master, you have opened my eyes.

I was foolish to think I would find the Mother in external things. I realise now that she has been within me all this while. I will create her temple of divinity within myself and pray and adore her there.'

Winter was at its peak. Raul snuggled deeper under his quilt to keep the cold out. He was drowsily reciting his Hail Marys when suddenly the room was filled with a bright light. It was the light of all lights and Raul had to cover his eyes with the crook of his elbows to shield himself from the radiance.

Gradually, as his eyes became somewhat accustomed to the effulgence, he saw a petite figure surrounded by a white and blue oval. She hovered above the foot of his bed, looking down at him.

It often happens in life that when you crave for something long enough, you don't instantly realise the moment when your desire has been fulfilled. Raul, who had hungered so much for a glimpse of the Mother, thought it was a dream and not the Madonna herself who was smiling down at him. He feverishly reached for the rosary he always kept under his pillow and started reciting his prayers as he rose to kneel in his bed. As he closed his eyes, a soft voice echoed in his mind:

'Raul, I have a task for you. Go to the rector and tell him to gather all my devotees inside the grotto and wait for further instructions there. Remember that they all have to be spiritually pure and that they believe in me and the Holy Trinity.'

With this, the dazzling vision slowly faded, and Raul was left drenched in perspiration despite the acute cold.

Quickly rising from his bed, his mind still in a whirl, Raul rushed to his mother and babbled that he had a message for the rector and ran out in the cold to the latter's house.

Jeanne Philippe was still reading prior to retiring when a dishevelled Raul knocked at his door. In words falling one over the other, he blurted out what he had experienced.

The rector took him to his study, made him sit and giving him a glass of water, asked him to slowly recount again all that had happened. By this time Raul was more composed and so related the incident with a measure of clarity.

'Gather the spiritually pure in the grotto?' exclaimed the rector. 'Why, Raul, the grotto can only accommodate around fifty or so. Surely you must be mistaken. Think carefully, my son, did you really see the Lady or was it something you conjured up because of your devotion to her? There is nothing wrong with that; we all tend to hallucinate at some time or another. But to imagine that the Lady actually gave some directions? Why, that is akin to Bernadette saying she wanted a procession to come to the place and build a chapel there!'

By now, a dishevelled Raul had acquired a measure of calm and was able to reflect on the episode in a somewhat detached manner. 'No, Reverend, I was neither asleep, nor was this a figment of my imagination. How else could I, while under the spell of the apparition, be surprised at her directions to gather *all* her devotees in the grotto? Even then, I thought she meant *in front of* the grotto, though that makes little sense. Tell me, master, what am I to do? Do you think I am perhaps losing my mind?'

'No son, if you can analyse the matter as coolly as you have just done, you are certainly not losing your mind.

Now it's not a question of what you should do, but of what I should do. My path is clear—we must immediately take this matter to His Eminence, the Bishop.'

With this, the rector bundled Raul in his creaky car and set off on the road to Tarbes. The 25-kilometre journey normally took around half an hour, but Jeanne Philippe made it to the bishop's lodging in much less time. Even then, it was almost midnight when they reached the house.

The Most Reverend, Pierre Abbey Giscard, the Bishop of Tarbes and Lourdes, did not sleep early and so was able to receive his visitors in his study. He personally brewed some instant coffee and then waited for the rector to explain the reason for this late call.

'A most unusual incident has happened in Lourdes, Your Reverence, and before it becomes public or goes further, I thought I would bring it to your notice and seek your directions. This is Raul Baptist, whose case I have discussed with you earlier. Following your directions, Raul has calmed down considerably from his earlier frenzy of adoration of our Lady and now has been praying to her in quiet meditation. Today he had a most unusual experience and I would recommend Your Reverence to hear about it directly from his lips.'

The two clergymen turned to Raul and waited for him to speak. 'Your Reverences,' he began, 'I know that in the past few months I have been a cause of concern to you both, and I am grateful to have received all the support from the church of my faith despite my fitful behaviour. As instructed by you, I have now started to pray to our most Blessed Lady within myself rather than look for her in external objects.

'Today I have been subjected to a vision I can neither explain nor deny but only describe to the best of my ability. While attempting to do so, believe me, I am filled with doubt and remorse that I may be ridiculed and mocked as one who has lost his mind. But I would be failing even more if I were to keep the matter to myself, and not do what the Blessed Mother asked me to. So, without further ado, I venture to state what happened.'

Raul went on to narrate his vision using all the faculties of memory at his disposal to recite the exact words and directions of the apparition. When he finished his narrative, he found himself bathed in perspiration as he waited for the reaction of the bishop.

In his long life as a servant of the church, Pierre Abbey Giscard was never surprised at the numerous situations he had been called upon to handle. Yet now, even he was shaken to the core. He was overcome with a great sense of déjà vu. Was this not an exact parallel to when Bernadette first approached the clergy with an account of her visions? The church had failed her then, but how was he to deal with reports of similar circumstances? He decided to question Raul closely of his account but, try as he might, Raul answered calmly and without contradiction.

'But, my son, how can we fit in so many people in the grotto?' he asked.

'I don't know, sir; I too am surprised. But those were the exact wishes of the Lady.'

The discussion went on late into the night before the bishop finally called a halt. He said he would visit Lourdes early next morning and made the others swear that the episode would not be discussed with anybody, not even Raul's family. It was a pensive duo that drove back from Tarbes.

❈

The next morning, Raul waited at the rector's house. He had had a torrid time trying to explain to his mother why he had rushed off to the rectory and returned so late at night. His silence, and the statement that all would be explained later, only left a curtain of tense silence behind. When the bishop came, the three went to the grotto to pray and seek guidance from Our Lady of Lourdes.

Raul had never seen the place so beautiful and peaceful as it was that morning. A wintery sun was out in all its finery and the grass glistened as the morning dew reflected its crystalline rays. The trees around the park were a profusion of sylvan greens while, on the edge, the River Gave de Pau genuflected joyously as it flowed past the grotto. Floating on the river were a few pairs of small ducks, calling to each other and racing to find early morning titbits. The grotto itself resounded with the sweet notes of the blackbird as it sang its hymns to the Holy Virgin with clarity.

The two clergymen and Raul knelt for a long time in front of the grotto before purifying themselves with holy water from the fonts. Raul went and brought a handful of candles from the stand nearby, putting in a few francs into the box as donation for the same. The three lit these candles in the row of shelves provided on the side.

Having completed these traditional rituals, Raul followed the bishop and the rector as they entered the grotto to get an idea of its size. The grotto was roughly 500 square feet, enclosed from all sides except the wide opening facing the river. Inside and to the left-centre was a glass-enclosed space, covering the spring that issued from the site that Bernadette had dug with her hands. Hanging on the walls inside were many crutches, sticks, surgical walkers, rosaries and other items left by those who were miraculously cured at Lourdes.

As the three emerged from the grotto, they knelt before the statue of the Lady, created all those years ago by Joseph-Hugues Fabisch in the niche surrounded by the bush of wild roses. The original rose bush at the time of the visitations had been destroyed by the crowds seeking souvenirs and a new bush had been planted in its place. As he looked up, Bishop Pierre Abbey Giscard gave a start and gazed long and steadfastly at the statue.

'Jeanne Philippe, I know that the domain office retains a copy of the original image of Our Lady created by Joseph-Hugues Fabisch in 1864. Raul, run as fast as you can and fetch it for me.'

Raul did as he was told, wondering why the bishop was so keen to have a copy of the image. It took some time to persuade the officials of the domain to part with it, and they did so only when they heard that the bishop was waiting at the site. As Raul unfolded the scroll on a bench in front of the statue, all three collectively gasped. While the original copy of the image had the Lady with her hands clasped together and a rosary hanging on the right arm, the statue they now saw had the rosary on the left arm with the right-hand lower down and pointing to the grotto!

❈

That night, it was the bishop's turn to receive instructions. These came in a realistic dream sequence as he fell into an exhausted sleep in Tarbes: 'A messenger will be coming to Tarbes with some friends from America. They will be bringing a large amount of equipment. The messenger will be wearing an ochre robe such as you see on pilgrims coming from India. You are to take them to Lourdes where they will stay with the rector. They will be working in the grotto and should be allowed to do so. They will carry further instructions with them.'

A second directive quickly followed: 'You have to collect as many of the faithful as you can to gather in front of the grotto, and to go inside after proper inoculation. Ensure that no evil mind enters the grotto.'

This message was similar to the one given to Raul; the bishop felt guilty that he had disbelieved the boy when he had first been brought to him. Matters had matured way beyond then and the bishop was only left wondering whether these preparations had anything to do with the fact that international relations had now sunk to a new low. However, leaving aside these mundane cares, he went about his given task.

With the permission of higher authorities, the Bishop of Tarbes and Lourdes called a congregation in the Basilica of the Immaculate Conception on a Sunday. It had been declared a special occasion to worship the Holy Mother. Thousands came from far and near and assembled to hymns of Ave Maria. The bishop in his address recounted the visions of Saint Bernadette and the miraculous events that had made Lourdes famous all those years ago. He asked the congregation whether they believed in the message of the Holy Virgin. The surprised audience all answered in the affirmative.

The bishop then said, 'The Lady has sent a test of your faith. All who believe in her are asked to assemble near the grotto in the next few days. Come with your families and bring with you articles of daily use. You will be given further instructions when you reach there.'

And so, it was that, beginning the next day, started a process soon to be named the final miracle of Lourdes. The bishop and his colleagues watched in amazement as the first twenty went into the grotto singing Ave Maria. Then the next twenty, and so on till more than a thousand had gone in. When they themselves entered the space, they found no overcrowding or shortage of space. The erstwhile tiny grotto was now of the size of the basilica above and even then, had room for thousands more! Everything was all so orderly. There was plenty of light, the holy spring was full of water and the faithful were as comfortable as if they had been out in the open. They did not know it then, but this would be their home for the next many years, saved from the doom the rest of the world would experience. And they had the protective shield thrown by Kalki acting through the divine intervention of the Holy Mother.

23

The Small Big Idea

SACRAMENTO

Ray took the last dregs of his morning coffee and fleetingly glanced at the newspaper headlines. The United States had walked out of peace talks with Russia and China over the situation in North Korea and there were accusatory fingers pointing all around. With all the major powers having their fingers on the nuclear arsenal, the chances for peace appeared distinctly bleak. Ray sighed and helped himself to the last sip from his mug.

Leslie Davis came into his office to confirm that the rest of the group would shortly be joining them in the conference room. Ray poured another cup of coffee for his companion and, because he wanted to discuss this with the team, asked Leslie for the latest progress on AI.

Pausing to collect his thoughts, Leslie said, 'Boss, not very much. AI is still a new area of application ever since 1955, when John McCarthy of Stanford University first coined the term to apply to a machine completing tasks, involving a certain degree of intelligence, previously deemed executable only by humans.

'Almost all AI used today is artificial narrow intelligence (ANI). This specialises only in one area that can be replicated indefinitely to equal or even exceed human intelligence; for example, games of chance on computers like chess, bridge and scrabble. Even specialised applications such as those used in cars, reservation systems for airlines or trains, the working of phones and facilities in them, and repetitive jobs in factories or commercial enterprises like maintaining manpower or payroll/pension records, patients' data in hospitals and so on are all ANI.'

'Yes, but what about building a computer to the next stage—artificial general intelligence (AGI), or as smart as humans in general and not just as a narrow speciality?' Ray asked.

Leslie shook his head. 'No chief, not possible so far, though that's what we are working on. The human brain is the most complex system in the known universe. It has trillions of neurons, each reacting differently in connectivity and response to each stimulus the brain receives from its innumerable sensory inputs. Trying to *reverse engineer* the brain's make-up and operation is the aim of our team.'

Ray hoped they had made some progress.

❀

'So, where are we now?' asked Ray, when they had all gathered in the conference room. Many had the ubiquitous coffee mug in their hands.

'Remember our goal is to try and create AGI in computers, such that machines can pass the Turing test. Just a quick recap—to pass the Turing test, a machine has to exhibit intelligent behaviour equivalent to, or indistinguishable from, that of a human. Give me some good news, guys.'

Sam Deakins, the expert in human brain scanning, was the first to speak: 'As you know, Ray, my team's been scanning the human brain to study its neural networks. We've been trying to figure how the human mind works and whether this process can be replicated in computers.

'The neural net paradigm is an attempt to emulate the computing structure of neurons in the human brain. Now, the human brain has about 100 billion neurons, each with over 1,000 synaptic connections to neighbouring neurons. With 100 trillion neural connections, each capable of 200 calculations per second (cps), we get 20 million billion brain impulses per second. This is the basic model of the neural network that is the source of human intelligence. The problem is, how do we get comparable computing capacity, even assuming that we can replicate the neural network in machines?

'Now, one way to express this computing capacity is in the total cps the brain can manage. You can come to this number by figuring out the maximum cps of each structure in the brain and then adding them all together. Experiments in this method have come to a rough ballpark figure of around 10 quadrillion cps. Currently, the world's fastest supercomputer can roughly match this capacity, but this is built at an immense cost, occupies huge space and consumes enormous megawatts of power.

'A linked, and perhaps more important, problem is that the neural networks are more complex and more varied than computers. Human thinking and, indeed, intelligence itself, jumps from one synaptic connection to the other as thought processes react to different stimuli.

The brain is composed of trillions of cells, each handling different sense inputs—hearing, seeing, moving, smelling, experiencing pain and so on. As we examine the parallel algorithms behind the neural system in different segments of the brain, we find that much of the neural network is devoted to simple life processes that are as varied as they are multidimensional.

'The task then appears to be to scan the entire brain and its neural system, then replicate that in machines with electronic circuitry of far greater speed and reliability. We are doing our best to do so, but it may take decades to create even the simplest machine of AGI. Whether that can be called endowing the machine with any element of consciousness is still a debatable question.'

This gloomy predilection cast a pall over the gathered meeting. Leslie decided to point out the only silver lining:

'Well, be it as it may, the good thing is that once we can create even the most rudimentary system, we can be assured that it will itself take over the task of reprogramming its design to improve its working.'

Ray nodded his agreement and added, 'We should always bear in mind that the first few steps are always the most difficult. The strength of a machine is that once it assimilates data, it can replicate it almost at the speed of light while, at the same time, improving on its design and architecture accurately and without tiring. By hypothesis, therefore, a machine that's empowered with consciousness will not stop at any level, but within micro-seconds attain superconsciousness. What happens then is a secondary issue. For the moment, let us continue with our task to make machines cognisant of human intelligence, and see where we go from there.'

Suddenly Ray Brown paused as if struck by a bolt of lightning. Slowly, he rolled over in his mind each of the words in his last uttered sentence.

'*Instead of teaching a machine to be as cognisant as man, why not teach man to be more cognisant of himself?*'

The Swami's words from the Hyderabad trip came back to him in a flash.

Quickly turning to Matt Spears, his specialist in human genetics, Ray asked, 'Matt, where are we on this question of using biotechnology for genetic engineering of the human body?'

Matt was taken aback at this query as he considered himself lower down the pecking order from the computer geeks who crowded the room. He was far removed from the world of machines, their microchips and electronic circuitry since he was basically a bio-scientist, more concerned with the anatomy of the human body than the means to replace it. But he was a specialist in genetics and knew more about the human structure than any of his colleagues.

'Genetic engineering has certainly taken huge strides in transforming our bodies, or at least many parts of it,' he started to answer. 'It has been used to cure diseases, alter genes that cause ailments, change physical parts of a body, and even improve mental faculties such as memory and intelligence. Genetic engineering has used titanium devices to replace our knees, jaws, spinal vertebrae and hips. Artificial arms, legs and feet are commonly in use and artificial hearts are being experimented on. There are synthetic vessels to replace arteries and veins, along with expandable stents to support for weak natural vessels such as those of the heart.

'The Human Genome Project will soon write down the genetic code that describes our DNA, chromosomes and basic cells. In the near future, we will design genetic therapies that target a long list of diseases and symptoms connected to ageing conditions. But to radically alter our cells—indeed the very way we think—we have to go inside the body, inside the brain, and reverse engineer the system from within.'

Matt was generally a man of few words. Even this clear-cut analysis seemed too long a diatribe to him. However, it was evident to everyone that what he had said was the kernel of truth. Silence reigned for a long time as everyone ruminated over what was required.

Suddenly, Gene Summers, the appropriately named expert on cellular technology, spoke up. 'Perhaps the answer to all that we have been discussing lies in nanotechnology. It's basically technology built on the sub-atomic level. We have found a key building material in carbon nanotubes (CNTs) that are allotropes of carbon with a hexagonal nanostructure. They are truly sub-atomic, with length-to-diameter ratio of up to 132 million:1. Owing to the material's exceptional strength, malleability and thermal conductibility, they are beginning to find application in shoring up the sturdiness of material for construction and industrial usage. They are being used in sporting equipment such as carbon-based golf clubs, tennis racquets, skis and bikes. In the foreseeable future, even spacecraft using nanotubes assembly will enormously bring down the weight, durability and cost of space flights.'

He looked excitedly around the room. It hit him that nobody was catching onto his chain of thought.

'My point is that billions of micro-mini electronic chips—encased in such nanotubes and linked for control, direction and movement to parent computers—could enter the body and alter the complete body chemistry *from within*. They would be nano-robots, or nanobots for short. Such nanobots will be the size of human blood cells, about seven to eight microns, or even smaller. They could be launched into our blood streams to rebuild cellular structures in our organs so that we could have refurbished kidneys, liver, pancreas, lungs, arteries and even hearts. The revolution in nanotechnology will ultimately enable us to redesign and rebuild, molecule by molecule, our bodies to banish the spectre of ageing and disease.

'Just look at another possibility—and now I am letting my imagination run wild—billions of such nanobots in the capillaries of the human brain can radically extend the way we think and thereby augment human intelligence. A new superhuman race will emerge and mankind will be changed forever!'

There was a stunned silence in the meeting. Ray was left with the ringing prophecy of the Swami in his head: man gaining greater cognisance of himself. To his colleagues he said, 'I think what Gene has spelt out is something that all of us should work towards. From now on, let this be our prime focus on AI. I want all of us to concentrate on nanotechnology and the creation of nanobots capable of circulating within the body.

'Sam, abandon your project into brain scanning and concentrate instead on getting whatever information you can on nanotubes. Leslie, you can work on the electronic microchip that can fuse with these nanotubes, and Mark can study on how we can use the nanobots to optimally alter genetic structure. This is an exciting adventure and I want to meet every week to review our progress.'

As he left Sacramento for his home in the mountains, the only thing that troubled Ray was whether his team would have sufficient time to produce results before the threatening war clouds overshadowed everything. However, he was an optimist and hoped that better sense would prevail over the warmongers of doom.

That night, as he tried to sleep with the rain tapping a staccato rhythm on his roof, Ray's dreams alternated with images of his team's failure to scan the neural networks of the brain, the shrill cries of war, the nanobots circling in body capillaries, and nanotubes endlessly wrapping themselves around electronic circuitry.

His fevered imagination finally found rest in the image of the Swami smiling at him and saying, 'Have no doubts, for you are on the right track; the consciousness in man has to increase manifold in order for him to realise the goodness within. A new order will emerge, cleansing the evil that surrounds society today. You and your team have been given a divine task. Arise, awake and stop not till the goal is reached.'

24

Sambhala

Bharat and Savitri had been working night and day on the task given to them by Lord Kalki. Savitri and Arjuna had mobilised the community for daily classes on information technology, with special focus on AI. Computers had been procured from Maheshwar and the local authorities ensured wireless connectivity. Many residents from Simdvipa had come to participate in the daily classes and soon it became a competition among the participants as to who was heading the class.

Meanwhile, Bharat and other leaders of the village had begun the task of deepening the caves in the forest. This was not particularly difficult since the caves were limestone, and not volcanic, in nature. The water in the caves was crystal clear and the stream widened as the cavernous structure was enlarged.

'Lord,' asked Bharat when Kalki appeared before him, 'Why is the government not engaged in these works? Would it not have been simpler if they had come to the aid of the village with all the resources at their command?'

'There are some things that have to be done by the faithful themselves, Bharat. This is one such venture in which only the spiritual can participate.'

And with this, Bharat had to be satisfied.

There was one area, however, which Kalki was yet to resolve and for this he sought the intervention of the Pawan Putra, Sri Hanuman.

'Mahabajrangbali, great Chiranjeevi, you are the perfect combination of shakti and bhakti, proving repeatedly your great strength and moral excellence in your profound devotion to Sri Rama. It was in recognition of these sterling qualities that Sri Rama had conferred immortality on you, so that you may watch over the preservation of dharma on earth.

'As my companion, you have witnessed Kali's advance. We need to purge this evil for the sake of the new Satya Yuga. You're aware that we have created many shelters around the world where the dharmic will go when evil is being destroyed. But there will be countless others who are isolated and beyond the reach of these shelters. Great Pawan Putra, I have a request to make of you. Please seek out such individual spiritual souls and whisk them to the shelters; I do not want the good to suffer the fate of the evil. Only you, with your divine insight and speed, can accomplish this task.'

Sri Hanuman bowed in humble salutation. 'Great Kalki, you are the personification of my *ishta devta* for me. It is only the deluded who see any difference between Sri Rama and you. So, Lord, it shall be my sacred duty to do as you desire. Those not in the evil net of Kali will certainly be saved.'

Saying so, Sri Hanuman bent to touch Kalki's feet and took off to fulfil his responsibility.

25

Race against Time

SACRAMENTO

Back in the laboratories of Ray Brown, it was a laborious and delicate task, with many dead-ends, pitfalls, twists and turns.

Gene Summers recounted the progress achieved in a review meeting.

'Matt and I have been working on nano-robotics together. Most of the basic structures we are trying to create through nanotechnology were articulated by K. Eric Drexler in his landmark book *Nano Systems: Molecular Machinery Manufacturing and Computation*, published in 1992. It spelled out the principles of the system and provided the roadmap for making them work. He spoke of a controlling computer and a molecular assembler that could be used to fabricate anything at the sub-atomic level. Actual experiments in the recent past have validated the success of Drexler's theories through practical design of molecular machines in constructing common items such as gears, electronic components, rotors and, more significantly, nanotubes.

'The problem is to extend the use of the molecular assembler into the biological area, but here also, some progress is notable. Various scientific laboratories are using nano-engineered assemblers to penetrate the cell nucleus and access the genetic information stored there. They have also been able to construct the amino acid sequence for an expressed gene while maintaining the genetic code in the nano computers. Changes in DNA could then be introduced to reprogramme the genes themselves. This could be used to defeat biological pathogens in the shape of bacteria and viruses by blocking any unwanted replication of genetic information. This is the first step in preventing ageing and getting rid of unwanted diseases.

'From this premise, we are studying how the process can be applied to neurons in the human brain. Reinforcing the neural network from within will alter the very way we think.

'Billions of assemblers in the shape of the nanobots will interact with the biological neurons. A new virtual reality, incorporating all the algorithmic neurological connections to our thoughts, our pattern recognition, our sense perceptions, our memories and emotions will emerge from within the nervous system. The biological and installed non-biological intelligence so created will usher in a new threshold of human consciousness.

'While we are now quite confident of the theory and are in a position to verify the practical experiments of other scientists, we are waiting for Leslie and Sam to come up with the production of the assembler units and microcomputers that can control the nanobots once they are introduced into the human body.'

Leslie cleared his throat, 'We already have prototypes of the nanotubes and, as everyone is aware, we are the leading centre for the most advanced micro electronic chips in the world.

'The problem was to scale down the circuitry to the molecular level. Honestly, we were originally stumped on this issue. However, Shiva Raghavan came up with a brilliant suggestion and we are now on a path-breaking trajectory. He suggested that we use the computer itself to design and create three-dimensional molecular circuits based on carbon nanotubes, that could process and switch signals at close to the speed of light. Our machines are being programmed into doing precisely this as they have the ability to reformulate designs to any desired outcome.

'Separately, Shiva is also working on algorithms that could provide the interface between the machine and nano-chips, so that their movement and direction can be controlled. I can confidently state that we will have satisfactory results very soon.'

At this point, Ray interjected. 'I am afraid speculation is not what we want. The growing crisis in international affairs may soon put paid to all our endeavours. Let us work night and day to find solutions. From now on, I shall be shifting to Sacramento to share in your efforts. Thank you, folks, for the strides you have already made.'

❁

A few more weeks of intensive work on their high-precision equipment showed some extraordinary results. Nanobots, controlled by external computers, were now commonplace in the company's laboratories. Except for the brain, considerable progress had been made in determining how they could be used to re-engineer virtually every system in the human body.

Matt Spears explained to the group, 'Let's start with the human digestive system. Man has to eat to survive, right? For centuries, the human species has depended on animal meat or available fruit, vegetables or grain to fulfil his dietary needs. In modern times, there is no shortage in food supply but, even so, essential nutrients can still be given intravenously to those who are too ill to eat.

'In other words, nutrients, drugs and other supplements can, even today, be introduced into the body to enable it to survive. Now, what if these essentials could be directly infused into the digestive tract through nanobots that will provide the exact amount of nutrients and the hundreds of phytochemicals needed to maintain a healthy balance in body chemistry? In one go, we would do away with the need to consume bulky amounts of food and, in the process, actually do away with the human alimentary system.

'Let us go one step further. The same system of accessing the bloodstream could also be used in redesigning the blood itself. The nanobots would be able to deliver scientifically enhanced red and white blood cells and platelets necessary for powering the human body. Pioneering research done by Robert Freitas, Jr, Professor at University of California, Berkeley, has shown that our red blood cells perform their oxygenating functions most inefficiently. He has redesigned them for optimal performance. He has shown that his robotic red cells could enable man to go for hours without the need for oxygen! The functioning of the lungs, and breathing itself, would be considerably reduced. The same would be true of micron-sized artificial platelets that would control bleeding a thousand times faster than biological platelets.

'Even more amazing is the theory that, if these robotic cells could have their own mobility, there would be no need of a heart to continuously pump blood to all parts of the body!

'Ray, we are fairly convinced that our theories are all workable. The problem is that we do not have a live biological system to validate our findings. Where do we find a man, or woman, who would be willing to undergo trials to test that their blood has really improved, or that their thinking has improved? We obviously cannot use animals or even localised cells to verify changes in their physical parameters. So how do we know what else remains to be done, or even if we are on the right track?'

There was considerable discussion on this very real problem. Suggested solutions ranged from using convicted prisoners to people who were brain dead. Since neither suggestion was wholly feasible, it was decided to carry on the research and leave the issue of testing for a future date. Leslie came closest to a possible solution by suggesting that perhaps the computer itself could show the success or failure of the trial, but even that was way off the mark.

❈

Kalki silently observed the developments in Ray Brown's group and was satisfied that they were on the right track. Perhaps they needed some catalyst to speed things up.

❈

Ray Brown was puzzled. As he entered his office, he found two people in ochre robes waiting for him. He was mildly irritated that the reception desk never informed him about them. Not only were these visitors unannounced, but they had also managed entry to his private place of work. He was also puzzled by the sweet fragrance pervading the place and the sense of peace that enveloped the strangers. He was strongly reminded of the atmosphere that had surrounded the Swami in Hyderabad.

'Ray Brown, forgive this intrusion into your private space,' one of them said while both rose from their chairs. Both the visitors had a strong and noble bearing and wore long strings of large brownish beads round their necks. Sandal paste was smeared across their foreheads, surrounding a red tilak that ran vertically to their hairline. Their hair was long and tied in a bun on the top of their heads. One of them had a long flowing beard while the other was clean-shaven. The most remarkable thing about them though were their eyes—unfathomable, timeless and all-seeing.

Ray politely smiled, while jogging his memory to check if he'd met any of them before. Turns out, he didn't even need to ask.

'We are travellers from afar in time and place and have been instructed to assist you in the remarkable work you and your illustrious team are doing here on the direction pointed out to you by the Swami in Hyderabad. My name is Parshuram and my companion is Vibhishana. We have observed how close you are to fulfilling the scientific objective of creating a new genre of human life. We are at your disposal in any manner you may so wish.'

Ray was momentarily rendered speechless. *Who are these two and how was it possible for total strangers to know of the work they were doing? More importantly, how can they possibly help in the tasks before them?*

He was sure he was not daydreaming. This was a mystifying situation and the most he could think of immediately, was to invite his guests to seat themselves. He began by offering them coffee or other refreshments which they politely refused. So, he came directly to the point. 'Please pardon my lack of comprehension; I am totally confused. You are obviously aware of our work and scientific research; how and why, I am at a loss to fathom. You have suddenly appeared before me and generously offered assistance. What am I expected to make of this? Even assuming I accept your credentials which, again, pardon me, I still have to be convinced of, what possible way can you help in our extremely difficult and delicate research?'

Parshuram shot him an understanding smile. 'There are few that are given an insight into the working of divine providence. Without going into the realm of deep philosophy, let's just say that God's will is a result of causality and that events in this whole cosmos are determined by various causes and their effects. All of creation, and its inevitable destruction, follow this self-same cycle of pre-determination. If you read our ancient Hindu scriptures, you will come across the theory of the yugas that extol the repeated cycle of ages and how one proceeds from one to the other.

'You must believe me when I say that the present age of evil is now drawing to a close, something that you must yourself be aware of. There will be some cataclysmic event, followed by a new age of truth, peace and development in which man will once again reach great spiritual heights.

'The great Swami you met in India was asked to select you and your team to be catalysts in this mission. We have watched with interest how you have come so close to fulfilling those expectations. Through your team's excellent groundwork there will emerge the superconsciousness. This will be the seed for the new age of man. There is still considerable work to be done and this is the reason we have been asked to assist you.'

This was still too much for Ray Brown to wrap his head around. Even though the stranger had spoken in a convincing manner, and even if Ray assumed much of it to be true, he still came back to his original query—who were these people?

He had hardly posed this question in his mind when Parshuram's whole body was enveloped in a blinding effervescence. He radiated incredible power that was both soothing and yet otherworldly. The vision lasted for no more than an instant, but it left a trembling and awestruck beholder more pliable than any word or speech could accomplish.

Parshuram answered this question, 'I am a messenger of the divine. Vibhishana is, like me, a Chiranjeevi, or what you might roughly translate as an immortal. We've been created to preserve dharma, the law of righteousness. Believe us that what we represent is the truth.'

Ray Brown opened his eyes. He hadn't realised they had been shut all this while. He found the two smiling, simple strangers standing in front of him again, looking as though nothing extraordinary had happened. Feeling desperately in need of refreshment, he poured himself a strong dose of coffee.

'This may still be some hallucination of a fevered mind, but tell me, what sort of assistance can you offer my team?'

Parshuram replied, 'I am leaving Vibhishana here—perhaps in a more acceptable attire for your team—to assist you in your research on robotics in the human bloodstream, not only on the genetic system, but also on the human mind. You may introduce him as a pioneering scientist from

India. Vibhishana will be able to inject the nanobots into his system without fear of any adverse effects and thus be able to validate the results of your experiments. When you are fully satisfied with the final trials, I shall come again to discuss further actions.

'And, by the way, I would recommend you read India's great epic, the Ramayana, to familiarise yourself with who Vibhishana really is, and why the great Lord Rama conferred the boon of immortality on him. Finally, before I leave you, may I request that this meeting be kept only between us?'

As Ray nodded his ascent, Parshuram and Vibhishana gradually faded from sight. A bemused Ray was left to wonder deeply about what had occurred.

❁

That it wasn't a dream or hallucination was proved the next morning, when Ray Brown found the 'scientist from India' waiting in his anteroom. Vibhishana now sported short, well-groomed hair and wore the clothes and long white gown used in laboratory work. The only noticeable feature that differentiated him from the ordinary were his piercing, knowledgeable eyes and the indefinable fragrance surrounding him.

As Ray hesitantly greeted him, Vibhishana put him at ease by asking if his appearance was suitable. Ray complimented him and assured him that he now would easily fit in. There remained only the question of a name. While Vibhishana was too long and complicated for the American tongue, its natural condensation to Vibhi seemed altogether too flippant. Ultimately it was decided that 'Dr Vibhishana

Swamy' was a sound balance and its invariable abridgement to 'Swamy' was entirely acceptable.

Ray introduced Vibhishana to his colleagues as a 'brilliant scientist from India', fully versed in Eric Drexler's work on nanotechnology and its application to the human genetic code. Dr Swamy was assigned to work with Shiva Raghavan on the interface of the nano-electronic chips to different organs of the biological system. The ultimate goal, to be shared by all members of the group, would be the introduction of billions of nanobots to interface directly with the brain's neurons to expand perception, memories and other cognitive functions.

Before joining in on the research, Vibhishana had, using his extraordinary powers of instant recall, totally familiarised himself with the latest information on nanotechnology, AI, the human genome, the genetics of the human body and its organs, as well as the neural networks of the brain. In any discussions within the group, Vibhishana was always a font of information and singularly creative in resolving different problems that arose. Very soon, Dr Swamy became the fulcrum around whom the entire research networked and progressed, often at breakneck speed till late at night.

❈

Michelangelo, the great Renaissance artist and sculptor had, while working on a marble block, observed that beauty and form were already enshrined within the block; all he had to do was to chip away the excess material and the form would reveal its full glory. The more the marble wastes, the more the statue grows.

Unveiling the secrets of the human mind is similar; the dark of ignorance has to be laboriously removed, layer by layer, through the tools of research and experimentation, to finally let the truth shine. The Adi Shankaracharya had pronounced that 'the truth of a thing is *tattvam*'.

This is expounded in a great verse in the *Mandukya Upanishad Karika of Gaudapada*:

> *Tattvamadhyatmikam drstva tattvam drstva tu bahyatah;*
> *Tattvibhutah tadaramah tattvadapracyuto bhavet*

> Having realised the tattvam that is residing within your own self, and realising the tattvam in external nature, becoming one with truth, taking delight in that truth, you never fall down from the truth.
>
> (Verse 2.38)

It is not possible to detail the thousands of experiments, even larger number of design changes, innumerable reverse-engineered prototypes, and equal number of dead-ends that the company encountered to reach the elusive tattvam but, at long last, Leslie interrupted Ray's reminiscing. It was well past midnight, but the man looked wide awake. He wasn't the only one; Gene Summers, Shiva Raghavan and Dr Swamy were in tow too.

Leslie placed a test tube in Ray's hands and said, 'Boss, this vial holds billions of nanobots that Swamy and Shiva Raghavan say are ready to be injected in the bloodstream to create the new superhumans of our race! We seem to be at the end of our quest but let's meet tomorrow to hear what Swamy has to say.' Ray looked at the tired group in front of him and murmured a few words of thanks before carefully placing the small vial in his locker.

'Leslie, let's sincerely hope that we have, at long last, found the final solution to the human race,' he said, trying to fit in some macabre humour. 'Let's meet tomorrow and see how we have been able to bridge the gap in testing it on a biological entity. Now go and get some rest.'

The end of a prolonged period of study, be it in pursuit of scientific discovery or even a simple school or college exam, always ends in a catharsis of sorts. There is a feeling of having scaled unknown heights to find that there is nothing beyond. Ray Brown marvelled at his determined band of men and remembered a stanza by Longfellow:

> The heights by great men reached and kept
> Were not attained by sudden flight,
> But they, while their companions slept,
> Were toiling upwards in the night

❈

Early next morning, as he was having his morning coffee, Ray was ruminating over the past few months of hectic activity. He was still puzzled at how the tests had been done and had just decided to call Vibhishana, when the latter materialised before him, bearing his same calm and unruffled demeanour.

'Ray Brown, my felicitations to you and your team for having accomplished a task it will take others many decades to achieve. You have in your possession the means to empower countless thousands that shall seed the coming age. Be not concerned about the efficacy of your results. I have personally tested them and have made minute adjustments to the system. In this, I have had the silent assistance of your most excellent colleague, Shiva Raghavan, who waits outside to meet you and give a fuller account.'

Ray quickly rose to call in Shiva and straight away sought answers. Shiva paused to gather his thoughts and then, with some trepidation, confirmed what Vibhishana had just told Ray.

'Boss, it began about a fortnight ago. Dr Swamy and I had just finished work handling the latest generation of nanobots, when he laughingly asked that I inject them into the vein on his arm. I was horrified since we did not know, at that stage, what the results would be. But he persuasively convinced me that he had undergone such tests before. "If I can survive the arrows of the fearsome Ravana, these are mere pinpricks in comparison," he had said.

'Something in the manner of how he said this weakened my initial resistance and I reluctantly injected the nanobot serum in him. Meanwhile I controlled their movements on the computer. Much to my relief, the stream of robotics had no adverse effect on Dr Swamy and, as a result, we learnt much about nanobot placement in the human body.'

Taking up the narrative, Vibhishana added, 'The only reaction we encountered was that the antibodies attacked the nanobots as a natural reaction of the body's immune system. But, with minute changes in the signal that the nanobots emitted, we not only solved the problem but actually converted the antibodies into allies, augmenting the body's resistance and preventing the onset of disease.

'Now, human biology has certain inherent deficiencies. Every genetic cell is built from proteins folded in one-dimensional strings of amino acids and these protein-based nuclei are singularly lacking in strength and adaptability. The nanobots redesigned the cells at the molecular level and rebuilt them with far more versatile and durable material. So, at the basic cellular level, the body got to have healthy high-performance organs. All these organic changes in the liver, kidneys, pancreas, spleen, lungs and heart are just as Gene

Summers and Matt Spears had theorised and have been captured on our monitoring computers for everyone to see.'

Leslie Davis, Sam Deakins, Matt Spears and Gene Summers had by now joined the meeting and had heard Vibhishana describe the biological changes in the body brought about by the nanobots. It was now time to describe the experiments on the brain and the team helped themselves to coffee as they waited for the explanation.

Vibhishana softly began his presentation. 'I would, at the outset, congratulate Sam Deakins for the pioneering work done on human brain scanning that has served as the basis for our own recent experiments. As outlined by him, the human brain has about 100 billion neurons, each interacting over 1,000 times with its neighbouring neurons and synapses, totalling about 100 trillion connections, each capable of simultaneous calculations. This massive *parallel* processing is the key to the strength of human intelligence.

'However, when you come to *sequential* thinking, you encounter the painfully slow speed of neural circuitry that is only 200 cps. The idea of introducing billions of nanobots into the brain was to increase this speed of connectivity through three-dimensional electronic circuitry to almost the speed of light. A new threshold of superconsciousness would thereby be achieved, reaching a level of awareness that sees beyond material reality and taps into the energy and consciousness behind that reality. Superconsciousness is this heightened awareness. Of course, all this was, in theory, known to all of you. The problem was how to verify human intelligence actually reaching this level of superconsciousness.

'In my country, India, the attainment of superconsciousness has been known since time immemorial.

Our scriptures talk of ancient rishis or sages who realised this state, called *nirvikalpa samadhi,* a heightened state of awareness where the ego and worldly reality have been dissolved and only consciousness remains. This was achieved through the practice of yoga, or physical exercises, and controlled breathing called pranayama.

'One of the methods is by raising the kundalini, an energy that lies dormant at the base of the spine, and channelling it upward through the spinal column to different levels and, finally, the brain, where superconsciousness resides. But the key still lies in meditation. As we delve deeper into the silence of meditation and experience enhanced peace, self-awareness, calm and bliss, we are on the threshold of the superconscious. The greatest scientist the world has known, Albert Einstein, defined it in the following beautiful words:

> The finest emotion of which we are capable is the mystic emotion. Herein lies the germ of all art and all true science.... To know that what is impenetrable for us really exists and manifests itself as the highest wisdom and the most radiant beauty, is the core of the true religious sentiment.

It was Leslie Davis who, on behalf of the whole by now thoroughly perplexed and fidgety team, asked Vibhishana, 'Yes, yes, Swamy, we understand all this and know what meditation can achieve. Even I, though not a particularly religious person, sometimes practise meditation to calm my mind when troubled. But what does this have to do with our experiments in nano-technology? You also speak of ancient Indian sages and their religious practices. What about modern times? Has superconsciousness been known in India at present?'

Vibhishana smiled quietly before answering, 'Leslie, I was only attempting to cover the entire spectrum of what is known today about the subject under discussion—superconsciousness. And yes, this subject is well known in India, with even the famous Beatles going to Maharishi Mahesh Yogi to practise transcendental meditation.

'But a more venerated person known to attain samadhi at will was Sri Ramakrishna Paramhamsa, whose ashram I believe Ray visited when he went to Hyderabad. This celebrated saint of mid-nineteenth century Bengal lived near Calcutta on the banks of the River Hooghly. He was a priest at the Dakshineshwar Temple and Swami Vivekananda was one of his prominent disciples. Sri Ramakrishna could go into samadhi at will, sometimes even without attempting to.

'Coming back to our own experiments, when Shiva Raghavan injected me with the nanobots and directed them to the brain, the electronic chips fired the neural circuitry to lightning speed and I began to experience that same pure consciousness that the sages must have felt.

'It is what our scriptures define as the state of *turiya* that cannot be experienced through the senses or known by comparison, deductive reasoning or inference. It is indescribable, incomprehensible and unthinkable through the logical mind. It is serene, tranquil, filled with bliss, and is one without a second.

'Regrettably, Ray, this state of the mind has not been caught in our monitoring computers because the computer cannot describe this in finite terms. You will have to take my word for it and, believe me, it is a feeling beyond all else and I still retain it!'

❀

During the following week, one by one, Ray's entire team was injected with the nanobots and their biological reactions captured on the computers. In each case, the body organs recorded vast improvement in disease resistance and non-ageing. The injection of the serum into the brain was left to the last and individual behaviour studied in personal reactions and on machines capable of high-resolution electroencephalography (EEG) recording electrical activity in the brain. All members of the group experienced enhanced levels of consciousness and a complete understanding of the effects of nano-technology on the brain circuitry. Their earlier doubts and hesitations were effaced by the new self-awareness.

It was this group of awakened men that gathered round Ray for a detailed de-briefing.

'Has it ever occurred to any of you what we have achieved here through this astounding research into human anatomy, even to the point of expanding the threshold of our thinking and consciousness? When I asked you to stop trying to make machines achieve AGI, and instead to concentrate on the biological parameters, what was the ultimate objective? Today we have in our possession the means to make a superhuman being with organs, blood and minds that would make him ageless and free from disease. He would want nothing of food and drink since he would be nourished internally by nutrient-infused nanobots. The question is why?

'Do we want to be the first to put this technology in the market? Yes, that would certainly make us instant billionaires and the toast of the scientific community till, invariably, someone improved on our design and made it better.

'No, gentlemen, that is not the purpose that was designed by people greater than I but who, I believe, control the very levers of human destiny. They certainly did not want the existing genre of humans, with all their avarice, violence and evil to be converted into uncontrollable superhumans wreaking havoc on the planet.

'Instead, and follow me closely here, we have been singled out to save selected humans from a looming global catastrophe that will occur in the near future.

'With your enhanced understanding, you will be aware of this but not the actual mechanics or details thereof. It will be a global operation and, when I am informed of our role, I will share it with you. In the meantime, may I request that you observe total secrecy on what has been achieved here?'

❀

Ray, Vibhishana and Shiva Raghavan were in the inner office when there was a brief burst of interjection, much as if a silent firecracker had fractured the room. Suddenly the three were joined by Parshuram, looking exactly as he had when he first met Ray. It took a while for the radiance to fade but his persona emitted deep contentment.

Vibhishana quickly presented Shiva Raghavan to him and Parshuram sagely nodded, 'My blessings, as you have helped us immensely in our task—from the moment you took Ray Brown to the math in Hyderabad and brought him to the presence of the Swami. You have also been a key figure in the great research conducted here.

'There remains but one major task in which all members of your team have to participate. Ray Brown, you are to send them, with whoever they want to take alongside, to different parts of the globe where shelters have been constructed deep within caves and underground caverns. Many thousands of selected people will have to live there for the next many years.

'Your colleagues will administer the serum to them and live with them for the duration. The nanobots will be controlled through your computers till superior consciousness makes this unnecessary. I understand that the nanobots, once introduced into the hosts, can alter specific organs to make eating, sleeping, oxygen dependency unnecessary. The chosen few and their progeny, with their new consciousness, will be seemingly ageless and will be able to endure the coming days of darkness.'

Ray Brown and Shiva were momentarily stunned at these directions, but never doubted that what Parshuram had stated was true. It is amazing how often one's perception, once released from ignorance, can still arrive at conclusions that initially seem way off the mark.

To Ray, the whole purpose behind their incisive research of the past many months now seemed clear. It was evident that some great calamity was to visit mankind. He could only surmise, not without reason, that it would be a nuclear devastation. Analysing the situation in this context, what Parshuram had spelt out made perfect sense. The only puzzling fact was why save only the spiritual? Why not shelters for everyone?

Parshuram read Ray's mind and replied, 'To save the whole of mankind would take many years of preparation, requiring millions of tonnes of the nanobot-enriched serum. And what if you administered the serum to the wrong type of person? Can you imagine the havoc a superconscious malevolent would wreak on an unsuspecting world? It would be like an ageless tyrant, forever lording the globe, and making certain that no one could ever get rid of him. No, the only guarantee of a new age of peace is that only the spiritual survive.'

With this issue resolved, the image of Parshuram faded, leaving just the three in the room.

❀

Despite whatever lingering doubts he may have had on the scale of operations, when Ray Brown met his colleagues again, he gave off a measure of self-assured confidence. Looking steadfastly at them he stated, 'I want each of you to prepare members of your team, their families, and of course your own, for a possibly protracted journey that will take you to different parts of the globe. These spots have been specially selected for this purpose. You will carry your immediate personal requirements and thousands of vials of the nanobots' serum, together with the computer equipment that will be needed, to inoculate a large number of people assembled at the sites. Any questions so far?'

Leslie Davis asked the obvious question. 'Why do we have to go? Wouldn't it be simpler for the subjects to be brought here, where the infusions can be performed in a controlled environment?'

Ray had anticipated this question and replied, 'Apart from the impossible logistics of transporting thousands of subjects from different parts of the globe to be brought and provided for here, and that too without attracting attention, there is need for engineering and scientific modifications to be made in the places where these people are located. For example, each site has to generate its own power supply from whatever source is available, and this can only be done once our teams get there and study what is feasible.'

'And what about our travel plans with family, equipment and personal luggage?' enquired Gene Summers.

Dr Swamy, who had so far remained silent, interjected here, 'I can assure you these details will be taken care of.'

Ray Brown summed it up. 'I am sure there will be many issues coming up in such a large operation. I am asking Leslie and Gene to draw up a master plan for this unusual exercise, emphasising only that on the success of this venture will depend the future of mankind. You have already played a stellar role in the design of the solution; let's now see to its fulfilment. We will meet as needed. Meanwhile, let's prepare large quantities of the nanobot brew, sufficient for our requirements, and maintain deadly secrecy over all we have done, or are about to do.'

26

The Comet

Kalki turned his mind to the comet that was still beyond the orbit of Pluto. It was travelling towards the distant sun at almost 60 kilometres per second. Even at this colossal speed, it would take almost four years before it came near the inner planets.

At present, it was a cohesive mass of ice chunks, rocks and frozen gases, bound together in a tight nucleus with ice—several metres thick—hidden beneath a surface crust. It would start losing its mantle only when well within the orbits of the gas giants. Then the sun's radiation would release the gases, sometimes in volatile outbursts the nearer it came, and the pressure of the solar wind would propel its lighter materials to form the tail streaming millions of miles behind the coma. But even now, the insidious tug of Jupiter was gradually having its effect. The comet was locked into a 1:11 orbital resonance with the planet; it completed one orbit for every eleven of Jupiter.

As he viewed this awesome instrument of destruction, as yet in the far reaches of space, Kalki's mind went to the objects of beauty that man had conceived down the years before evil had captured his creative mind. There were marvels of design like the Taj Mahal in Agra, the Acropolis in Athens, the Duomo in Florence, the Great Wall in China or even the Pyramids and the Sphinx of Egypt. There were religious sites round the world such as the Kaali Temple in Dakshineshwar, Kashi Vishwanath in Varanasi, Notre-Dame in Paris, the Kaaba in Mecca, She Dagon Pagoda in Yangon, Angkor Wat in Cambodia and so many others where the faithful went for peace and to seek salvation.

Kalki also remembered the sylvan beauty of the forests surrounding Sambhala and the wild denizen of the woods that had so befriended him in his childhood. He determined that no harm would come to the animals, birds and marine life as they would be a necessary part of the new Satya Yuga. Nor would the beauty and biodiversity of the great mountain ranges around the globe be destroyed in the coming calamity.

With his infinite power, he would throw a cloak around these monuments, religious sites, mountains, forests, birds, animals and the oceans to preserve and protect them through the darkness that was to come. Kalki reasoned that any evil lurking in these places would not survive the years of doom except as determined by him.

It is a wonder how, once divine providence shows the way, even the most herculean of tasks becomes well-ordered and easy to implement. So, it was with Arjuna, Bharat, Sonam Rabgye, Imran, Raul, the Sangharaja and the many other leaders of the exclusive masses, gathered round the shelters prepared. Sri Hanuman and Parshuram were the designated instructors and appeared before each in the form of their individual ishta deva, be it Lord Kalki himself, Guru Padmasambhava, the Said ul Auliya, the Maitreya Buddha, or the many other revered spiritual prophets of the communities.

The message given to each was similar: 'You are the appointed leader of your flock and have done admirable work in that which was pointed out to you. These caves and underground retreats have been constructed for the purpose of affording you shelter for the coming many years, when the world around you shall witness annihilation on a scale never seen or imagined before. Horror and destruction will sweep the land as if the very furies of the Armageddon have been let lose all over. Let not your minds despair, but have faith, for you are the chosen who shall see the end of darkness and the dawn of the new age. Remember that at all times, the flock under your guidance should keep faith in the one and only God, and that the curse of evil is kept away from their hearts and mind. For any who do not adhere to these instructions, the retribution shall be swift, and they shall be banished into the dark outside.

'In the coming days, messengers of the divine shall be visiting you. You will welcome them and their families, for they will be staying with you. They are experts in AI and shall be using their equipment to inoculate your people with life-giving drugs that will obviate the need for food and nourishment, eliminate disease and improve the capacity of the mind. They will carry computers and other machines to run on micro hydel units operating on running water. Prepare the groundwork for these water conduits so that you will have enough energy to last the period of darkness. You are never alone and we will answer any call through your power of meditation. Be of good cheer.'

With these directions, the visions faded and the community leaders were left to carry out what they had been told. Their main task was to ensure the construction of small but hardy viaducts to channelise the flow of water at a pace necessary to run the hydel machines, but through experimentation and with the specialised guidance of the scientific teams when they arrived, this mission was successfully implemented.

27

The Final Lap

Back in Sacramento, Ray Brown and his colleagues were finally able to assemble over thirty teams for travel to different parts of the globe. To gather together their families, equipment and baggage was no mean exercise and required the combined effort of all. The assembly of the families was particularly difficult. Invariably questions arose:

'Is granny coming with us?'

'Can we take our pet dog along?'

'Why can't my friends accompany me?'

The answer to these and other queries was always the same.

'Daddy has to go on an important mission and is taking us along for a holiday. You will be back soon.'

At least in the case of the elderly and the household pets, Sri Hanuman was there to whisk them away to the designated shelters.

❀

Sri Hanuman, Parshuram and Vibhishana carried Ray Brown's teams and their families to their designated shelters in the blink of an eye. The scientists set up their equipment inside the caves, closely watched by the curious onlookers. By now, each of the shelters had sufficient electricity from the hydel sets. It was transmitted through cables to the farthest depths of the caverns. Once the scientists arrived, improvements were made on the generating systems so that there would be no shortages during the period of darkness.

Arjuna, Bharat, Imran, Raul and Tashi Tshering were the first to be inoculated. Ray's teams followed the injected nanobots on the master computers to channel them to different organs. When no adverse effects were noticed, the others in the congregations were subjected to inoculations in small groups. The same procedure was followed in all the other shelters, with the community leaders being the first to be tested.

By now, the scientists, who had also injected themselves and their families, knew that the serum was working and that their heightened perception was capable of dealing with any minor fault occurring. Not that any did take place and so, within a short time, all residents of the shelters carried the miracle of the serum within their bodies. Strange as it seemed to the crew from Sacramento, there was not a single mishap reported from anywhere. Had they but known, the Chiranjeevis were monitoring the entire exercise to ensure its complete success.

28

Path of the Comet

The comet was now well inside the orbits of the gas giants and began to feel the light tug of Saturn as it passed near the ringed beauty, still 245 days from its scheduled rendezvous with Earth. Though far from the warm embrace of the sun, its solidified outer structure was imperceptibly loosening in the pull effected by the ringed planet's immense gravity.

It was not, however, until it was approaching the orbit of the mighty Jupiter that the comet was first sighted as a tiny blip on the world's probing telescopes. At its discovery, the comet was a nineteenth magnitude object, as yet not displaying any of the characteristics that would make it famous later. But within a few weeks, and around 130 days from the Earth, it had brightened perceptibly. Comets possess highly volatile ices such as carbon dioxide and carbon monoxide, that turn directly from solid to gas (or sublimate) at much lower temperatures than water ice. So, long-distance comets tend to brighten relatively far from the sun, when these ices melt and release large quantities of dust and gas.

Now, after a journey that had spanned almost a third of the way to the nearest star, the lonely traveller was awakening. The make-up of its materials, including carbon, hydrogen, oxygen and nitrogen, were signs that it formed about 4.5 billion years ago, along with the rest of the solar system.

Nature is a master architect in creating beauty out of nothing, even if that beauty is ephemeral and all consuming. So, it weaved the innocuous dust particles and volatile gases ejected from the nucleus into crystalline objects of colour and shape, as the comet crossed the asteroid belt between the orbits of Jupiter and Mars.

The immense dust trails appeared pale yellow, like straw, especially closer to the comet's fuzzy head where dust production is greatest. The increased solar radiation created a plasma tail that pointed directly away from the sun, and the carbon monoxide ions caused these gases to glow blue. Ion tails may also have cyanogen and diatomic carbon molecules, which both glow green when the sun's light energises them.

Using the braking power of Jupiter's gravity, Kalki had slowed the speed of the incoming projectile to almost half of its original, so that the people of the Earth witnessed at leisure this sign of divine retribution.

As the comet came closer, a huge white coma of fluorescent gases and dust enveloped the nucleus and flared to the side and behind the racing object. Man's imagination had always seen faces and forms in clouds, but these were always momentary spectres. This comet was different: its coma resolved itself into the shape of a white horse, its tail and mane whipped back as in a galloping steed. In time, the imaginative could also make out a figure seated on the horse, carrying what was clearly a flaming white sword in its hand. People recalled the words in the *Book of Revelation*:

And I saw heaven open, and a white horse appeared. Its rider is called Faithful and True; justly he judges and wages war. His eyes are like a flame of fire, and on his head are many diadems with a name inscribed which no one knows except himself. The robe he is wearing has been dipped in blood: and the name by which he is called is The Word of God.... And out of his mouth issues a sharp sword...."

(*Book of Revelation* 19, 11-13)

It was only now that the global astronomical and scientific community awoke to the fact that the path of the comet was likely to interject that of the Earth. The world forgot its petty quarrels in the face of this colossal danger. Ray Brown, before he mysteriously disappeared, had suggested the comet be named Kalki and the name had stuck. Precise calculations of its speed and orbit had been fed into powerful calculators in NASA and the Space-Guard systems, only confirming what was now obvious: Kalki was certain to collide with the earth.

The scientific community had, of course, been aware of the danger of comet/asteroid strike for many years. As astronomers around the world increasingly worried about Kalki, their minds went back to another unique event in the history of science: the first ever globally witnessed collision of a comet striking the solar system's largest planet, Jupiter.

The comet Shoemaker-Levy was first spotted in March 1993 with an orbital speed of 60 kilometres per second, circling Jupiter every two years. It was believed that the body had been captured by the giant behemoth at least a couple of decades earlier and had last made a close approach to Jupiter on 7 July 1992. It was at a distance of approximately 71,400 kilometres above the cloud tops, when the comet was broken into at least twenty-one pieces by the planet's tidal gravity. Due to the immense pull, which changed the orbits slightly, on the next approach to Jupiter, the pieces impacted the planet.

Comet Shoemaker-Levy experienced one of the most spectacular ends that humans had ever witnessed. From 16–22 July 1994, twenty-one separate fragments of the comet ploughed into Jupiter's whirling typhoons, leaving dark blotches where the comet smashed through the tenuous medium. Despite the gaseous clouds miles above the planet, huge fireballs erupted, carrying material whipped away by the terrifying winds in Jupiter's upper atmosphere.

The gargantuan mass of Jupiter seamlessly swallowed up the pieces of Shoemaker-Levy in 1994. The impact scars disappeared many years ago and scientists declared that Jupiter's atmosphere had suffered no permanent effects from the collisions. But what would be the fate of lesser planets had such an event befallen them? The world was soon going to find out.

For many years following Shoemaker-Levy, astronomical scientists were busy researching techniques to deflect or destroy these objects once it was determined that there was a possibility of impact on Earth. Asteroids posed the more immediate danger as there were plentiful more on near-Earth orbits. The first step was to find and track them in order to determine if their circuits interjected that of the Earth. Programs such as Spacewatch and Spaceguard were created to detect, by 2008, 90 per cent of near-Earth asteroids over a kilometre in diameter.

It became apparent that there were fewer options with short warning times and larger objects, and more options with additional warning time and smaller objects. Obvious techniques were to use space rockets to either destroy or nudge the incoming threat using strike force or nuclear devices for this purpose. Most deflection efforts for a large object require from a year to decades of warning, allowing time to prepare and carry out a collision avoidance project, as no known planetary defence hardware had yet been developed.

For long-period comets, however, there was no known technology to counter the massive speed and size of the incoming object. Moreover, the warning time was already too late to prevent collision.

Comet Kalki had already crossed the orbit of Mars and was only 120 days away from impacting Earth.

29

Mount Kailash

His preparations almost over, Kalki retired to Mount Kailash. Meditating on Lord Shiva and Devi Parvati, he waited patiently for their permission to speak. At last Mahadev opened his eyes and, with a gentle smile, asked, 'It is truly a celebrated moment when we are blessed with darshan of the force behind creation itself. You are most welcome, Lord Kalki. How may we be of service to the avatar of Lord Vishnu Hari?'

Kalki remained in his kneeling position before Shiva-Parvati before replying, 'Great Lord of the Tandava, the occasion has come when you, as the supreme architect of pralaya, must step forward to end this creation. Lord, this is the role prescribed in the blessed Trimurti, where Lord Brahma is the creator, Lord Vishnu, the preserver and you, my Lord, the destroyer.

'As my divine guru, you had instructed me on my role as the tenth avatar of Vishnu. With your blessings, the task I was given has been nearly accomplished. It needs your final touch to be fulfilled. Lord, I await your command.'

Mahadev smiled to himself for he knew Kalki's boundless knowledge and recognised that this request was only meant to seek his blessings. 'Blessed Lord Kalki, you are fully aware that creation, or srishti, itself can never be destroyed for it is the imperishable Brahmand of which you and I are an integral part.

'The venerated Trimurti is a manifestation of that creation, everlasting and ethereal; it has no beginning and no end. It is only the world of man that is subject to *trikaal*, the three divisions of time: past, present and future. That is subject to the theory of chaturyuga. As the presiding deity over the Kali Yuga, you, Lord Kalki, are responsible for its destruction and the ushering in of the new yuga cycle. It is so prescribed by dharma; it is so proclaimed in our scriptures. Devi Parvati and I are mere spectators in this great drama. Lord Kalki, you have our blessings to perform your designated role.'

Lord Kalki bowed low with joined palms and accepted the divine benediction.

30

The Looming Oblivion

When faced with disaster and death, the human mind tends to become numb, the body and limbs feel paralysed, and one feels enveloped in a gloom that denies searches for escape. And when none present themselves to the distraught senses, sheer panic sets in. So now panic set in the world over as man sought to evade the catastrophe that was upon him.

And yet, even now, his thoughts were enmeshed in his prized possessions on earth—his loved ones, his properties, the wealth he had acquired in his craven lust for gold, and meaningless trinkets of gems and precious stones. Many buried them in whatever hideout they could find. Many others fled with them to whatever places they thought safe. The super-rich boarded their yachts and went on the high seas, thinking this would provide them protection.

Those who were powerful leaders of nations and communities sought shelter in the numerous dug-outs they had prepared for their nuclear adventure. Many countries on both sides of the divide had constructed fallouts against radioactivity during the Cold War. Apart from underground buildings, mass-transit and subway tunnels were strengthened to serve as bomb and fallout shelters.

Their objective was to save high-ranking national figures from exposure to deadly radiation. But they also served a military purpose, that of launching effective counter attack on the enemy. Government and other leaders now rushed with their pathetic possessions to evade the comet. They were yet to realise the scale of the disaster or the long period of darkness that was to follow.

The comet was now only thirty days away.

❈

Kalki made some last-minute changes to the comet's trajectory so that its speed was now only 15 kilometres per second and its orbit adjusted so its main bulk would strike on the barren tundra landscape. Because of the flaring coma, the comet had also lost over 90 per cent of its mass. This would significantly lessen the global impact as its size was now only 1,500 metres across of loosely bound ice, dust and gas that it was rapidly even now shedding the closer it got to Earth.

Kalki knew this would save considerable marine life and isolated forest cover. Over the remaining forests, animal life, mountain ranges, historical and holy sites he threw his mantle of cover. He ensured that there would be enough humus in the forests to provide fodder and water to the animals for a few years, till the Chiranjeevis could make alternative arrangements. Through his infinite mind's eye, he could see that the shelters constructed for the spiritual were now functioning properly and were in the process of being sealed.

❈

The comet was just two days away, or slightly more than half the distance to Earth's satellite, the moon. With its giant white coma, now clearly depicting a rider flashing a mighty sword astride a white stallion, it was a vision to behold. But there were none to appreciate its beauty, or the beauty of its flaring tail, as it gradually rose over the evening sky. It still gave no sign of any deadly design as it drew ever closer to its target. By the next evening, it was brighter than the full moon and cast a spectral shadow over the barren and deserted land. Now the effect of the Earth's gravity pulled the comet in faster, as if pulling a reluctant lover into a final embrace that had been tortuously withheld for ages.

31

Doomsday Strike

As the comet struck the outer limit of the thermosphere, for the first time since birth, it felt a slight tug of resistance that increased significantly every millisecond of its vertical entry. Still it plunged on, punching a hole a kilometre wide through the stratosphere, generating temperatures so high that the air itself started to burn. The heat and sound waves produced were powerful enough to incinerate an area covering a tenth of the continent below.

When it hit the ground, rock turned to liquid and spread outward in rippling waves, not freezing until it had formed a crater 70 kilometres across. The bulk of the nucleus tunnelled down 4.5 kilometres into the Earth's surface and ejected material in a fireball that reached nearly as high as 10 kilometres and was visible almost 1,000 kilometres away from where it ascended. The ejector cloud that was formed was about 64 kilometres high, over seven times the height of Mount Everest. It disbursed incandescent dust, ash and stony material into the upper atmosphere. While the heavier pieces fell back to the ground in whistling missiles, the bulk of the cloud circled the earth, blocking light from the sun and creating darkness at the peak of day.

The comet's impact triggered seismic shocks that were recorded round the globe. While the earthquakes were not of an intensity that could cause serious damage, the shifting of the ocean's tectonic floor resulted in massive tsunamis that battered the coasts around the Pacific, Australian and Arctic rims, and the Mediterranean, Caspian and Black seas. The Ring of Fire of active volcanoes around the Pacific felt the pressure from the strike and belched their contents of scorching lava, ash and other noxious material to saturate the searing heat of the ejector cloud. Within an hour of the comet strike, kilometre-high tidal waves had washed away the eastern seaboard of America, large parts of Europe and North Africa. Within three hours, it had flooded all the land on the western rim of the Pacific and Australia.

The churning ejector cloud was carried along with the gale-force winds of the upper atmosphere. As the volcanic ash and dust added to its bulk, in a short while it covered most of the globe. The cloud picked up moisture from the oceans and its colour changed to a menacing violet-black. It was also charged with static electricity from the moving particles and huge bolts of lightning flew from the mass, charring forever man's pathetic sources of electrical power. He could well wail, as had Axel Munthe centuries ago:

> The night will be dark for there will be no stars overhead
> and no hope for a dawn....it will be lonely to be dead
> but it cannot be much more lonely than to be alive.

The rain that precipitated did little to salve the burns below; on the contrary, it was rain like never seen before: acid rain caused by the flaring of nitric and sulphur oxides inside the blazing cauldron of the cloud.

So now, a perpetual haze enveloped the skies and hid the sun for days, months and years. The continents were dimly visible through the smog but their outlines were blurred and indistinct. For a long time, the earth, cocooned in the sweltering cloud, faced a thermal nightmare. Temperatures rose to bake its surface with unrelenting fever. But weather never remains unalterable, and as the heat of the engulfing cloud slowly dissipated through the thermosphere, a numbing chill descended, converting the land into a cold replica of a long-forgotten ice age.

32

The New Satya Yuga

On the world once known as the earth, the exposed few still alive were slowly dying out. There was nothing left in them to live for. In the corpse light of the dying land, the remnants of mankind that had miraculously survived the hammer blows of the comet strike, shuffled about the frozen landscape, desperately foraging for anything to battle starvation. They would not have long to wait. A towering silence now filled a land that had, for so many centuries, known the cacophony of tumultuous activity. Soon that silence was to become absolute, save only the sounds that nature created in short outbursts.

It was time for Kalki to remove his cloaks of protection and lead the spiritually pure to a dawn of the new age.

Appendix I

THE CYCLE OF YUGAS

In the Hindu pantheon of Time, creation (*srijan*) and destruction (pralaya) are the two inevitable sequences in the life of cosmic reality.

The *Vishnu Purana* maintains that the creation and destruction of the universe is a cyclic process, lasting 24 million years, corresponding to a day (kalpa) and a night (kalpa) in the life of the creator, Brahma. The universe is, thus, in a state of creation for 12 million years and in a state of dissolution again for the same period. Each kalpa consists of a *mahayuga* of 1,000 yugas, and therefore, each yuga has a duration of 12,000 years.

> *When the universal spirit wakes, the world revives; when he closes his eyes, all things fall upon the bed of mystic slumber. In like manner as a thousand great ages constitute a day of Brahmá, so his night consists of the same period; during which the world is submerged by a vast ocean. Awaking at the end of his night, the unborn, Vishnu, in the character of Brahmá, creates the universe anew …*
>
> (*Vishnu Purana*, Book VI, Chapter IV, p. 645)

According to the *Vishnu Purana*, each yuga follows a descending ratio of 4:3:2:1 in terms of time as well as the quality of life prevailing in it. The yugas are termed Satya (or Krita), Treta, Dvapara and Kali, beginning with creation in the Satya Yuga and ending with dissolution in the Kali Yuga.

Now, there is a slight addition in the periodicity of the yugas due to the following:

> *The period that precedes a yuga is called a Sandhya, and it is of as many hundred years as there are thousands in the yuga; and the period that follows a yuga, termed the Sandhyánsa, is of similar duration. The interval between the Sandhya and the Sandhyánsa is the yuga, denominated Satya, Treta, Dwapar, and Kali, constitute a great age, or aggregate of four ages: a thousand such aggregates is a day of Brahma.*
>
> (*Vishnu Purana*, Chapter III)

The 10 per cent of time added for each sandhya and *sandhyánsa* in a yuga, thus, gives the following calculation in the *Vishnu Purana*:

Satya Yuga	4,000 years	
Sandhya	400 years	
Sandhyánsa	400 years	… 4,800 years
Treta Yuga	3,000 years	
Sandhya	300 years	
Sandhyánsa	300 years	… 3,600 years
Dwapar Yuga	2,000 years	
Sandhya	200 years	
Sandhyánsa	200 years	… 2,400 years
Kali Yuga	1,000 years	
Sandhya	100 years	
Sandhyánsa	100 years	… 1,200 years
	12,000 'divine' years	

The Purana then goes on say that these are 'divine' years and each divine year comprises 360 years in the life of ordinary mortals. Therefore, if these divine years are converted into years of mortals, the timeline of yugas consist of:

Satya	4,800 x 360 = 1,728,000 years
Treta	3,600 x 360 = 1,296,000 years
Dwapar	2,400 x 360 = 864,000 years
Kali	1,200 x 360 = 432,000 years
	… 4,320,000 human years

There are two basic flaws in the theory of the yugas as it has been expounded in the Purana.

First, the conversion of divine years into human years by a multiplication factor of 360 sends all recorded history into an unrecognisable past.

It is now universally accepted that the genus homo sapiens evolved from the earlier generation of neanderthals and homo erectus less than half a million years in the past. They are believed to have originated around 200,000 years ago along the drift valley in Africa. The oldest fossils of earliest man date back to only around 160,000 years ago.

These primitive humans lived in small bands as nomadic hunter-gatherers who, despite the benefits of fire, were still marginal creatures. It was only between 70,000 and 30,000 years ago that new ways of thinking and communicating, or what is called the *cognitive revolution*, enabled man to emerge to higher rungs in the survival chain. Through better interactive communication, humans were able to transform their social structures, increase trade and business and spread survival techniques, especially relating to agriculture, to diverse social groups. Settled agricultural practices meant settled communities and the first human dwellings, and then villages came into existence.

Earth's first known civilisations arose between 4000 and 3000 BC at Mesopotamia (Sumer) in the Middle East, ancient Egypt, the Indus River Valley in India and China. It was only around 1500 BC that advanced civilisations in the Middle East, Iran, India, China and Greece came about and entered the pages of recorded history.

There is, therefore, little ground for accepting that the Satya Yuga existed 1.7 million years ago when man was just about entering the caveman age. Nor that the great maharishis/Brahmarishis of the Treta Yuga arose from marginal creatures roaming the land as nomads. Or that Sri Ramachandra blessed the earth with his footsteps a million years ago at the end of the Treta Yuga. Or that Sri Krishna lived more than 430,000 years in the past at the close of the Dwapar Yuga.

There is, on the contrary, acceptable data regarding the period of the Bharata War in which Sri Krishna was intimately involved. The Panchalas (connected to Dronacharya and King Dhrupad), the Pauravas (Bhishma and the Kauravas/ Pandava line) and the Yadavs (Sri Krishna's people) were historical lineages connected to events in Gangetic North India. We are told that these kingdoms had their interplay around 1400–1000 BCE, the approximate time of the Bharata War. Therefore, we can assume this as the time when Sri Krishna blessed the earth with his presence.

What then is to be made of the huge time lines for the ages suggested in the Puranas? Sri Yukteswar Giri, the guru of Yogananda Paramhamsa, in his book, *The Holy Science*, has given a rational explanation. He believed that:

> … the wise men of the time … fancied that 1200 years, the real age of Kali (yuga), were not the ordinary years of our earth, but were so many *daivya* years (years of the gods), consisting of 12 day months of 30 daivya days each, with each daivya day being equal to one ordinary solar year of our earth. Hence according to these men, 1,200 years of Kali Yuga must be equal to 432,000 years of the earth.

In other words, the writers of the Puranas incorrectly multiplied the timeline of the yugas by a factor of 360 to arrive at the large timescales mentioned in the *Vishnu Purana* and other literature.

Second, there is no convincing argument why the yugas should have a descending timeline ratio of 4:3:2:1.

The world over, when we talk of cyclical ages, the cycles comprise equal time units. The Zoroastrians believe that the world lasts for 12,000 years, which is divided into four equal ages of 3,000 years each. The ancient Greeks, the Mayans and the Incas all believed in time cycles of equal length. Two of the most respected astronomers of ancient India, Aryabhata and Pulisa, believed in a yuga cycle that consisted of four yugas of equal duration of 3,000 years each.

We are left with the conclusion that somehow the fact of *the decline in virtue* over the ages in a given ratio was also taken to mean *a decline in the time factor* of the yuga by the same ratio.

There is, therefore, the fact that the yugas in the yuga cycle are of equal duration, and that the 4:3:2:1 sequence may have been a mathematical manipulation that crept into the doctrine sometime prior to 500 CE. It is reasonable to assume that this manipulation was introduced because people were inclined to believe that the duration of a yuga should decrease in time in tandem with the decrease in virtue and human longevity from one yuga to the next.

The theory of the yugas is a unique account of the development of man and how his stature, character and make-up suffered noticeable decline down the ages. The emphasis here is not on the material but rather the spiritual and moral fibre of life—compassion, righteousness, purity of mind and inner growth—that man has increasingly lost.

During the golden age of Satya Yuga, when sages roamed the earth, the world was at its peak in terms of truth, virtue and bliss, having people of character grounded in staunch spiritual values. The *Srimad Bhagavatam* states:

> *In the Krita Yuga, Dharma (virtue) exists for men complete in its four limbs, viz., austere penance, internal and external purity, compassion and truthfulness. In the other yugas, even as unrighteousness advances, virtue diminishes by one limb successively.*
>
> (*Srimad Bhagavata Mahapurana,* Book III, Discourse XI, 21)

Their physique reflected their inner strength and they were powerfully built, tall and good-looking, youthful, energetic and vigorous. They were models of devotion and cared for each other and all of god's creations, leaving little scope for conflict, injury, killing or tension.

As the age advanced, it was blessed with great teachers and sages like Parshuram, Vasistha, Visvamitra, Atri, Agastya, Bharadwaj and Kashyap, many of whom survived to guide the next yuga. These spiritual giants left indelible marks on polity, the state, the flow of religion and the ethical standards of the people.

Great ashrams spawned the land and were home to religious churning, intellectual ferment, character development and nation-building.

The climate reflected the mood of the people and the weather was always calm and pleasant. Because man worshipped nature and lived harmoniously with it, there were no droughts, floods, earthquakes, storms or other forms of natural calamity.

Disease and illnesses were rare and it is said that the average age of man was 100,000 years in this atmosphere of truth and perfection.

The Treta Yuga basked in the reflected glory of the preceding age. Purity, compassion and truthfulness still underscored human relations even though virtue itself had diminished by a quarter. Perhaps the presence of the great sages imparted a measure of continuity. They were, after all, the font of religion and spirituality and, under their guidance, ashrams and gurukuls flourished, providing moral and ethical education to the people.

The emphasis was heavily on the citizens' obligation to society and to each other. While this did foster loyalty towards one's own, in the wider context, feelings of differentiation slowly permeated the thinking of men. This led to the emergence of social groups, tribal loyalties and territorial boundaries. As this process matured and then accelerated, kingdoms, nation states and kingly rulers came into being.

At the beginning of the Treta Yuga, the desire to form civil society was motivated solely by the need to ensure common protection and orderly development. But soon, ambition and greed propelled these social groups to organise themselves in aggressive bands, seeking expansion of territory and the fruits thereof.

There were still, however, model leaders and kings such as Raghu, the founder of the Ikshvaku line, Raja Siradhwaja (better known as Sita's father, Janaka) of Mithila, Dasaratha of Ayodhya, Bali of Kishkinda, Lord Parshuram of Kanyakubja, Kartavirya Arjun of Mahishmati and many others that fought only to protect the weak and destroy evil.

Above all, the Treta Yuga saw the towering presence of the seventh avatar of Vishnu, the Maryada Purushottam, Sri Rama of Ayodhya. This led to the destruction of evil and the establishment of a just and equitable society. The concept of Ram Rajya was a singular contribution of the yuga to the political landscape of land.

By the end of the Treta Yuga, the weather started to change as nature and its inhabitants came under attack. Disease too made an appearance and life expectancy was not what it used to be. Ultimately, the conquests and killings had their impact, with the average lifespan of humans coming down to around 10,000 years.

The Dwapar Yuga was a time of half virtue and half sin. This was a period when man's individual identity got increasingly submerged in the collective consciousness of different races, religions, languages and lifestyles. From this eddy of patriotic fervour, communal commitment and blatant aggression, emerged powerful kingdoms and principalities, and inevitably, conflict came to play an increasing role in the tide of history.

This was the age characterised by the great Bharat War described in the Mahabharata, that saw both virtue and sin attain their sharpest contrast in men's behaviour. The valour and courage of Arjuna, the evil of Duryodhana and Shakuni, the virtue of Abhimanyu, the misplaced loyalty of Karna, Bhishma and Dronacharya, the battle between truth and the urge to gamble in Yudhishtra, and the overall desire for territory and empire, paint a vivid mosaic of human psyche.

Lord Krishna was the dominant figure of the age and as the eighth avatar of Vishnu, participated in all major developments—political, religious and social. He was a towering personality, who balanced the forces of virtue and sin and showed, by his own example, what life on earth should be. His great discourse with Arjuna, the Pandava Prince, in the Srimad Bhagavad Gita, is a monument of spirituality, detailing the nature of all existence and the right manner of attaining the ultimate pinnacle of freedom through adhyatmik vikas. The Dwapar Yuga is said to have ended with the destruction of the kingdom Dwarka and the passing of Lord Krishna. By then, of course, the portents of the grim future were already at hand and the average age of man had been reduced to a few centuries only.

The Kali Yuga that follows is the age of darkness and ignorance. Sin totally overtakes the forces of virtue and integrity and we leave it to the great epic, *Srimad Bhagvata Mahapurana,* to tell us its grim reality:

> *So long as Lord Sri Krishna, the husband of Lakshmi, touched the earth with His lotus feet, Kali was powerless to subdue this planet.*
>
> *Persons learned in ancient history maintain that the age of Kali set in on the very day, nay, the very moment, Sri Krishna ascended to his abode in heaven....*
>
> *Truth, piety, fortitude, glory and prosperity departed from the earth along with Him.*
>
> (*Srimad Bhagavata Mahapurana*, Book 12, Disc. 11, 29-33)

Appendix II

THE CHIRANJEEVIS

Indian scriptures such as the Ramayana, Mahabharata and the Puranas mention seven (sometimes eight) immortals, or Chiranjeevis, destined to have extended periods of life. An ancient sloka, used as a prayer in many households in India seeking long life and divine benediction, runs as follows:

Ashwatthama Balir Vyaaso Hanumanshcha
Vibhishanaha Krupascha Parshuramascha
Saptaitey Chiranjivinaha

Of the seven, only Ved Vyasa and Parshuram are gifted with immortality from birth; the first, as the divine scribe recording all events since the beginning of time, and the second as the supreme exponent of martial arts that he bestowed on select disciples. Ved Vyasa would record the deeds of the Kalki avatar while Parshuram would be his chief preceptor.

Ashwatthama, said to be a Rudra avatar of Lord Shiva, was the tragic son of Dronacharya, the martial guru to both the Kauravas and the Pandavas. Handsome beyond compare, with a ruby shining on his forehead, he was gifted as a warrior and greatly extolled for his virtue. The treacherous killing of his father by the Pandavas changed all that. Dronacharya, who otherwise could not be defeated on the battlefield, was fed the rumour that his son Ashwatthama had been killed. Not believing this canard, Dronacharya went to Yudhishtra, who had been given the appellation of *dharmaputra*, the paragon of virtue, who could never tell an untruth, and asked him to validate the killing. The Pandavas had earlier killed an elephant also named Ashwatthama, and so Yudhishtra replied:

'Ashwatthama hato'

Ashwatthama has been killed.

And then, under his breath, he said, *'Naro, wa kunjarowa'*

Man, or the elephant.

Hearing only the first part, and struck by mortal grief, Dronacharya laid down his arms and was beheaded by Drishtadyumna as he knelt on the ground and prayed for the moksha of his son. When he heard of the foul manner of the killing of his father, Ashwatthama was filled with blinding rage and resorted to revenge by killing all the sons of the Pandavas as they slept in their camp at night, an act of adharma that led Krishna to curse him to live for 3,000 years with suppurating sores all over his body and forehead, emitting a foul stench and shrieking out of fear for mercy. It is said that his figure haunts abandoned temples in the forests along the River Narmada and that his agony will find deliverance when the Kalki avatar releases him from his curse.

The epic of King Mahabali relates to the fifth avatar of Lord Vishnu, the Vamana Avatar. King Mahabali was the great grandson of Hiranyakashipu, and the grandson of Prahalad. He was a just and noble king of the beautiful state of Kerala and greatly respected by the people for his wisdom, piety and generosity. To test his philanthropy, Vishnu, disguised as a poor but handsome dark boy, approached him and asked a boon of three footsteps of land. An amused Mahabali readily granted this request. At this the Vamana avatar grew to his full height, covering the earth with one step and the heavens with the other. He asked Mahabali where he could play his third step and the king offered his own head. The Vamana's third step pushed Mahabali into *patala*, the netherworld, but his humility won over Vishnu who granted him immortality and the boon of once a year coming to his kingdom. The festival of Onam, celebrated every year in Kerala, is a tribute to the sacrifice of King Mahabali and people in the state make elaborate preparations to welcome a king affectionately called Onathappan.

In the Mahabharata, Sage Kripacharya occupies a pride of place as the Kul-guru of the Kauravas and Pandavas. Other than Bhishma, he commanded the greatest respect for his learning, wisdom and impartiality. After the Great Bharat War, Kripacharya was chosen as the teacher for Parikshit, the son of Abhimanyu, and the future king of Bharata. He was granted immortality by Lord Krishna but plays no part in the life of Kalki.

The personality of Hanuman as the quintessential worshipper of Sri Rama is one of the fascinating studies encapsulated in the Ramayana epic. It has led to the popular belief that Hanuman will be a part of humanity as long as the story of Rama lives and that at any devotional rendering of the Ram Katha, Hanuman will always be present. An embodiment of strength, piety, intellect and devotion,

Hanuman was blessed as a Chiranjeevi to preserve dharma on earth and to serve the Kalki avatar in his task.

Hanuman's contemporary and fellow immortal was Vibhishana, the brother of the demon king of Lanka, Ravana. Vibhishana was a devotee of Vishnu and a counterpoise to the evil of his brother. His defection to the side of Sri Rama was a defining moment in the Lanka war. After Ravana's defeat, Vibhishana was appointed King of Lanka and granted the boon of immortality to continue the fight against evil.

Appendix III

KAALI AND KALI

Kaali is the supreme mother goddess, the *Adi Shakti* or *Adi Parashakti,* worshipped by many devotees as the ultimate creator of the cosmos. In her many forms as Devi, Uma, Parvati, Durga or the terrible Kaali, the mother goddess is the counterpart of Lord Shiva and it is their union that leads to Creation. Kaali as creator is, therefore, the universal form of the supreme reality or Brahman itself. It is she who dwells in all creatures as the atman, as the centre of knowledge, as consciousness, as intelligence, and as emotion. She is also the ultimate protector and represents the force of the divine when directed against evil.

There is a scientific reason for the worship of Adi Shakti. From the instant of creation, everything that exists is a manifestation of pure energy. This energy, or what is called shakti, is the life force behind the atman, and shakti worship is thus the purest and most direct form of communion with the Brahman. Obviously, shakti cannot be worshipped in its amorphous nature; so, tradition has devised that it is worshipped as the Mother Goddess named Kaali.

Hers is the cosmic womb that gives birth to the universe. She not only begets the creative reality out of darkness, and hence the name Kaali, but also resides in it as infinite consciousness—call it what you will, God or Brahman, or *Satchidananda* (Being-Consciousness-Bliss) or just the Supreme Being.

Of all the forms of Devi, she is the most ferocious to look at and yet the most compassionate, loving, tender and easily accessible to her devotees. She is, therefore, prayed to as the great protector who can provide cover against any form of evil and demonic forces.

Is it not, therefore, supremely ironic that her sweet, powerful and all-protective name should have even a remote phonetic likeness to that of Kali, the destructive male demon, the very incarnation of pure, unadulterated evil and the presiding deity of the Kali Yuga?

It is said that at the moment of creation—and since this was *all creation*—there also came into being *maleen pataka* or the personification of sin, Kali, having a black complexion and symbolising quintessential evil. The *Kalki Purana* lists the lineage of Kali as follows:

> *The name of sin personified was Adharma (irreligion) whose wife was Mithya (falsehood) and a son named Dambha (pride), always a picture of anger and energy. Dambha had a sister named Maya, and within her womb, he begot a son named Lobha (greed), and a daughter named Nikrti (cunning). Lobha begot a son named Krodha (anger) and a daughter Himsa (envy). It was from the womb of Himsa that Krodha begot a son named Kali.*
>
> (*Sri Kalki Purana*, 1, 15-18)

Kali is always seen to be holding his genitals in his left hand. His complexion is very dark, like black ointment that has been mixed with oil. Kali's abdomen is like that of a crow, his face is frightening to behold, and his tongue is red and full of greed. His appearance is fearful and a bad odour emanates from his body. Kali is fond of playing chess, drinking wine, enjoying the company of prostitutes, and associating with evil merchants.

This was the description in the *Kalki Purana* of the destructive progeny of Kali:

> *... who were all blasphemers of genuine religious principles. All these relatives of Kali were the destroyers of sacrifice, study of the Vedas, and charity, because they transgressed all the Vedic principles of religion. They were reservoirs of mental distress, disease, old age, destruction of religious principles, sorrow, lamentation, and fear.*
>
> (*Sri Kalki Purana*, 1, 4-22)

King Parikshit, grandson of the mighty Arjuna, and the son of Abhimanyu and Uttara, had inherited the throne at Hastinapur after his granduncle, King Yudhishtra, left for his heavenly abode. One day, whilst he was travelling along the River Saraswati in his 'well-decorated chariot driven by dark horses and bearing an ensign with the devise of a lion', he chanced upon a strange scene. He saw a person, bearing the insignia of royalty, mercilessly beating a white bull and a cow. The bull had been so traumatised that it could only stand on one leg and the cow, lean and thin and hungry, was bereft of her calf. King Parikshit was filled with anger and, stringing his bow from his gold-plated chariot, challenged the so-called king to account for his tyranny.

It so transpired that the white bull was Dharma (god of virtue) who had lost his three other legs of austerity, purity and compassion, being left with truthfulness as his sole support. The cow was the good Mother Earth who grieved at her barren and fruitless nature deprived of the bounty she used to offer earlier.

King Parikshit comforted the two and restored the three lost legs of the bull—penance, purity and compassion—and the fruit-bearing capacity of the cow. He then drew his sword to dispose of Kali, 'the spring of unrighteousness', who had been posing as a king. Seeing Parikshit's determination, Kali threw himself at the mercy of the king and begged for his forgiveness.

Now King Parikshit was 'kind to the meek and hospitable to those who sought his protection' and so, instead of ridding the world of an unspeakable horror, he banished him from the kingdom of Hastinapur to go and live in places inhabited with the five vices of falsehood, intoxication, passion, slaughter and animosity.

The chakra of karma always comes full circle and eventually no person can stop the relentless tide of time. It so came about that Kali was thus needlessly spared and, in a short while, again began his depredation into the lives of men that, in course of time, covered the whole globe.

Notes

BROWN DWARF

The universe is full of the most amazing phenomena, each more stunning than the other. It is estimated that one-third of the stars in our galaxy are either binary or part of a multiple-star system orbiting a common barycentre. Seen through a telescope or even a pair of binoculars, some of these—such as Mizar in the constellation of Ursa Major, Albireo in Cygnus, or Alpha Centauri, the nearest star to our sun—resolve into jewelled pinpricks of light, spectacular to behold.

The question is then often asked: why is our sun single or does it also have a binary we are not aware of? And it is in this context that the issue of brown dwarfs become relevant. Simply put, brown dwarfs are 'failed stars', stellar objects with mass generally between ten–ninety times the size of Jupiter. These objects are below the critical mass necessary for continued gravitational collapse leading to pressures and temperatures causing thermonuclear fusion at their cores. The cold vacuum of space dissipates their heat and, on account of their low temperatures and small sizes, brown dwarfs have low luminosity, which makes them extremely difficult to observe. Richard A. Müller at the University of California, Berkeley, has suggested the *Nemesis hypothesis*, in which the sun could have an as-yet-undetected companion brown dwarf, whose periodic disturbance of the Oort cloud and its subsequent effect of sending comets hurtling towards the inner solar system could explain an apparent 26 million year regularity in human extinction events.

THE OORT CLOUD

The Oort cloud, first theorised by the Dutch physicist and astronomer, Jan Hendrick Oort, is believed to be a thick shell of rock and icy debris that surrounds our solar system a third of the way from our sun to the nearest star, Alpha Centauri. Although no confirmed direct observations of the Oort cloud have been made, it may be the source of all long-period comets entering the inner solar system. The trillions of particles theorised to be constituting the cloud are the remains of the disc of protoplanetary material out of which the sun, planets, moons and asteroids were originally formed. This disc, once closely surrounded the sun in the early days of planetary evolution, was scattered subsequently into interstellar space by the gravitational effects of the gas giants, particularly Jupiter.

KALKI AVATAR

The birth of the Kalki avatar as the tenth incarnation of Lord Vishnu is foretold in the *Vishnu Purana*:

When the practices taught by the Vedas and the institutes of law shall nearly have ceased, and the close of the Kali age shall be nigh, a portion of that divine being who exists of his own spiritual nature in the character of Brahma, and who is the beginning and the end, and who comprehends all things, shall descend upon earth: he will be born in the family of Vishńuyaśas, an eminent Brahman of Sambhala village, as Kalki, endowed with the eight superhuman faculties. By his irresistible might he will destroy all the Mleccha and thieves, and all whose minds are devoted to iniquity. He will then re-establish righteousness upon earth; and the minds of those who live at the end of the Kali age shall be awakened, and shall be as pellucid as crystal. The men who are thus changed by virtue of that peculiar time shall be as the seeds of human beings, and shall give birth to a race who shall follow the laws of the Krita age, or age of purity.

(*Vishnu Purana*, Book 4, Chapter XXIV)

The *Bhagavata Mahapurana* also states:

Lord Vishnu, adored of the whole animate and inanimate creation, and the soul of the universe, appears in this world of matter, for protecting the virtue of the righteous and wiping out the entire stock of their karma and thereby liberating them. The Lord will appear under the name of Kalki in the house of the high souled Visnuyas—the foremost Brahmana of the village of Sambhala...

(*Srimad Bhagavata Mahapurana*, Book 12, Disc II, 17-18)

The *Sri Kalki Purana* is devoted to the birth and life of Lord Kalki and is the inspiration behind many of the episodes in this book. As mentioned in the introduction to the Purana: *'Exalted personalities (such as Vyasadeva, the author of the Purana) can see everything, past, present and future. For this reason, there is no fault in narrating these future events as if they had already occurred.'*

The location of Sambhala and Mahishmati is a matter of conjecture. While in the Puranic legend, Sambhala, near the Haihaya kingdom of Mahishmati, is the birthplace of Lord Kalki, the Buddhist Kalachakra traditions associate Sambhala as the kingdom of Maitreya, the coming Buddha. In recent times, many have tried to identify Sambhala with the mythical paradise kingdom of Shangri-La, somewhere in the Himalayas. Incidentally, however, the *Kalachakra tantra* also mentions a Kalki king from Sambhala who will vanquish the forces of evil to usher in a Golden Age!

Though the exact location of Mahishmati is uncertain, it was the centre of southern Avanti, divided by the Vindhyas from northern Avanti with its capital at Ujjaini. Mahishmati was situated on the banks of the River Narmada and was the stronghold of the Haihaya monarchy and its famous king, Kartavirya Arjuna, who is said to have even imprisoned Ravana.

CHICXULUB AND MASS EXTINCTION

Near Gubbio in Italy, there is an exposed and extensive limestone rock formation of many layers that represent millions of years of the earth's early history. While excavating here, geologist Walter Alvarez found a thin layer of clay that separated the cretaceous from the tertiary rock formations. This same layer of clay has marked what has come to be known as the K-T boundary in many parts of the world—Spain, Denmark and New Zealand.

What was significant was the known fact that the K-T boundary marked the most famous extinction of all time—the end of the great dinosaurs. This was borne out by the fossilised shells of creatures found above and below the layer of clay, the lower or older layer containing much larger fossils than the younger layer above. Surprisingly, the thin layer of clay held no fossils at all, *as if in that period Earth was without life!*

Walter Alvarez was then joined by his father, the famous physicist Luis Alvarez, and their enquiry yielded the amazing fact that the thin layer of clay contained an abnormally high level of iridium. Now iridium is one of the densest metals in existence, rarely found in random layers of clay. Its properties of density and weight had made it descend the crust of the earth to the core when the planet was still molten. While, however, rare on earth, meteorites, asteroids and comets are rich in iridium as they are from the earliest days of creation. Based on this premise, the Alvarez' proposed their hypothesis in June 1980 that a large asteroid had struck earth at the K-T boundary causing worldwide catastrophe and killing off most of the then life forms.

It was only eleven years later, in 1991, that a team of scientists proposed that the 180-kilometre-wide crater near the village of Chicxulub on the Yucatan Peninsula in Mexico was the K-T impact crater. Coincidentally, the crater had been discovered earlier at the same time as the Alvarez' report by two geologists, Glen Penfield and Antonio Camargo, working with the Mexican oil giant PEMEX, but they had been forbidden to release this data.

It was only in 2016 that a scientific project drilled deep into the peak ring of the Chicxulub impact crater to obtain rock core samples from the site of the impact. The samples confirmed that the rock had been melted instantaneously from its normal state into its present form by immense heat and pressure. The peak ring had an abundance of granite not usually found in sea-floor deposits, but had been ejected to the surface from deep within the earth by the colossal force of the impact. The asteroid created a 120-mile ring, burrowing 30-40 kilometres into the crust and throwing trillions of tons of rock, dust and sulphates into the atmosphere that would have affected the climate globally and caused worldwide extinction of life.

DASAVATARA

The concept and stories of the Dasavatara, or the ten avatars of Lord Vishnu Hari, are integral to Hindu religion and are contained in many sacred texts such as the *Vishnu Purana*, *Srimad Bhagavata Mahapurana*, the Ramayana and Mahabharata. In fact, the *Bhagavata Mahapurana* refers to twenty-two avatars of the Lord but says these are merely a few of the innumerable appearances of the divine in mortal form.

The *Garuda Purana* (Chapter V111, X-XIII) lists the ten principal avatars as follows:

1. *Matsya* (the fish)
2. *Kurma* (the tortoise)
3. *Varaha* (the boar)
4. *Narasimha* (half man-half lion)
5. *Vamana* (the dwarf)
6. *Parshuram*
7. *Sri Rama* (king of Ayodhya)
8. *Sri Krishna* (king of Dwarka in the Mahabharata)
9. *Buddha* (The Enlightened Sakyamuni)
10. *Kalki* (the destroyer)

Matsya

The narrative of a great deluge sent to cleanse the earth of sinners and save only those that can be accommodated, along with seed plants and animals, in a giant boat built by a saintly figure, is a common theme to many civilisations such as Mesopotamia, Sumeria, Greece and, of course, the expansive Genesis account of the flood and Noah's Ark.

The story of the Matsya avatar recounted in the *Matsya Purana* is similar. It is set at the end of the Satya Yuga when evil had begun to influence the lives of people and it had become necessary to flood the earth and rejuvenate it. The guidelines for doing so had been given by Lord Vishnu to Brahma, the creator, in the form of the Vedas, the four principle books of Hinduism. However, when Brahma was asleep, a horse-headed demon named Hayagriva stole the Vedas and hid himself deep in the oceans of the earth.

Meanwhile, a pious king named Satyavrata, the king of pre-ancient Dravida, and a devotee of Vishnu, was washing his hands in a river when a little fish swam into his hands and pleaded with him to save him from predators. Satyavrata, filled with compassion for the little fish, put it in a jar, which it soon outgrew. From there he transferred it to a tank, then the river and finally the ocean. The giant fish revealed itself as Vishnu and told Satyavrata that a deluge will occur within seven days that will destroy all life. He is instructed to build an ark to take all varieties of seeds, animals and the saptrishis and ride out the deluge in the boat. The Matsya pulls this boat with its horn to the high Himalayas. When the storm ended and the water subsided, Vishnu told Satyavrata that, as Vaivasvata Manu, he would be the father of future generations. Matsya killed Hayagriva and returned the Vedas to Brahma with whose help Manu began the task of regenerating human civilisation.

Kurma

As the second avatar ofVishnu, Kurma appears in the form of a tortoise or turtle to support the foundation for the cosmos and the cosmic churning stick, Mount Mandara, when the ocean of life is stirred between the devas and asuras. The symbolism here is that Vishnu provides the foundational support for any sustained creative activity whether it be good or evil in the shape of the nectar of immortality or the poison of destruction.

Varaha

To rescue Mother Earth, Bhudevi, from the predations of the demon Hiranyaksha, who threw her to the bottom of the primordial cosmic ocean, Vishnu takes the form of a boar in his third avatar, the Varaha, who jumps into the ocean, kills the demon and lifts prithvi up in its tusks to restore it in its rightful place in the universe. In the Puranas, Mother Earth is portrayed as being susceptible to those who would recklessly exploit her. The Varaha is her saviour, bringing order out of chaos, destroying the defilers, and reviving the earth.

Narasimha

Vishnu appears as half lion and half man to save his disciple Prahalad from the atrocities of his father, the demon king Hiranyakashipu, who had gained special powers from Brahma that he would not be killed by any human or animal, inside or outside any residence, in daytime or at night, nor on the ground or in the sky. Vishnu, as Narasimha, killed

Hiranyakashipu at twilight (when it is neither day nor night) on the threshold of a courtyard (neither indoors nor out), and with the demon on his thighs (neither earth nor space). The Narasimha avatar restored dharma on earth by destroying a supposedly indestructible symbol of evil.

Vamana

The story and appearance of the fifth avatar of Vishnu is significantly different from those of his earlier incarnations as a giant fish, a massive tortoise, the great boar or the terrible man-lion; instead he appears here as a dwarf in human form born to the great sage Kashyapa and his wife Aditi. Nor is his task the destruction of any evil or wrongdoing but rather the emancipation of a wise and just king to his rightful place in the paradigm of nature. King Bali was the grandson of Prahalad and succeeded to the demoniac throne of Hiranyakashipu. Bali was a Vishnu bhakta and the embodiment of righteousness, piety, charity and goodness. He was a wise and noble king and, in his rule, people were treated with justice and fairness.

Once, on the bank of the River Narmada, he was performing the Ashvamedha yagya, when Vishnu as Vamana walked into the *yagnashala*. Blinded by his effulgence, the king washed his feet and sprinkled the sanctified water on his own head. He then offered the young Brahmin anything he desired. All that Vamana asked for was land measuring three paces of his foot. When a surprised Bali willingly agreed to this seemingly innocuous request, Vishnu arose as a giant, measuring the entire earth with one step and entire sky with the second. When he asked the king where he should place his third step, Bali humbly offered his own head. Pleased by Bali's self-sacrifice, Vishnu offered him permanent protection under his holy feet in the nether kingdom of Suthala which is ever free from disease and want, defeat and distress.

King Bali was also given the status of a Chiranjeevi and the festival of Onam marks his annual return to be among his beloved people.

Parshuram

Parshuram as a Chiranjeevi has been a virtual sutradhar, not only in this book but all down the pages of history from the earliest Satya Yuga to the close of the present Kali Yuga. His story has been interwoven with the story of Kalki.

Parshuram is the first avatar to figure in recorded history and, because of the definitive role he played in the Bhrigu-Haihaya conflict, the epoch itself is termed the Parshuram period between 2550-2350 BC.[1]

Sri Rama

For pious and devout Hindus, the seventh avatar of Vishnu, Sri Rama, is widely worshipped as God incarnate and his legend is woven in stories, bhajans and plays in virtually every village in India, Nepal and Southeast Asia.

The divine story of Sri Rama was first recounted in Valmiki's great epic, the Ramayana, in Sanskrit, and has since been the inspiration behind many classics in different languages. Perhaps the most beautiful rending of it, in pure love and bhakti, is the *Ramcharitamanas* by Goswami Tulsidas. Written in Awadhi, it made available the story of Rama to the common man to sing, meditate and perform on. It

[1] R.C. Majundar (General Editor), *The Vedic Age: The History and Culture of the Indian People,* Bharatiya Vidya Bhavan, 1996, pp. 283-285.

heralded the tradition of Ramlila, the dramatic enactment of the text performed before millions in places throughout the length and breadth of India.

It is written that Valmiki himself learnt of the legend of Sri Rama through his query to the exalted sage, Maharishi Narada, to whom he asked:

Sampratam asmin loke kah gunavan kah ca viryavan
Dharma jnah ca krta jnah ca satya vakyah drdha vratah ca
Kah ca charitrena yuktah kah sarva bhutesu hitah
Kah vidvan kah ca samarthas kah ca eka priya darsanah
Kah atmavan jita krodhah kah dyutiman anasuyakah
Samyuge devah ca kasya jata rosasya bibhyati

Who in this world is virtuous? Who is powerful and knows dharma?
Who is grateful, truthful and of firm vows?
Who has good character traits? Who is kindly disposed towards all living beings?
Who is learned and competent? Who has an appearance uniquely pleasant?
Who is self-possessed and has controlled his anger?
Who is brilliant and non-envious? Who is feared even by the demi-gods when engaged in the battle?[2]

Narada Muni replied:

Ye bahavah gunah tvaya kirtitah durlabhah ca eva
Aham buddhva vakswami mune taih narah sruyatam
Ikshvaku vamsa prabhavah niyatatma mahaviryah dyutiman dhrtiman
Vasi Ramah nama janaih srutah

[2] Demian Martins (trans.), *Mula Ramayana,* as narrated by Narada Muni to Valmiki, Jiva Institute, Vrindavan, 2015, Text 2-4.

These many qualities you mentioned are certainly
very difficult to be found.
O sage hear about a person who has them, for having
known Him myself, I shall now tell you.
There is a very powerful person born in the dynasty of
Ikshvaku, known by the people as Rama.
With restrained mind, He is resplendent, steadfast and
self-controlled.[3]

Struck by this description of the *Adipurush*, Valmiki was inspired to write about him and did so in the epic running into 24,000 verses. The Ramayana covers Sri Rama's birth and childhood, his training under Sage Vishwamitra, the Swayamvara and marriage to Sita, Princess of Mithila, and his heart-rending banishment to the forests for fourteen years due to the connivance of his stepmother, Kaikeyi. In the Dandaka forest, Sita is kidnapped by Ravana, King of Lanka, and Sri Rama, aided by *vanars* and others, is forced into a war with him leading to the killing of Ravana, recovery of Sita and return of Sri Rama to Ayodhya as king.

This brief synopsis of the divine life of Sri Rama seems utterly inappropriate in the context of the beautiful Ramkatha known in every village and household in India, making him the most worshipped incarnation of Lord Vishnu.

Sri Krishna

If Sri Rama is the most admired and worshipped avatar of Vishnu, Sri Krishna is certainly the most loved. He is loved as the babe of Yashoda Mai, the naughty and playful

[3] *Mula Ramayana*, as narrated by Narada Muni to Valmiki, translated by Demian Martins, Jiva Institute, Vrindavan, 2015, Text 7-8.

cowherd of Gokul, the eternal prankster weaving his spell on the hearts and minds of his fellow cowherds and *gopis*, the incomparable flautist mesmerising the world with his music or displaying his infinite power even as a young child lifting the mountain in Vrindavan. Sri Krishna's divine leela marked the first phase of his life where he symbolised eternal love for all who came in touch with him. When he left for Mathura to fight with and kill his evil uncle Kamsa, he embarked upon a socio-political life that was to leave an indelible mark on the religion, philosophy and history of India.

Sri Krishna emerged as a revered leader for all who came in touch with him. He established a strong Yadava kingdom and built the city of Dwarka as its capital. He participated in all the leading events of the time: the growing hostility between the Kauravas and the Pandavas that was to end in the great Bharat War; the killing of Sisupala and Jayadratha; saving Draupadi from the *chirharan* and, finally, acting as the charioteer of Arjuna at the battlefield in Kurukshetra. It was here, between the forces of the two combatants, that he narrated the Song Celestial, or the divine Bhagavad Gita, that has for centuries been the purest enunciation of the Vedanta philosophy, the very heart of the Hindu way of life.

While in its setting and dialogues, the holy Gita is Sri Krishna's instructions or *upadesha* to Arjuna, it is in fact a universal message to all people on how to live their lives, how to become strong and shun weakness, how to act without seeking rewards for that action, how to move, talk and behave as *stitahpragna*. This contains the science of human depth dimension yet unknown to modern physical science.

Sri Krishna thus gradually leads Arjuna, and all of us, on the path of adhyatmik vikas, or spiritual growth, and proves to be the perfect avatar for the modern age. As he so beautifully expresses it:

Matah parataram nanyat kincidasti Dhananjaya
Mayi sarvam idam protam sutre manigana iva

There is no reality higher than me, Dhananjaya,
In me all this manifested world is strung together
like so many pieces of gems on a threaded garland
(*Sri Bhagavad Gita*, Chapter 7, 7)

He was learned, caring and kind, infinite within himself, yet acting as a normal being. He was the shining light of his time and it is for this reason that the *Bhagavata Mahapurana* states that the evil age of Kali dawned the day he departed for his celestial abode.

Sri Buddha

Sri Buddha is by far the most 'human' of the avatars of Vishnu. He was not born with divine powers but as a normal yet much-loved prince of the Sakya tribe of Kapilavastu, a small kingdom on the border of India and Nepal. His mother, Maya Devi, was actually travelling in a litter to her mother's home to have her baby when she was forced to give birth to him in the forest grove at Lumbini, one of the sacred sites in the kingdom. Unfortunately, Maya Devi died soon after childbirth and Siddhartha, as he was named by his father, King Suddodana, was brought up by his mother's sister, Mahaprajapatid.

At the official naming ceremony for his son, Suddodana consulted astrologers to read the baby's birth charts, and was surprised to hear from them that his son would not rule over the Sakyas but hold dominion over the four corners of the earth. Dissatisfied with this apparently contradictory prediction, Suddodana consulted Asita, an ancient holy man living in the kingdom, and asked him about Siddhartha's future. As Asita knelt before the baby to have a closer look at him, the baby's foot touched the hermit's head. At this, the ascetic seemed to crumble and copious tears rolled down his cheeks. On regaining his composure, he told Suddodana that his son would not be master over any earthly kingdom but would rule his own soul and, more significantly, teach others how to do so. He would be a Buddha, or an enlightened one, and Asita's only sorrow was that he would not live to have his darshan.

Gautama was so affected by the mysteries of life that, at the age of twenty-nine, he quietly left the palace, his wife and child, and went into the forests as a wandering ascetic to seek the path to salvation. He practised spiritual exercises on the bank of the River Neranjara where he sat under a pipal tree and went into deep meditation determined to seek the way out of suffering. After forty-nine days under the Bodhi tree, he awoke as the Buddha or the Enlightened.

The knowledge he attained was a profound insight into life and the essentials that define it, the nature of suffering and the causal relationship that binds man to his karma, and the way to liberation by following the correct path. These came to be known as the Four Noble Truths and the Eightfold Noble Paths.

The Buddha, after introspection, decided to preach this path to end the cycle of rebirth to others, and his first discourse was at the deer park at Sarnath in Varanasi. His followers, called the sangha, continued to grow and came to include his father, King Suddodana, his wife Yashodhara, and his son Rahul. For the next forty-five years of his life, the Buddha continued to preach his doctrine of love and right action in the Gangetic plain, the kingdoms of Magadha, Kasi, Kosala, Vaishali and the foothills of the Himalayas, including Nepal. The message was simple as it was direct and shunned the metaphysics and rituals that religion had come to mean in those days.

The Buddha attained *mahaparinirvana* or final moksha at Kushinara in the Kosala kingdom, now in Uttar Pradesh. His serene features, captured in paintings and statues, full of calm composer, peace and nobility are found all the way from Afghanistan, the Indian peninsula, Southeast Asia to the Far East, all the way to Japan.

Kalki

The tenth and final avatar of Vishnu, Kalki, will manifest to destroy the evil of the Kali Yuga and usher in the next yuga cycle of Satya Yuga with a new breed of enlightened men.

THE HOUSE OF THE VIRGIN IN EPHESUS

The house of the Virgin in the wooded hills above Ephesus does actually exist as described in the visions of Anne Catherine Emmerich and is a place of remarkable peace, quiet and serenity. It's a simple stone structure of great antiquity and her tiny room has been converted into an altar that gives off immense spiritual vibrations to all who enter it. The author was surprised to find, in the small clearing as you approach the ancient building, a sunken pit containing what was clearly a stone *yoni,* an unmistakable sign of the Mother Goddess.

COMET SWIFT TUTTLE

Comet Swift Tuttle has been taken as the model of the comet in this book. Discovered in 1862, the comet has a nucleus of 26 kilometres, orbiting the sun every 133 years at a speed of 60 kilometres per second, or more than 150 times the speed of sound. If a comet of this size struck Earth, the energy of the impact would be 300 times that of the Chicxulub asteroid that wiped out the dinosaurs. Last seen in 1992, Swift Tuttle is expected to cross Earth's orbit on 14 August 2126 at a relatively safe distance of 23 million kilometres. This will, however, dwindle to around 1 million kilometres in 3044 which, in astronomical terms, is a very close passage. Considering the changes that can happen to its orbit by the jets of gases released as it approaches the sun, or the gravitational effects of the sun or the giant planets, Swift Tuttle remains the single most dangerous extra-terrestrial object known to humanity.

Bibliography

A. Ferdinand Herold, *The Life of Buddha: According to the Legends of Ancient India*, translated from the French by Paul C. Blum (Albert & Charles Boni, 1927).

Abbe Francois Trochu, *Saint Bernadette Soubirous* (Tan Books, Saint Benedict Press, 1957).

Abdullah Yusuf Ali (trans.), *The Holy Quran* (Kitab Bhavan, 12th edition, 2017).

Alan R. Hildebrand, Glen T. Penfield, David A. Kring, Mark Pilkington, Antonio Camargo Zanoguera, Stein B. Jacobsen and William V. Boynton, 'Chicxulub Crater; a Possible Cretaceous/Tertiary Boundary Impact Crater on the Yucatan Peninsula (Mexico)', *Geology*, Vol. 19, Issue 9 (1991), pp. 867-871.

Anne Catherine Emmerich, *The Life of the Blessed Virgin Mary: From the Visions of Ven* (Tan Books and Publishers, 1970).

Bhikkhu Bodhi (trans.), *Discourses of the Buddha, Anguttara Nikaya* (Wisdom Publications, USA).

Bhumipati Das (trans.), *Sri Kalki Purana* (Jai Nitai Press, 2006).

Demian Martins (trans.), *Mula Ramayana, as narrated by Narada Muni to Valmiki* (Jiva Institute, Vrindavan, 2015).

Edward J. Thomas, *The Life of Buddha* (Motilal Banarsidass Publishers Private Limited, 2017).

Eugene Poulin, *The Holy Virgin's House*, translated by Ivi Richichi (Arikan Yayinlari, 1999).

H.H. Wilson and John Murray (trans.), *Vishnu Purana*, *Shanti Parva* (Bhandarkar Edition, 1840).

J.P. Vasvani, *Dasavatara* (Jaico Publishing House, 2018).

James Barrat, *Our Final Invention* (Thomas Dunne Books, St. Martin's Griffin, New York, 2013).

Jan Hendrik Oort, *The Structure of the Cloud of Comets Surrounding the Solar System and a Hypothesis Concerning Its Origin* (Bull Astron Institute, Netherlands, 1950).

K. Eric Drexler, *Nano Systems: Molecular Machinery, Manufacturing, and Computation* (Wiley Interscience, 1992).

Luis W. Alvarez, Walter Alvarez, Frank Asaro and Helen V. Michel, 'Extraterrestrial Cause for the Cretaceous-Tertiary Extinction', *Science*, Vol. 208, Issue 4448 (6 June 1980), pp. 1095-1108.

Maurice Walche (trans.), *Discourses of the Buddha, Digha Nikaya* (Wisdom Publications, USA).

Nick Bostrom, *Superintelligence: Paths, Dangers, Strategies* (Oxford University Press, 2014).

R.C. Majumdar (General Editor), *The Vedic Age* (Bharatiya Vidya Bhavan, 1996).

Paul Brunton, *A Search in Secret India* (Random House, 2003).

Ray Kurzweil, *The Singularity Is Near* (Penguin Books, 2006).

Richard A. Müller, *Nemesis: The Death Star* (Weidenfeld and Nicolson, 1988).

Romain Rolland, *The Life of Ramakrishna*, 24th reprint edition (Advaita Ashrama, 2014), Preface.

Shastri C.L. Goswami (trans.), *Srimad Bhagavata Mahapurana*, 2 volumes (Gita Press, 2017).

Swami Sri Yukteswar Giri, *The Holy Science* (Self-Realization Fellowship, Los Angeles, California, 1984).

Swami Vivekananda: Complete Works, Volume 111, Eighth Edition.

Therese Taylor, *Bernadette of Lourdes*, anniversary edition (Bloomsbury Publishing, 2008).

Glossary

aarti	prayer sung in praise of a deity at the end of worship
aanchal	corner of a sari
Aayushmaan bhava	May you be blessed with long life
adharma	irreligious
adhyatmik vikas	spiritual development
ahuti	symbolic flame taken around to give blessing
amshika avatar	partial incarnation
angavastra	a stole draped over the shoulder
batashas	crystallised sugar sweets
Bajrang Bali	an epithet of Lord Hanuman
bhajan mandli	prayer group
Bhudevi	Mother Earth
Brahma	God-head
Brahmarishi	highest level of sainthood
Brahmaloka	abode of the gods
Brahmand	the cosmos

Brahmastra	divine weapon of Lord Brahma
charan-kamal	lotus feet
chirharan	disrobing
Chiranjeevi	immortal
chulah	fireplace for cooking
damaru	small hand-held drum
dandavat	the act of prostrating oneself in reverence
dakshina	offering
dharmic	religious
dhyan	meditation
dohas	sacred hymns
Dzongkha	Tibetan dialect spoken in Bhutan
gangajal	holy water from the Ganges
Gajraj	bull elephant
guggul	incense gum
gurukul	personalised teaching institutes
haizza	cholera
havan kund	the place where the sacred fire is lit
honi	an occurrence bound to happen
ishta devta	personal deity
kalpa	a measurement of time in the life of Brahma
karma yogi	one who has done good deeds
karmabhumi	place of action
kamandal	hand-held water carrier associated with sadhus

khadaons	wooden foot slippers
khartal	musical instrument with a wooden clapper
leela	divine play
lori	lullaby sung to a baby
Madhyadesh	central land, referring to the kingdoms of the Indo-Gangetic area
maiya	mother
Mahadev Mahakal	an epithet of Lord Shiva
maryada purushottam	the ultimate man; an epithet of Lord Ram
majira	a type of musical instrument
manvantara	time period
mahavakya	great utterance
manuśraddhādeva	the first Manu designed as a leader of man
namkaran	naming ceremony
nityoham, shuddhoham	(I am) everlasting, ever chaste
budhhoham, muktoham	ever learned, ever free
nirvikalpa samadhi	the highest stage of samadhi
paschataap	suffering performed as retribution
parashu	hand-held battle axe
param saubhagyavati bhava	forever may you remain married; a blessing given to a married lady
param dharma	the absolute truth
param purush	great person akin to godhead
parmanu shakti	nuclear energy

Pawan putra	son of the wind, an appellation given to Lord Hanuman
patala	the netherworld
Pranav	the sacred sound Aum
prithvi	earth
poorna avatar	a full incarnation since birth
putra kameshti yagya	religious ceremony seeking birth of son(s)
rajabhishek	coronation
Ramkatha	story of Lord Rama
Ram Rajya	rule of Lord Rama
rishiwar	saint
rudraksh	ripe seeds from the genus *Elaeocarpus* widely used as prayer beads
sadhvis	a female sadhu or holy person
samagri	sacred mixture used in ceremonials
Sanatan Dharma	perineal true way of life
sandhya	evening; also, the period that precedes a yuga
sandhyansa	period that follows a yuga
saktyavesa-avatar	partial manifestation of avatar
saptrishis	the seven sages
shashtang dandavat	prostrating oneself on the ground in reverence
Shantipath mantra	a peace invoking prayer
shakti	power

shankh, chakra, gada, padam	conch shell, revolving disc, mace and lotus in Lord Vishnu's four hands
Shanti path	peace invocation
srishti	cosmic creation
srijan	creation
siddhic	extra-sensational powers
sijda	bending over and touching the forehead to the ground in prayer
Solasa Mahajanapada	the sixteen great republics of ancient India
soma-rasa	nectar
stitahpragna	person of steady wisdom
sudarshana chakra	spinning disc-like finger weapon
sushumna	spinal channel
sutradhar	a storyteller stringing together a narrative
swayamvara	the ceremony where a bride can choose her own husband
tandava	the dance of Lord Shiva that is supposed to destroy creation
tapas	ascetism; cleansing inner self
tattvam	the truth
trishula	trident
trikaal	the three divisions of time—past, present, future
turiya	state of pure consciousness
upadesha	instructions
vanar	monkey

yagya	sacrifice
yagnashala	place of sacrifice
yatri	traveller
yogic shakti	strength borne out of yoga